Praise for Nicolas

Burn It All Down

"Audacious, addictive, highly entertaining —UNFORGETTABLE!"

—**James Patterson,** *New York Times* bestselling author

"A fast, fun, and unforgettable debut."

—**Steven Rowley,** bestselling author of *The Guncle*

"Riotously funny and packed with heart."

—**Hannah Orenstein,** author of *Meant to Be Mine*

"Entirely too much fun."

—*Good Housekeeping*

"Wild [and] delightful."

—**PopSugar**

"Side-splitting."

Shelf Awareness, Starred Review

"Hilarious."

—*Booklist*

"Just the summer read you've been craving ...a fiercely funny novel."

—*Real Simple*

the gay best friend

A Novel

NICOLAS DIDOMIZIO

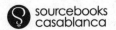

sourcebooks
casablanca

Published by Sourcebooks Casablanca, an imprint of Sourcebooks
P.O. Box 4410, Naperville, Illinois 60567-4410
(630) 961-3900
sourcebooks.com

Cataloging-in-Publication Data is on file with the Library of Congress.

Printed and bound in Canada.
MBP 10 9 8 7 6 5 4 3 2 1

For Graig

june

The Bachelor Party

1

I always thought it would be difficult—or at least somewhat dramatic—to cancel a wedding.

But no. So far the experience has followed the same pattern as any other dull errand of modern adulthood. Robotic emails, forced signatures, inexplicable fees. The world hasn't stopped spinning, my fiancé hasn't had a total emotional meltdown, and exactly zero vendors have begged us to reconsider. One person's pain is just another person's paperwork.

"Oh, babe." Kate carefully strokes the stem of her turmeric-ginger martini glass as I sulk beside her. "You sure you're okay?"

I take a swig of carrot-cucumber gin and sigh from my bamboo barstool. Kate insisted we meet at Cocktailia, which is somehow *not* the name of a gay porn sci-fi spoof but instead a vegan cocktail lounge in Tribeca. It's trying hard to be a spa— trickling fountains in the walls, stone decor on the surfaces, an omnipresent whiff of eucalyptus in the air—but the food sucks and the drinks taste like grass-fed donkey piss. I appreciate Kate's attempt at ushering zen into my life, but I'd kill for a beer and some chicken wings right now.

"Why do people keep asking me if I'm okay?" I respond. "I'm fine! Totally, extremely, deeply *fine*."

I've been totally-extremely-deeply-fine for two weeks, three days, and four hours now—and yes. I'm counting.

I can guarantee that Ted is, too. Even if his reason for doing so is less because he's heartbroken and more because he's a finance bro who just gets off on counting shit. He's probably already calculated a target time line to start dating again based on "what the research says" about how to optimally rebound from a five-year relationship.

"You don't sound fine, Domenic." Kate squints at me. "You don't look fine, either. Have you been sleeping, like, at all?" She digs into her leather Balenciaga and pulls out a makeup compact and tiny spray bottle. "Here. Facial mist infused with Vitamin C and hyaluronic acid—a total miracle serum. Give yourself a spritz."

I crack open the compact and inspect myself in the little round mirror. I don't see anything wrong at first—just my usual dark features, thick eyebrows, five o'clock shadow—but then I notice the bags under my eyes. When did I become a bags-under-the-eyes person? I snatch the spray bottle from Kate's hand and go to town on my face.

"Jesus, Kate!" My eyelids squeeze shut, which only makes the sting worse. It's like I just voluntarily pepper-sprayed myself. "This stuff is toxic!"

Kate stifles a laugh. "I said a spritz, babe. Not a full *Flashdance* drenching."

I take a deep breath and dab my eyes with the little napkin from beneath my drink. It's unclear if the tears I'm crying are all facial mist-induced or if there are some Ted-related ones in the mix, too. I'd guess the distribution is about eighty-twenty.

Okay, fine. Seventy-thirty.

Sixty-forty.

Okay! Fine! Fifty-fifty, final offer.

Kate rubs my shoulder, pure pity radiating from the tips of her manicured fingers. "What can I do to help? Anything? What about the vendors? Do you need me to get on the phone with—"

"We've already handled everything." I perform a blasé shrug—as if I didn't just sob into a cocktail napkin at happy hour. As if I couldn't care less about losing the one person (and corresponding life event) I've staked my entire sense of self-worth on for the past five years. "We have a *spreadsheet*."

I explain to her that, when we first started planning our wedding, Ted created a shared Google Doc for us to track each part of the process. And that within hours of our breakup last month, I got a Gmail notification that he had made several edits—adding a new column next to each vendor to indicate who was responsible for handling the cancellation, along with a P&L tab to track any refunds we were entitled to against the sunk costs of lost deposit money.

"That is some cold serial killer shit," Kate says. "So there's nothing I can do? You're sure every task on the spreadsheet is covered?"

"Mhmm." I wince as I recall completing the last—most humiliating—one over the weekend. "I finally dealt with the worst of it on Sunday. The STDs."

Kate's lashy eyes widen. "Dom? Babe?"

"Save the Dates," I clarify. "Since we'd already sent them out last November, I had to contact the printer and have them send out *un*-STDs."

Kate pretends to shiver. "Please stop saying STD."

"Oh, stop acting like you've never had one."

"I haven't!"

"Really? Not even one of those antibiotic-curable ones?"

"Okay, fine." She lowers her voice and leans in. "Chlamydia. Freshman year of college."

"Shut up! Me, too!"

It's amazing I can laugh about it now. At the time, I thought it was a death sentence—convinced the antibiotics wouldn't work and I'd gradually slip into madness over the years. But now a decade has passed, and I'm still (mostly) sane. So at least there's that.

"Twinsies!" Kate proclaims. "As per usual." She swallows the rest of her martini and composes herself. "Now let's never speak of that again."

I nod and smile, leaning into the air of feigned vapidity between us. Our usual dynamic, which, frankly, I've missed all night. "What the hell am I drinking right now?"

"It's a self-care cocktail, honey." She twirls a lock of her strawberry-blonde hair. "So herbal. Gwyneth turned me onto this bar when she came to the office for her beauty feature last month."

She is indeed referring to the Gwyneth. As a senior beauty editor at Vogue, Kate frequently rubs elbows (and makeup brushes) with a who's who in fashion and entertainment. Normally I'd get excited about the name-drop and beg her to give me the latest Goop scoop—but in this case it just kills my buzz. Because thinking of Gwyneth makes me think of the Iron Man franchise, which she starred in, and which is Ted's favorite. I sat through so many viewings of Robert Downey Jr. in that ridiculous armor suit over the years, hating the movies but loving the idea that I was watching them with my—

You know what? I should probably just leave.

I signal the bartender for one more drink and then the check. "I'm gonna head home after this round. Still have to pack my bags for the weekend."

"Oh. Right." Kate's exposed shoulders tense all the way up and her voice descends an octave. "About that..."

"We agreed we weren't gonna do this," I warn her before she can go where I know she's going. "The only way I can throw Patrick's bachelor party this weekend *and* go to your bachelorette party next month is if we have a strict don't-ask-don't-tell policy on both sides. You two have to trust each other."

I was hoping she'd have learned this lesson after the last time she tried to use me as her own personal Patrick nanny cam, back in September when he and I went to the Giants season opener in Jersey. He promised Kate he'd stick to light beer (he was driving)— except he didn't tell *me* that. So when Kate texted me at halftime and casually inquired about his latest beverage—a double IPA—I told her the truth.

They fought for the entire following week, and somehow it was all my fault.

"It's not that." Kate gulps the rest of her herbal martini and throws her head back. She makes a weird guttural sound like she's mustering up the strength to dive into an ice-cold body of water or something. "Okay, so, between you and me?"

"Always."

"I'm thinking of calling it off."

"Your bachelorette party?" I ask. Because surely she can't mean—

"The wedding," she confirms.

"What?" She has to be kidding. "You have to be kidding!"

What kind of bride would tell the *best man* that she's thinking of canceling the wedding just one night before he's supposed to throw the groom a joyous bachelor celebration at his family's beach house?

"I'm not! It's just...seeing how easy it was for you and Ted to cancel your wedding is making me realize that maybe I still have time to change my mind." Now that she's broken the honesty seal, she's speaking as casually as if she were contemplating the return of a recently purchased love seat. "I love Patrick so much, but—"

"This is absurd." Kate can't leave Patrick! They're a flawless pair. Blonde beauty guru with dewy clear skin and handsome sports attorney with flawless bone structure? It doesn't get any more *New York Times* Vows section-y than that. Which is exactly why I spent the better part of my twenties desperately searching for the gay equivalent of it. And exactly why losing Ted was such a blow: I now have to start the search for a picture-perfect husband all over again. "Patrick adores you."

"Because I've always made it so easy for him," she suggests. "Think about it. What if he only proposed to me because I was all 'cool girl' in the beginning? *I* was drinking beer and going to Giants games with you guys back then. And you know how much I hate gluten and football! I just did what he wanted, always so careful not to complain or nag or force him to do anything *he* didn't wanna do." She takes a breath. "Ever since we got engaged and I started asserting myself, he's begun to show his asshole side."

Okay—she's not entirely wrong. That IPA debacle *was* shortly after Patrick proposed. If it had happened before, she probably would have let it go without saying a word. I even remember Patrick saying as much at the time.

"Patrick isn't an asshole," I assure her. "He's just getting used to you having strong opinions. Or any opinions."

She ignores me and continues. "Last Thursday he didn't get home from happy hour until after midnight—never texted, nothing. And when I asked him why he was out so late, he accused me of being insecure and paranoid. And you know I'm not that girl.

But after he said it, I was like...*should* I be that girl? Sometimes he just sucks at communicating with me."

I lean forward. "He's—"

"It's just who he is. If I marry him, I have to accept it. The question is, do I want to accept it? Because I know there are guys out there who are sensitive and in touch with their emotions—" She cuts herself off and takes a centering breath. "I'm sorry to put all of this on you. I know you're going through a lot right now. And I know you're technically Patrick's best friend."

"Right," I deadpan. "Technically."

She always does this when she wants me to take her side. Suggests that the "best friend" label between Patrick and me is just a technicality, the result of our twenty-plus years of shared history and not an indication of how close we actually are.

The sad part is that it's kind of true.

Sometimes I wonder if Kate is the only reason Patrick and I are even still friends in the first place. We drifted fully apart in college—I came out of the closet; he joined a fraternity— and it wasn't until he started dating Kate in law school that we reconnected. She and I instantly bonded over our shared obsessions with *Sex and the City*, tacky chain restaurants, and Drew Barrymore's personal journey—and we've been best friends in our own right ever since.

"You've never had an issue trusting him before," I remind her. "Why don't you trust him now?"

Kate lowers her head and rubs her temples in thought. When she finally springs back to life—her hair falling back in waves over her shoulders—her eyes glow with a newfound light. As if she didn't just admit that she's thinking of leaving the man she's supposed to marry in two months. It's enough to make me wonder if the whole thing was just a pretense.

"I'm nervous about the bachelor party," she says. *And there it is.* "You know how he can be around his other friends. They're absolutely primitive…"

She pauses before swooping in for the kill. "Which is why I need you to keep him in check this weekend. No getting blackout drunk, no strippers, no drugs—"

"Drugs?" I literally couldn't even tell the difference between a gram of cocaine and a teaspoon of Benefiber. And I take that shit daily! (Benefiber, not cocaine.) "Don't be silly."

"I know *you* would never initiate any of those things," she says. "But sometimes you act different around Patrick. I'm worried you'll go along with whatever he and the guys want you to do."

This might be a little true—I've been following Patrick's lead for over two decades at this point—but if Kate's worried that his lead will be so twisted this weekend, then why isn't she having this conversation with *him*?

"You've seen the itinerary I made," I remind her. "It's jam-packed. There won't be time for anyone else's plans." I pin her with a stern look. "Damn. I can't believe you'd construct an entire relationship crisis just as an excuse to ask me to babysit Patrick all weekend." Especially considering the very real relationship crisis I've just been through. The timing feels more than a little insensitive.

She throws a hand up. "I didn't. I really am having second thoughts." She pauses. "But obviously I'm hoping Patrick will be good this weekend and prove that I am making the right decision by staying with him." She pauses once again. There's a flash of hurt in her eyes—like she might be genuinely trying to open up about a real problem—but it's gone before I can tell for sure. She's back to her typically breezy self within seconds. "You know what I mean?"

"Kate," I begin, "if you need to talk—"

"What I need is to know this weekend is going to go well."

Before I can respond, my attention is hijacked by an attractive gay couple that plunks down at the bar across from us.

Speaking of the *Times* Vows section—these two are practically ripped from the pages of its most recent token-gay-feature spread. Fit bodies, neat hair, smooth skin, clean smiles. There's an effortless energy of affection between them that suggests they truly love being in each other's company, which makes me want to vomit directly into the zen waterfall beside me. I'm completely removed from Kate's wedding drama and viscerally reminded that *I'm* the one who just lost my happily-ever-after. I can't even stand to look at them—or her, at this point—so I throw some cash on the bar and jump down from my stool.

Kate's eyes widen. "Babe? You still have half your drink—"

"It's getting late," I tell her as I scan the room for its nearest exit. "Don't worry about the bachelor party. Nothing bad is going to happen."

2

Something bad is going to happen. I wish I didn't have this thought right now, but I do. It's been buzzing around my mind all day, like a bitchy little bee. And it's only gotten louder (and bitchier) since I arrived at the Coopers' beach house in Mystic, Connecticut, a few moments ago. Something bad is going to happen this—

Stop! I swat it away, glance around the lavish kitchen—a crisp playground of quartz and oak and stainless steel—and tell myself to think good thoughts. This is a bachelor party I'm throwing, after all. It's supposed to be fun. It's *going* to be fun.

Where the hell is the groom, though?

I send him an ETA-inquiring text and slink down the hall into the great room.

This space epitomizes the ambiance of comfortable luxury I've always relished as a guest of Patrick's—all brilliant natural light and sturdy designer furniture. There's a mile-high stone fireplace decked out with nautical décor that's just authentic-looking enough to indicate it wasn't purchased at HomeGoods but was instead bought at auction from some bougie charity event at nearby Mystic Seaport. One wall features a giant brass helm, another displays a mounted antique lifeboat, and I honestly wouldn't be surprised if these items were salvaged from the actual Titanic.

But the room's true centerpiece is a dazzling white Steinway & Sons grand piano. It glistens under the exposed wooden beams of the vaulted ceiling, bringing me right back to the summers of my childhood. Begging me to sit down and play it.

I can still hear Mrs. Cooper's elegant voice in my ears as I brush my fingers across the keylid. "Thank God *you* have such a talent for the instrument," she'd always say. Then she'd shoot a glare at Patrick, who refused to take a single lesson. "Otherwise I'd never even bother getting this thing tuned."

My shoulders relax as I settle onto the bench, my mind flipping through the possibilities of what to play. The lush sonatas I'd memorized as an undergrad music major, the complex chords I struggled to master during my stint in a jazz trio, or the simple pop songs I used to indulge in as a guilty pleasure between classical lessons. My hands ultimately decide for me; I anticipate the sound of an opening riff as my fingers creep into position.

But then I snap out of it and stand up before hitting a single note.

Better to resist. Over time, I've found it's easier to deprive myself of the feeling of making music altogether than to get a taste and be reminded that my daily life has absolutely no room for such childish pleasures. I'm a lawyer, not Elton fucking John.

So I traipse around the rest of the empty house instead.

This sprawling coastal New England oasis—what Patrick's family matter-of-factly calls their "summer home"—has been the definition of paradise for me since I was eight years old. And not just because the fancy piano provided a melodic alternative to the dinky Casio keyboard I had at home. It was everything. The air, views, countertops, area rugs, flower arrangements, glassware, lighting, pillows.

My God, the *pillows*.

I'm not talking about, like, pillows in pillowcases that you would actually sleep with. I'm talking about expensive decorative pillows in various shapes and sizes, arranged in tasteful profusion, forming a sort of puffy mountain at the head of a duvet-draped California king bed. The kinds of pillows you'd see in the master bedroom of an upper middle-class couple in a Nancy Meyers movie from the early 2000s. You know the scene! The husband and wife passionlessly transferring the fluffy accents from mattress to floor, one by one, right before bedtime, as they fight about whether or not he's screwing the babysitter.

As a scrubby kid from a single-parent household, I was obsessed with those pillows—along with all the other subtle markers of wealth that the Mystic house has always possessed. Spending time with the WASP-y Cooper clan was like teleporting into a Ralph Lauren catalog. One day I'd be miserably spectating a game of bocce ball on the tiny patch of dehydrated grass behind my dad's aging ranch; the next I'd be partaking in a polo-clad badminton tournament on the lush greens of the Coopers' property, the shimmery ripples of Mystic Harbor washing ashore every few seconds on their private beach just down the hill.

The transition between worlds always felt so Cinderella-esque. I frequently marveled at how lucky I was that the one and only Patrick Cooper had chosen me as his best friend.

Not just best friend, but *hand twin*—a designation that happened during a sleepover one night when we stumbled upon an episode of *Friends* in which Joey freaked out after encountering a man whose hands were identical to his.

Patrick and I promptly compared our own hands and gasped upon realizing that we too were a perfect match, both in size and finger-to-knuckle-to-nail proportion. Something about it felt like fate. At least to me.

From then on, we'd often put our palms together, fingers extended, anticipating the day when one of us would outgrow the other. I got a small thrill every time we confirmed the day hadn't yet come. There was nothing I cherished more than having this one real thing in common with Patrick. Like, sure, my existence was infinitely less charmed than his...but our *hands*.

We kept this bit going all the way until the summer before high school, when we were finally forced to drop it after a heated scuffle left Patrick's hands temporarily mangled.

It was all my fault. Some bully in Patrick's neighborhood had been relentlessly harassing me on AOL Instant Messenger (remember AIM?) that summer—apparently I had bumped into him in the hallway on the last day of school—and I dished the harassment right back, calling him every name in the book from behind the protection of my dad's crappy HP desktop screen.

I had assumed our beef was strictly virtual, but it turned out he wanted to kick my ass in real life. So much so that he confronted Patrick about it one day during a neighborhood run-in.

Patrick told him to just drop it already, but the bully persisted—making fun of me for being poor (the worst insult of all amongst our peers at the time) and fat (listen, what closeted gay kid *wasn't* a little chubby in the early aughts?)—which prompted Patrick to get physical. He threw the first punch, followed by the second, third, fourth. The altercation shut the bully up for good, but it also left Patrick's knuckles severely bloodied.

Later that week, during a stay at the Mystic house, my stomach churned with shame for being the cause of such a violent episode.

"I'm so sorry," I told Patrick from across our sandy beach chairs. "I didn't realize he was so serious about wanting to fight me."

Patrick brushed it off with a shrug. "That punk had it coming. No way in hell I was gonna let him talk about you like that, man. I know you'd do the same for me."

The shame knot in my stomach tightened. If I couldn't even fight for myself, I knew it was highly unlikely I'd ever be able to do so for somebody else.

"Definitely," I said anyway.

"How cool is this, though?" Patrick extended his hands out in front of us, scabby and bruised from combat, and threw a small punch into the air. "I'm like Mike Tyson."

"Yeah." I forced a small chuckle, but the sight depressed me as I put my own (intact, pristine) hands out next to his. "But I guess we're not hand twins anymore."

We sat in silence for a few moments after that, listening to the waves crash. Despite his nonchalance, I still stewed with fear that this incident would lead him to question our entire friendship. High school was just weeks away. Patrick was already stronger, hotter, richer, and butcher than me—clearly bound for a life of popularity that I could only hope to achieve by way of association. Why should he keep me around?

He eventually perked back up and kicked his feet out of the sand.

"What size shoe are you?" he asked. "Let me see your feet…"

I kicked mine out. "Nine. Why?"

"Me too!" he said with a kind smile—squashing my insecurity with a small but life-affirming gesture of loyalty. "Foot twins."

I would've been elated to know then that—despite our temporary estrangement in college—our friendship would survive all the way to his bachelor party weekend, right here at the same house, on the same beach. The thought warms me up as I glance down at my now-adult-size-twelve feet. I dig my toes into the sand, take in the clear blue sky, and text him again.

Still no ETA.

My gaze shifts over to the lighthouse-shaped shed at the edge of the Coopers' property, which I hold for several moments. An entirely new wave of memories washes over me. Patrick and I used to love camping out in that lighthouse, swapping secrets like baseball cards for hours before falling asleep to the sound of the water.

An image begins to surface from one night back in tenth grade, when—

3

~

*C*ome here, baby!"
My nostalgia trip is interrupted by Steven Tyler's bombastic voice in the opening bars of Aerosmith's "Crazy."

I whip my head around and see present-day Patrick—a pulsating Bluetooth speaker in one hand, two bottles of Amstel Light dangling from the other—barreling down the lawn toward the beach. He's wearing his Nantucket Reds shorts, Sperry boat shoes, and nothing else. The sight of his effortlessly strong chest and stomach makes me wish I could magically undo all the post-breakup binge eating I've engaged in over the past month.

"What's up, brother?" His voice booms over the music as he places the speaker down on one of the nearby stone steps. "Sorry I'm late." He cracks the beers open with his key chain and tosses one my way. "How you doing? You look good. Fuck Ted, am I right? He's the worst."

I love this about him. I've spent countless hours agonizing over every detail of my failed engagement—desperate for reasons and explanations and justifications—but somehow Patrick can distill the entire thing down to three little words: He's the worst.

It's liberating! Even if it's not exactly the full truth.

"The absolute worst." A chuckle sneaks out of my mouth as

I say this. My anxiety already abates around Patrick. It's just the two of us tonight; I can start worrying about bad things happening tomorrow. "So what took you so long?"

He reclines in the maroon Adirondack chair next to me. "Thought I could squeeze in a half day at the office, but you know how that goes. Calls, contracts, bullshit. Retired NFL players having existential meltdowns." He takes a swig of beer. "Fun never ends."

"Don't remind me." I squirm at the thought of my own stack of paperwork awaiting me at the office on Monday. "Nice song choice, by the way."

"Yeah, man." Patrick runs a hand through his golden-brown hair. "It came on during my drive up from the city and I was like, 'Oh, shit!' Remember how obsessed we used to be with this music video?"

Of course I do. "A classic."

"We *loved* those chicks—"

"Alicia Silverstone and Liv Tyler."

"And our pact that I was gonna get with a girl like Alicia, and you were gonna find a Liv." Patrick playfully punches my arm and laughs to himself. "Guess one for two isn't so bad."

What I didn't tell Patrick back then is that my eyes were actually focused on the hot young farmer the girls went skinny-dipping with. That scene where they stole his clothes and forced him to chase after their car naked? Whew! The ultimate homosexual awakening.

"One thing's for sure," I offer. "Kate is a total Alicia."

"Isn't she, though?" Patrick tilts his head back in pride. "If anything, Kate's even *more* gorgeous."

This is good. Patrick is acknowledging that he finds his future wife attractive. Surely he will have no desire to employ the services of a sex worker this weekend.

"So anyway," he continues. "I took a gander at the itinerary you emailed us." His voice almost flips into a laugh at the word *itinerary*. Probably not a great sign. "Methinks we may need to make a few adjustments."

"What do you mean?" I do my best to match Patrick's jokey tone. "I covered all the bases. Golf, beer, gambling..."

"You sure did." He takes a swig from his bottle. "But come on, man. You have us watching all four days of the Travelers Championship. It'd be nice to actually *play* some golf one day."

"I figured you'd want to watch Bucky on TV—since he can't be here in person and all."

"Bro," Patrick deadpans. "Don't tell me you still have your stupid thing against Bucky."

"I don't have a thing against Bucky," I insist. "I just think it's interesting that he's the only groomsman who declined my invitation."

Patrick rolls his eyes. "I know you're not that into sports, but Bucky is an *elite* golfer right now. He was in the top half of the leaderboard at the Masters! He can't be missing tournaments just to party with us. That'd be, like, forfeiting potentially millions of dollars. Plus he'll lose his PGA Tour card if he doesn't play in enough events."

Here he goes again. Acting like Bucky is some kind of god just because he swings a golf club around on TV every weekend. Meanwhile, I was promoted to senior counsel two months ago—but did he gush to his other friends about that? No. (The fact that I hate my job notwithstanding...it was technically still an accomplishment.)

"Yeah, no. It's fine." I dig my feet further into the sand. "We can book a tee time. I don't know if I'll play, but you and Wilson and Greeny can—"

"We'll figure it out," Patrick says. "That's not what I was talking about anyway. I couldn't help but notice that your schedule has one, uh, glaring omission."

"What do you mean?" I ask—desperate for him to answer with something like "you forgot movie night" or "we should do a wine tasting" or "the Sunday brunch menu is all breakfast and no lunch." (But I mean, really. What kind of cretin actually cares about the "unch" in brunch?)

"I'll give you a hint." His mouth stretches into a smirk. "It rhymes with...knits."

"Um." I rub my eyes in an effort to unsee the giant fake breasts that have just bounced into my mind like a pair of self-dribbling basketballs. "I don't follow."

"Cut the shit." Patrick laughs, revealing some new crow's feet around his eyes. They're handsome on him, even if they do slightly remind me of Ted. "Listen, I don't really *want* strippers myself—the entire concept is weird. Who wants to pop a woody surrounded by their closest friends?" He laughs again. "But with the crew that's coming here this weekend, we have to accept that it's inevitable. I can't stop Wilson from doing what Wilson is gonna do."

"But Kate!" I protest. "You promised her we'd keep it clean."

"I was worried this would happen." Patrick stands up and squeezes my shoulders from behind my chair. "Okay. So remember in high school, before you were gay?"

"I was gay in high school," I tell him. "I just wasn't out."

"You know what I mean." He tightens his grip. "I'm just trying to remind you of a time when you were better at adhering to Bro Code—one of the most important rules of which is *don't tell wives and girlfriends incriminating shit*. Bros before hoes."

"That is such a juvenile and sexist little idiom." I try to sound assertive, but it's no use. Patrick's display of dominance makes me feel twelve years old again. Like we're playing Truth or Dare by flashlight in the lighthouse shed. "Kate would be crushed if she knew there were women here this weekend." I consider going into detail about how she literally threatened to cancel their wedding over this, but think better of it. "And she's gonna ask—"

"That's exactly why you need to do me a solid here. She trusts you. If you tell her nothing happened, she'll believe it." Patrick's fingers are basically melded into my clavicle at this point. "I love Kate—obviously. I would never do anything to hurt her. But this is just one of those situations where what she doesn't know won't hurt her."

Perhaps that's true, but what about my karma? While I understand what Patrick is saying about Bro Code, lying to Kate would be betraying a totally different code to which I'm also bound. The fact that I'm gay and friends with his fiancée should exempt me from Patrick's antiquated gender expectations altogether.

"Come on," I attempt. "Kate's my…"

"I've always had your back."

"But—"

He somehow manages to squeeze even harder. "Dom."

And that settles it.

I'll just have to suck it up. Regardless of our differences, Patrick's right. He has always been there for me. He's gotten into *fist fights* for me—the AIM bully incident was just the first of several in which he had to step in after I talked shit I couldn't back up with my own knuckles. (Listen, I was an angsty teen.) I owe him.

Plus his death grip is telling me I don't have a choice in the matter, anyway.

"Alright, man." I wriggle free and stand up to face him. "Fine."

"You have to say it," he demands.

I'm an inch taller than him, but somehow he towers over me.
"Say what?" I ask.

"That you won't tell Kate anything about this weekend." All jokiness has vanished from his voice. He's not messing around. "What happens in Mystic..."

"Stays in Mystic." I swallow the boulder of dread that's been forming in my throat and take a breath. I knew something bad was going to happen this weekend. And it's only Wednesday. "Got it."

4

Four hours and twice as many light beers later, I'm finally buzzed enough to entertain a conversation about the whole Ted thing.

"I still don't get it," Patrick says through a mouthful of meat lover's pizza. He's perched on the kitchen counter while I pick at my slice from a barstool at the island. "You guys were together for so long. Almost as long as me and Kate."

"Would've been six years in September." It's amazing I can say this without bursting into tears. I've had several variations of this same conversation with Kate over the past month, and the crying usually starts once we get to the part about how I've wasted nearly half of my adult life on one man. But Patrick and I have never cried in front of each other, so this time I just fake a laugh and trivialize my pain into a stupid little punch line. "To think he dumped me over a damn *spider*."

"Kate told me about that." Patrick scratches his right nipple—he still hasn't put a shirt on, and honestly I feel like he's just showing off at this point—and shakes his head. "Unreal."

Spidergate started innocently enough. I was getting ready for bed while Ted stayed up to watch the end of a Red Sox game in the living room. Pretty standard weeknight for us.

But then I noticed there was this big, satanic-ass spider just chilling on our bedroom wall—mere inches away from our new Pottery Barn headboard. And I hate spiders. Who doesn't? They're creepy, hideous, cursed—basically what I imagine gonorrhea would look like if it took on a physical life-form.

So I did what I always used to do in those types of situations: sprinted into the living room and ordered Ted to kill it for me.

Once upon a time, he'd have laughed off my hysterics and obliged. Which is why I fell in love with him in the first place, because he didn't have the same silly fears as me. But this time he decided to use it as an opportunity to pour gasoline all over our relationship.

"Go to bed." He didn't even take his eyes off the ball game. "I'm sick of enabling your bullshit."

My heart plummeted. "I don't know what I did to piss you off, but can you please just kill it? You know I won't be able to go to bed until that spider is—"

"Then kill it yourself!" he snapped. "Jesus Christ, Domenic. The world doesn't revolve around you and your ridiculous anxieties."

The conversation escalated into an all-out battle from there. Ted spat out a whole laundry list of reasons he had grown to loathe me over the past couple years. He said I was so controlling that I basically treated him "like a piece of AI software." He claimed our shared money troubles were all *my* fault because I didn't understand the concept of living within my means. And then he blasted me for having a "pathetic" obsession with measuring my life against those of our well-off straight friends. Apparently Ted didn't even want to propose in the first place; he was just acquiescing to all the naggy marriage comments I'd started making once Patrick told me he was proposing to Kate.

These were all versions of fights we'd had many times before, but this was the first time they were all lined up together in such a neatly targeted stampede.

And the worst part was that by the time I stormed off and returned to the bedroom, the spider was gone! So then I had to go back into the living room and start a whole *new* fight about how Ted's tirade against me had led to its escape from my view—and so now there was no way I was gonna be able to sleep (ever again), and also we'd probably have to burn the house down.

Ted shook his head in exhaustion and said those eight little words that threw my entire life off track. *I don't think we should get married anymore.*

Sometimes I wonder what would've happened if I hadn't gone back out there. What if I had just swallowed my fear and gone to bed? Would Ted have slept it off—like he usually did—and been okay in the morning? Would I have been saved the humiliation of having to personally cancel on multiple wedding vendors and over a hundred guests? Obviously he'd been unhappy for a while—"I don't think we should get married anymore" isn't exactly a spur-of-the-moment kind of remark—but still. I had assumed we were on the same page in thinking we could wait until *after* the wedding to address our growing incompatibility.

"Dom?" Patrick shocks me back to the present moment by jumping off the counter and pressing an ice-cold beer against my neck. "Lost you for a second there, bud."

I snatch the beer from his hand and take a big, desperate gulp. Patrick squints at me in pity with those amber eyes of his.

"Can I give you some advice?" he asks, launching directly into said advice before I can answer the question. "Stop thinking about everything so much. Some stuff you just can't control. No matter how hard you try."

"Are you saying I shouldn't *think* about the fact that my fiancé left me less than five months before our wedding? Are you saying I drove Ted away because I was too controlling? Are you saying—"

"No, no." Patrick chuckles as if I've just proved his point. Which I suppose I have. "I'm just saying that you've always had this tendency to worry about the worst possible thing happening before it ever even happens. It's highly unproductive."

"That's not true."

"Dude," Patrick says. "Last week you went and got an ultrasound of your nutsack—"

"I thought I felt a lump on one of my balls!" I interject. "How was I supposed to know it was just...the other ball?"

"That would probably be most people's first assumption!" he says through a full-on laugh. "Like I said. You're always worried about the *worst* possible thing happening. You gotta stop doing that."

"Yeah." I guess he's mostly right. "But also..."

"What?"

"The worst possible thing *did* happen." I shift in my seat. "Ted left me."

This takes the air out of the room, and we sit in silence for a few very depressing moments.

It was stupid of me to embark on this conversation with Patrick. It's easy for him to never expect the worst, because the worst just naturally avoids him. His life has always been like that—charmed, easy, hashtag blessed.

I know because I've spent the majority of *my* life trying to keep up with him. Sometimes literally; we both ran track in high school and I was always placing behind Patrick. I can still see him galloping ten feet ahead of me—his tan biceps and strong shoulders peacocking amongst the scrawny teenage limbs of our competitors—before cruising past the finish line like it was his bitch. Meanwhile, I hobbled past that thing like I was *its* bitch, depleting every last morsel of energy in my body just to finish eight runners after him.

That's how it's always been with us. The things that have come easily for Patrick have required herculean strength and sacrifice on my part. All those years I spent in the closet—twisting myself into a zillion excruciating knots—I was trying to embody an image of straightness that Patrick was simply born with. All those semesters in college and law school amassing a six-figure mountain of student debt, I was trying to attain an education that Patrick's parents simply covered with a quickly forgotten check each year. All those nights I pestered Ted about marriage—eventually driving him away entirely—I was trying to score the same happily ever after that Patrick was all but guaranteed the moment he met Kate.

All that trying and trying and trying only for Ted to dump me *because* of it. I might as well have never tried at all.

"Thanks for the pep talk." I get up to sit on the counter beside him. "But enough about that asshole."

Patrick's gaze is so buried in his phone that he barely even notices my presence next to him. Whatever he's reading, it must be good. Or bad. I can't really tell from his expression, which is more blank than anything.

"Holy shit," he finally mutters under his breath.

"What?" I ask.

He hands me the phone.

It's open to a tweet from *Golf Digest*:

Bucky Graham pulls out of this weekend's Travelers Championship at the last minute, cites health emergency.

5

I swear I don't hate Bucky.

I barely even know him, really. We've always inhabited two very separate sectors of Patrick's life. In the decade since Patrick first ~~replaced me with~~ befriended him, I've hung out with Bucky a total of four times.

I can say that conclusively because I've counted. It's hard not to remember being in the presence of Bucky Graham. Perfect Bucky with his perfect smile and perfect golf swing and perfect ass that looks *particularly* great on TV in his Nike golf pants and— damnit! The man is extremely hot. Maybe I do hate him. He's confident, rugged, Southern. The opposite of me.

Last fall he posed for a series of pictures in *ESPN Magazine*'s Body Issue—their annual celebration of the human form in which professional athletes pose naked—and I can't even tell you how many times I self-loathingly jerked off to them over the past year. I mean, my sex life with Ted had atrophied into nonexistence a while ago, but still. How twisted is that? Fantasizing over entirely non-sexual pictures of my best friend's *other* best friend.

But regardless of my mixed emotions on Bucky, I obviously wouldn't ever wish him physical harm.

Which is why it's so alarming to see this headline about him suffering from a sudden medical emergency. Especially since Patrick—who happens to be Bucky's lawyer—didn't even know anything about it until seeing it online. He has since disappeared into the master suite to make a handful of calls to Bucky and the rest of his management team, leaving me to twiddle my thumbs in the living room until there's an update.

I stare at the local news—muted on the fireplace-mounted flat screen—and contemplate what the hell might've happened. Some kind of accident? Bucky's in amazing physical shape. And golf isn't exactly the most injury-inducing sport in the world. It's an old people's game! So this is all just very weird.

Before I can think too hard about it, my phone spasms with a call from Kate.

I should probably be concerned that it's only the first day of the party, and she's already calling me to check in, but instead I'm relieved to have someone to talk about this whole Bucky thing with.

"Oh my God, hi." I can feel my voice switching gears. All day and night I've been talking to Patrick in subdued, relaxed, low tones—avoiding effeminacy as much as possible. Now that I have Kate on the line, my accent is going up a half-step, and I'm low-key mimicking the Valley Girl cadence she's known for. Neither voice is entirely *my* voice, but for some reason all I know how to do is go to extremes to fit in with whomever I'm talking to at any given moment. What does my true voice even sound like? Ted is probably the only person who would know the answer to that. "What's going on with Bucky? Do you know what happened?"

"No! That's why I'm calling." Kate's energy is a fifty-fifty mixture of gossip and concern. "Patrick's not picking up his phone. What are you guys even doing right now?"

"He's been trying to get a hold of Bucky, but I don't think he's had any luck." I then remember that Bucky's girlfriend

Trista—a professional swimsuit model (of course)—is one of Kate's best friends. "What did Trista say?"

"She's freaking out. She had a job in Miami this weekend, so she didn't go up to Connecticut with him for the tournament. She found out about this from a *tweet*."

"Us, too. So weird."

There's a moment of awkward silence before Kate switches the subject.

"So how's it going so far?" she asks, a hint of interrogation in her voice. "How's the Mystic house?"

"We've just been hanging out, talking. Drinking beers. Eating pizza." I realize how boring this sounds, which is...perfect. Exactly what Kate needs to hear. "I'm sure this is how it will be tomorrow night. And Friday night. And Saturday night."

"Ha. Right." Kate scoffs. "With that crowd?"

"Yes, with that crowd!" Let's see how many white lies I can tell without sounding suspect. I need the practice. "Patrick and I had a whole discussion with Greeny and Wilson on FaceTime earlier. Everybody loved the chill itinerary I put together." One. "We all agreed this weekend is going to be a tranquil little beach retreat." Two. "We didn't even get any craft beers or hard liquor! Light stuff only." Three. "So this is *basically* going to be a dry event—"

"You sound suspect," Kate says. I guess three is more than I would've expected from myself. "What's going on? Are the guys asking you to lie to me? Is *Patrick* asking you to lie to me? Oh my God. He's going to cheat on me with a—"

"Do you hear how insecure you sound right now? Snap out of it!" I demand. I hate that I'm invalidating her (somewhat warranted) feelings, but I can't allow them to escalate. The last thing I need is her sending Patrick an accusatory text because I sounded shady on a phone call we shouldn't even be having. "He would never cheat on you."

I feel some relief in knowing that I ended on what feels like a genuine truth. Regardless of what else he might do this weekend, I'm positive Patrick loves Kate too much to cross the line into infidelity.

"That's what I've always thought," Kate says. "But—"

"Stop worrying so much. You're worse than *me*."

She takes a few deep breaths.

"You're right," she finally concedes through a sigh. "I don't know what's going on with me, Dom. I do trust Patrick. He isn't who he used to be back in college."

"Exactly." I have no idea how long this sudden burst of enlightenment will last, but I'll take what I can get for now. "He's a good guy."

"I'm sorry for putting you on the spot like this," she says. "And I'm sorry for unloading on you at drinks last night. That wasn't cool of me. I know you and Patrick are close, and you have your own stuff going on with the whole Ted thing. I shouldn't have said anything."

It feels so good to have a chance to clear the air that I immediately accept her apology without a second thought. "Don't even worry about it. It's not like I didn't get where you were coming from. I wasn't always the most secure partner with Ted."

Kate laughs. "Remember when he went on that March Madness trip with his undergrad friends, and you were *convinced* they were having a secret gay orgy in the hotel room? Even though they all had literal wives at home?"

I cringe-chuckle. "God, that's embarrassing. I was so paranoid for no reason. Ted was an emotionless prick at times, but a cheater he was not." I pause for effect. "And neither is Patrick!"

"I know," she says. "Honestly? I think it's just the other guys I'm worried about. Deep down I've always known they're the types who would throw a totally inappropriate bachelor party one day, but now that the party is happening, I guess I'm not as comfortable with it as I always thought I'd be."

"Well, it's just Patrick and me tonight." I walk over to the wall-spanning living room window and stare out at the harbor. The water is an eerie shade of onyx, glistening in the moonlight. I remember Patrick's warning to me earlier—Bro Code—and suddenly feel indignant on Kate's behalf. Unease spreads in my chest as I consider what would happen if Kate's and my roles were reversed right now. If Ted had ever asked her to lie to me, I'd fully expect her loyalty to fall on my side. "But when the other groomsmen get here, I promise I won't let things get out of hand. Okay? If you don't trust them, you can at least trust me."

Kate exhales. "Thanks so much for having my back on this, babe." Her breathing steadies to the point where I can no longer hear it, an encouraging sign that I've tamed the beast. Even if I had to dig myself a hole by doing so. "You're such a good friend."

Guilt rises in my throat as I absorb the compliment.

6

Despite its grandiosity, there are only four proper bedrooms in the Mystic house: a giant master suite on the first floor, a slightly smaller "second master" upstairs, and two kid-sized guest bedrooms tucked around a shared bathroom down the hall. All four are drowning in beachy yet elegant décor (lots of sailboats), freshly laundered linen everything (even curtains), and an abundance of those useless pillows I've always loved so much (of course).

As the groom, Patrick is staying in the primary master this weekend. As the best man, I snagged the second master upstairs. And then the little bedrooms in the guest wing will be occupied by one groomsman each. It's a neat fit—everyone in his own room—which is why I was actually a bit relieved when Bucky said he couldn't make it this weekend. Having more people than beds is always a recipe for disaster. Especially for the odd man out. It encourages this attitude of, like, *I'm crashing on the couch anyway, so I might as well get extra wasted!* And we don't need that kind of energy here this weekend.

Except now it looks like we might have it after all.

"It's perfect." Patrick leans against the dresser in the corner of my room. "He's already in Connecticut for the tournament, anyway."

I sit up in the bed. "He's healthy enough to come *here*, but not healthy enough to play golf? What the hell even happened to him?"

"Strained his lower back."

"That qualifies as a 'health emergency'?"

"His doctor told him it was important to rest before it gets worse." Patrick shrugs. "I know, man. It's random. He's played through back pain before and been fine. So this must be worse than he's letting on."

"If it's worse than he's letting on, he shouldn't come!"

"Why?"

"All the rooms are taken." I feel like Cher in *Clueless* when she threw her dad a fiftieth birthday party and it was total chaos because *people came that, like, did not RSVP*—I'm totally buggin'. "And someone with a bad back can't be sleeping on a couch."

"It's not a big deal," Patrick says. "He can just crash with me in my bed. Or one of the other guys can take the couch. We'll figure it out."

"But—"

"Dom. What was I just telling you earlier? You gotta stop worrying so much. Just go with the flow." He sits down to join me on the neatly made, impossibly lush bed. "This is going to be great. The guys are gonna freak when he shows up. I can't even remember the last time we've all been in the same room together."

I heave a resigned sigh. "You know what? Maybe I should just go home."

I know this is an overreaction—I'm not sure where the impulse to go all scorched-earth even came from—but now that I've said it out loud, I realize that leaving early may actually be the perfect solution to all my problems. If I'm not here for the debauchery, then I'll never have to lie to Kate about it. Ignorance will be bliss.

And do I really need to be here while Patrick reconnects with his old frat buddies, anyway? Being an outsider gets old quick. It'll probably be more fun for all of us if I just remove myself from the situation entirely. Then I can go back to the city and continue mourning my breakup all weekend while mindlessly perusing Grindr and sobbing into a pint of Talenti gelato. Not that those things are necessarily *fun*, but at least they're safe.

"You can give Bucky this room." I enthusiastically gesture around at the space like I'm a real estate agent trying to sell him on his own house. "I barely know him—or the other guys—anyway. You should enjoy each other's company this weekend. You and I can do our own thing some other time."

"Dude!" Patrick says. "What are you even talking about? Don't be ridiculous."

"Seriously, it's cool." I grip a handful of duvet and make a note to really enjoy the one night I'm going to have in the ultra-comfort of this room. I'll keep the window open and let the waves soothe me to sleep. "I can leave in the morning before the guys arrive."

Patrick's face falls. "Don't do this. I know we've drifted in and out over the years, but come on. I have more history with you than I do with any of the other clowns coming up here this weekend. This is my bachelor party, and you're my *best man*. You can't go home just because Bucky may or may not show up tomorrow. I need you here."

It's nice to know he's not flushed with relief at the thought of me stepping aside so he and his bros can have a proper rager, but also: shit. He has a point. This is a major life event, and I can't bail on him because of a single unexpected guest.

"You're right," I concede. "That was a dumb suggestion. Of course I'll stay."

"Yeah, you will." Patrick smiles, slaps my thigh, then jumps up off the bed. "I really hope Bucky comes so you can at least get to know him better. You're my two best friends. It's crazy that you've never really partied together."

Isn't that kind of your fault? I think but don't say.

For the past five years, my time with Patrick has been strictly limited to the context of couples' activities—him and Kate, Ted and me. And even back when I was single, I rarely got invited to go along with Patrick and his buddies on their adventures. I've always been squarely in that very particular role of "childhood best friend from home."

"You guys just might hit it off!" Patrick continues.

"I'm sure we have a lot in common," I say through clenched teeth. Something tells me Bucky's presence is going to make the threat of bad things happening this weekend several times worse than it already was, but it's clear I don't have a say in the matter. "It'll be great."

7

It's not even ten in the morning yet, and all ~~horsemen of the apocalypse~~ groomsmen have arrived—the deep cacophony of their ball-busting voices traveling all the way up to my bedroom. Bucky's Southern drawl in particular stands out. I knew Patrick was full of it last night when he framed Bucky's attendance as something that "may or may not" be happening.

But here's the bigger problem. These jerks got here *three* full hours ahead of the start time I put in the itinerary. They were supposed to show up at lunchtime, when I planned to have a full spread of lobster rolls and fries from Abbott's ready on the back patio. It was going to be the official kick-off meal of the weekend—complete with a craft IPA tasting and a basket of custom beer koozies that say PATRICK'S LAST BREW BEFORE "I DO."

Now—to quote Cher Horowitz once more—I have to *haul ass to Abbott's, redistribute the food, and squish in an extra place setting.*

I take the longest shower of my life before getting dressed and tiptoeing downstairs to the kitchen.

The first person to notice me enter is cocky hedge fund manager Mike Wilson, known as just "Wilson." Quickly followed by Greg Green, a.k.a. "Greeny." In painfully cliché frat tradition, they all go by their last names. It occurs to me that I'm in for a weekend in which Patrick is incessantly referred to as "Cooper" and "Coop."

"There he is!" Wilson greets me in his Mark Wahlberg-ian Boston accent. He looks the same as he does in the nonstop couple pics his wife Melanie posts on Instagram—sleepy eyes (a random scar under the left one), hair in a clean fade, permanent smirk. "Diva Dom! I haven't seen ya in, what? Over a year? How's it hangin', buddy?"

Of course I don't get a standard last name moniker. Instead I'm stuck with Diva fucking Dom. All because the first time Patrick introduced me to these guys was years ago on a camping trip in Vermont, where we all shared a big tent—half of which was taken up by their modest sleeping bags while the other half was occupied by my queen-sized, full-height air mattress. How the hell was I supposed to know that comfort wasn't allowed on camping trips? (And I was the poor one, while they all came from money! I still don't understand why they chose to subject themselves to that kind of torture for no reason.)

"It's...hangin' fine." I give Wilson a fist bump and pour myself a cup of coffee. Caffeine to fuel the hypermasculine energy I'll need to muster to fit in with this crew. "Hey, fellas."

I exchange awkward high fives with Greeny next, who's also hovering by the kitchen island.

"We were listening to your app on the way up here," he says to me. "I noticed a glitch on the—"

"Not my problem." The last thing I feel like doing is pulling up my work email and notifying the UI team of yet another bug. "I'm just the music rights attorney."

Greeny smiles at my cantankerousness and lightly punches my shoulder. "Right on, man. I feel you."

I take a chug of coffee—gripping the mug more firmly than I normally would, because God forbid I sip daintily around these two—and address them both in a deep mumble. "So what brings you guys up so early? I thought you weren't coming until lunch."

"It's Coop's epic bachelor bacchanal!" Wilson says. "We gotta soak up every moment." He points over at the door to the master. "Especially now that our main man was able to join."

So that's where Bucky and Patrick are. Probably going over lawyer–client stuff in the wake of Bucky's dropout from the tournament.

Wait. I squint at him. "Did you just refer to Bucky as the *main man*? You guys know this is Patrick's bachelor party, right? Not his."

Wilson rolls his eyes. "You know what I mean. Graham is a *god*, dude. Do you know how hard it is to play at his level? He's one of the best in the world!"

"This year especially," Greeny adds. "His drives have been insane. His putting game is better than anyone else's on tour. He's gonna win the Open, I can feel it. Our guy was so close at the Masters."

I swear to God—these guys idolize Bucky even more than I've idolized Patrick over the years. And they're so transparent about it! It honestly makes me wonder if my insatiable appetite for male approval is actually not a gay thing at all, but instead just a guy thing. Or maybe it's a guy thing exacerbated by the fact that I'm gay.

"Tough break with his back, then." I place my empty coffee cup down on the quartz countertop. "We'll have to take it easy this weekend so he can recuperate."

Greeny brushes off the suggestion. "He'll be fine."

"After tonight, he'll be more than fine." Wilson chortles and slaps my arm. "Don't tell Coop, but we have a little surprise coming to the house later. An early wedding gift, if you will."

Tonight? I thought I had until at least Friday or Saturday to worry about the threat of surprise strippers.

"I'm pretty sure Patrick already knows about what you have planned," I tell them. "He made sure to warn me last night."

"He *thinks* he knows," Wilson whispers. His resting smirk has taken on a particularly devious quality. "But he has no idea."

"So what is it?" I ask.

His smirk goes crooked. "Don't worry about it. You'll find out soon enough."

This prick. It's bad enough he went behind my back to plan an entire night at a party he knows I've already organized—but now he won't even tell me what those plans are? If I were a confrontational person, I'd slam my coffee down and demand a little respect.

But instead I just fake a laugh and excuse myself to the bathroom down the hall. Maybe taking a moment alone will help me devise a way to thwart Wilson's agenda without actually having to challenge him directly.

The door to the powder room stops halfway in my attempt to swing it open, and it's not until I see the back of Bucky's tanned neck that I realize I just slammed it against his ass.

He flushes the toilet immediately and steps out into the hallway. He's wearing a standard outfit—white Nike polo, gray golf pants, navy Callaway hat—but the masculine contours of his body still manage to announce themselves through the fabric. It takes superhuman strength for me not to picture him naked the way I tend to do whenever I catch a glimpse of him on TV.

"If it ain't the best man himself!" he says through a welcoming grin. "You swung that door open mighty hard. You tryin' to put a blister on my butt?"

"Sorry," I stammer. "Didn't know you were in th—"

"My fault, I should've locked it." He extends a hand in my direction. "Good to see ya, bud."

"Yeah. I..."

...am still stammering.

Get it together, bitch.

"Likewise," I finally mutter.

Bucky draws attention back to his hand. "Don't leave a brother hangin' now!"

I have a sharp revelation that he didn't use the sink when he rushed out of the bathroom just now, but for some reason I'm still incapable of formulating a sentence. So I oblige and give him an awkward high five slash handshake. Did I just six-degrees-of-Kevin-Bacon touch Bucky Graham's...bacon? I believe I did.

"Alright, then." He clicks his tongue and chuckles. "I reckon I'll get back to Coop and leave ya here to drain the lizard."

By the time my mind catches up enough to ask myself what the hell just happened, he's gone.

8

"S omething is super weird about this." Kate's voice is incredulous through my car speakers. "He's too hurt to golf, but he drove up to Mystic to party with you guys all weekend? Aren't people with back injuries supposed to stay horizontal or something?"

"It's not that weird." I turn left on Fishtown Road, en route to pick up the lunch platters from Abbott's. "His injury is bad, but it's not so bad that he can't hang."

Meanwhile, I completely agree with Kate. Something is very weird. Back at the house, Bucky was a paragon of health. No back brace, no limp, no groaning in pain. The man took a door-slam to the ass and didn't even flinch.

"Trista thinks it's very suspicious," Kate says. "She said that when he had a herniated disc last summer, he was doing several hours of physical therapy per day. And he still didn't miss any tour stops. If he was truly injured, there's no way he would spend four days drinking in Mystic. It would be career suicide."

"Why would he fake it, though?"

"Trista thinks he might be in trouble with the PGA or something and the injury is just a front to save face." She pauses. "By the way, Bucky's been completely ignoring her. Leaving all her messages unread. She is *livid*. She was wondering if you might be able to ask him to—"

"No way!" I can't believe she's asking me to do this. But then again, I can. I should've known that, by acquiescing to her demands last night, they'd soon increase in scope. "I can't have all the guys thinking I'm communicating with their wives and girlfriends all weekend. I shouldn't even be talking to *you* right now."

"What is that supposed to mean?"

"Nothing—I'm just saying it's not my place to intervene. I barely even know either of them."

Kate stays silent for a moment, and all I can hear is the clacking of her computer keys in the background.

"Hello?" I ask. "I'm almost at Abbott's. I gotta go."

"Sorry—multitasking. I have this dumb feature on a new Olay serum due in twenty. The product sucks ass, but they're our biggest advertiser, so...guess who's getting a glowing Kate Wallace review in *Vogue*?" She sighs. "Shoot me."

Normally her lack of focus might bother me, but right now it comes as a huge relief. *Saved by the serum.*

"Oh, honey," I tease. "No amount of product could conceal a bullet wound."

"Funny."

"Did you hear me before?" I ask. "I gotta go."

"Fine, okay." She's huffing. I can't tell if her annoyance is on account of me or her current deadline. "But just remember: you *are* going to be back in that house with me and Trista—*and* Melanie—next month. And I can't help it if we'll all have questions about what our husbands and boyfriends did this weekend."

On second thought, that serum didn't do shit to save me.

"Are you serious right now?" I ask her. "I thought we agreed last night that you had nothing to worry about with Patrick. Now your entire coven is expecting me to spy on *their* men, too? Come on."

"So we're witches because we want to know what our men are doing behind our backs this weekend?" she sneers. "Check your misogyny, babe."

"Not until you check your ridiculous insecurity!" I hiss before hanging up without saying bye—an act of hostility I'd typically never even contemplate, let alone execute. But there's no getting through to her at this point. Now that Trista has reason to distrust Bucky, the two of them are going to be stewing and speculating together for the entire duration of this event. And I refuse to establish myself as a spy for the entire bridal party.

In a huff, I finally pull up to Abbott's.

I take in the coastal New England charm of the place—a homey waterfront lobster shack adorned with white shiplap siding, decorative buoys, rows of picnic tablecloths—and actively feel the frustration leave my body. It would be impossible to stay pissed in this environment.

I'll never forget the first time I ate here.

It was a middle school summer. Patrick's parents took us for lunch one afternoon after a long morning of playing on the beach, and I fell instantly in love with lobster—both the taste and everything it represented to me at the time. A twenty-dollar sandwich? The height of luxury! As far as I was concerned, we might as well have been eating Chanel scarves.

"You want another one?" Mrs. Cooper asked me after noticing how ravenously my first was inhaled. "Go ahead."

Her nonchalance toward the cost made me question everything I'd ever known.

The following weekend at home, I asked my dad if we could go out for lobster rolls sometime. He laughed in my face.

"What'd you just ask me?" he said. "Who the hell do you think we are? The Rockefellers?"

"Just one each," I clarified.

Apparently my child-logic had determined that if the Coopers could afford multiple servings, surely we could afford a single.

"You've been spending too much time with those Mystic snobs." He scratched his chest through his tank and took a swig of Budweiser. It was just the two of us at the table, as he was between girlfriends at the time. "Now shut up and eat your ziti."

A typical exchange in the Marino household. While I viewed the Coopers' lifestyle as aspirational, my blue-collar father simply dismissed them as out-of-touch rich people who "wouldn't know real work if it bit them in the ass."

I think we both felt inferior to them, really, but expressed it in opposite ways. Dad doubled down on his belief that people like them and us were entirely different species whereas I went all-in on my quest to become one of them. Nothing scared me more than the thought of growing up and living life the way my father did: always angry, tired, stressed, or on the clock. I appreciated the concept of hard work, but he took it to an extreme that seemed more like suffering. And for what? To pay a cable bill.

Hence my white-collar career path. Hence the vast majority of significant life decisions I've ever made.

But the cruel irony is that, even though I eventually managed to become a lawyer, my student loan payments and high living standards have rendered me just as broke as my dad was growing up. In some ways, more so. He was at least able to afford a down payment on the shitty little ranch I grew up in. Maybe I should've figured out how to be happy with a plate of ziti after all.

But I still can't resist splurging on lobster every chance I get.

Which would explain why I just purchased two large platters

of ten rolls each, despite the fact that there are only five of us eating lunch today. This kind of excess is simply what the Mystic house calls for. And participating in it right now almost makes me feel like I've finally fulfilled my dream of joining the Coopers' ranks—at least if I don't think about the forthcoming credit card bill.

I jump into my car and head back to the house with the provisions. Kate calls me again, but I send her to voicemail. In a way, I'm glad our call ended so acrimoniously earlier. I clearly conceded a bit too much last night. Maybe now that I've drawn a line, she'll back off for a while.

The guys are playing cornhole in the front yard as I pull up. The first thing I see is Bucky—biceps bursting from shirt sleeves—winding up and tossing a bean bag across the lawn. He sinks a three-pointer.

Back injury, my ass.

I give Kate's voicemail a listen before stepping out of my vehicle.

"*Why did you hang up on me like that? We need to be on each other's sides here, Dom.*"

Her voice reeks of desperation. "*You* need to be on my *side.*"

She pauses, takes a breath. "*I didn't want to say anything, but you should know...*"

She pauses again, takes another breath, as if the thing she plans to say next is combustible and she's having second thoughts about lighting the match.

But then she does. "*I'm the reason Patrick made you best man. He wanted to pick Bucky, but I told him it would be so wrong to do that to you, especially when I knew you were gonna make him your best man after you and Ted got engaged...*"

Her voice shakes. "*I'm sorry.*" It's clear she already regrets stooping so low—but the damage is done. "*I'm just trying to say that, if it comes down to picking sides, I have always been on yours. So I hope you would do the same for me.*"

9

So. First Ted reveals that he didn't want to propose to me—but did; and now I learn that Patrick didn't want to make me his best man—but did. All the men in my life, just throwing me bones out of pity. I must be a special strain of pathetic.

But I'm not going to let this unravel me.

Maybe Kate is lying about Patrick—tugging at my insecurity until it finally snaps and gives way to a full, unforgiving report on his behavior this weekend. But why go to the extreme of fabricating such a specific best man backstory? That's a wholly unnecessary level of manipulation, especially for someone who has no real reason not to trust her fiancé in the first place. Unless there's some kind of drama going on between them that neither has told me about. I guess that would explain why Patrick is equally as paranoid about me talking to Kate as she is about him misbehaving.

You know what? These bitches need couple's counseling. I shouldn't have to be thinking about any of this. I should just be enjoying my lobster roll and Narragansett.

Which I'm going to do.

Starting now.

"Good call on lunch," Wilson says. He and I are sitting together at the outdoor stone bar in the backyard. The other guys are eating their lunch inside, presumably while watching the first round of the golf tournament. "That little shack makes the best lobstah rolls I've ever had. And you know the wife and I visit her family in Maine all the time. The rolls I've had up there don't compare. Weird, huh?"

"How is Melanie?" I ask. "I haven't seen her since the Super Bowl party last year."

"She's fine." Wilson takes a swig of beer. "She still loves *you*. Can't wait for the bachelorette party. I think she's more excited to see you than she is to see Kate."

I flinch at the implied compliment. "I'm sure that's not true."

He shrugs and our conversation falls into an easy silence. It occurs to me that if it weren't for my friendship with Patrick, I'd probably never find myself sitting outside eating lunch with someone like Wilson. But I'm enjoying it. There's something so straightforward about interacting with men like him. I'm still a little on guard after our last conversation, still aware that I'm clearly adjusting to his energy more than I am expressing any of my own, but his energy is so easy that I don't mind. It must be so uncomplicated inside his head. I'm jealous.

"So what's the deal with Bucky?" I ask him. "Is he okay?"

Wilson wipes his mouth after throwing back a swig of shandy. "The guy's a beast. He's probably in so much pain right now, but you would never know it. He's got that mental toughness."

Or he's just not actually in pain.

"He was asking about you earlier," Wilson says.

"Me?"

He nods.

"Bucky was asking about me?"

He nods again.

"Why? What'd he say?"

He shrugs. "He thought you were acting weird around him."

Alright. Scratch what I just said about Wilson being uncomplicated and easy to talk to. This conversation suddenly feels like a trap. Why would Bucky have said anything about our (extremely brief) interaction earlier?

"How was I acting weird?" I ask.

"He didn't say."

Something about his tone gives me the distinct feeling that I'm the butt of an inside joke I know nothing about.

"I barely even saw him!" I snap. "And I had to take a piss. What? Was he upset I didn't immediately greet him with unbridled praise for how great his golf swing is? I figured you guys gave him enough of that already."

Wilson bursts into spontaneous laughter. "I don't think he meant all that much by it. But damn, bro. Tell me how ya really feel."

"You suck," I say in as light a tone as possible.

He just smiles and then yawns. "Time for a nap. Gonna need all the sleep I can get if I wanna rally later."

My shoulders tense up at the reminder.

But then my phone buzzes in my pocket, which makes me think back to Kate's voicemail. And you know what? Fuck it. I gave her every assurance last night—but it still wasn't enough for her to back off today. She's descended into a level of emotional manipulation I had no idea she was even capable of. At this point I hope something *does* happen tonight so I can be the clearly better person by not using it against her like she's using Patrick's best man decision against me.

So it's settled. I'm gonna take Patrick's advice and just go with the flow—screw his perfect marriage.

I lost *my* perfect marriage; why should Patrick and Kate get to keep theirs? Tonight I will summon my inner bro. I will not only encourage the debauchery—I will participate in it.

"I'm gonna take a nap, too." I get up from my seat and give Wilson a fist bump. "I can't wait to see what you've got up your sleeve."

10

~

The first thing I see is the gun.

An actual gun! Just tucked into a holster in his belt, the way you see on the belts of cops—except this guy is most definitely not a cop. His back is ramrod-straight, and his expression is icy-stern. He must be…a bodyguard? A pimp? Oh my God. Forget literally everything I said earlier about summoning my inner bro and being a willing participant in tonight's debauchery. This was a mistake.

My itinerary has gone up in flames, and it's only the first official night. We're supposed to be playing a five-person game of Texas Hold'em right now, and instead there is a stern man—*a stern man with a gun*—standing in the foyer of the Mystic house.

Everything escalated so quickly after I woke up from my nap.

I came downstairs—groggy, because I took half a Tylenol PM in order to *actually* get my brain to shut up enough for a nap—and the house was empty. It was seven o'clock. I looked outside and saw the guys sloppily throwing bags at the cornhole boards, which clearly indicated they'd been drinking for hours and were probably already hammered.

So I went outside and took three massive gulps from a bottle of Skrewball peanut butter whiskey left out on the bar. I wasn't kidding when I decided to get royally blotto tonight. But now—three hours, eight light beers, nine cornhole games, four shots, and one *armed security detail* later—I am having serious regrets.

"Where are the girls?" Wilson asks the gun-toting, mustachioed mystery man. Greeny is standing behind him like he's ready for a rumble. Me? I'm leaning against a nearby oak console table, trying to will myself into invisibility.

"Girls are in the car," the man replies. He looks about forty and kinda like my dad twenty years ago—tall, sturdy, hairy. Except my dad never carried around a firearm whilst making stripper deliveries. "Pay first, play later."

I quietly tiptoe out of the foyer and then run out into the backyard to find Patrick and Bucky shooting the shit in the Adirondack chairs on the beach. I'm just drunk and terrified enough to not care about coming off as a square or a spy or whatever else they'll probably think I am right now. "You guys!" I say through heavy breaths. "We have a problem."

They both stand up and face me.

"What happened?" Patrick asks. "Is everyone okay?"

"Everyone's fine—for now. But the guys ordered strippers and now there's, like, a *man* in the foyer. And he has a gun! Strippers aren't supposed to have armed security with them, are they? I sincerely doubt he has a license for that weapon! This all seems very precarious."

Patrick shakes his head in disapproval. "Jesus Christ. I knew they'd do this, but I thought they were at least smart enough to go through respectable channels. They probably found these girls on Craigslist or something."

"Craigslist?" I ask. "But this is the Mystic house."

"Y'all—I really shouldn't be here for this," Bucky says in his deep Southern lilt. His face looks ruggedly handsome in the glow of the moon, which is just annoying. "Those girls might recognize me and sneak pictures."

"Dude, you're not Justin Timberlake," Patrick cracks. "I doubt they'd—"

"Still, man." Bucky's clearly not amused. "I got enough bad press right now with my injury and all that. And Trista'll be madder than a hornet in a Coke can if she finds out about this."

"The bodyguard wouldn't let the girls inside before we paid," I tell them. "But what if it's all a con? What if there aren't any strippers at all and he just takes the money and runs? What if he shoots us all dead?!"

Right as I contemplate the headline of GOLF STAR BUCKY GRAHAM AND FOUR OTHER RANDOM ASSHOLES SHOT DEAD BY CON ARTIST POSING AS STRIPPER BODYGUARD, a blast of goofy cheers erupts from up the hill at the outdoor bar.

The patio lighting illuminates the silhouettes of Wilson and Greeny popping a bottle of Moët with two scantily clad women—one in a tiny dark bandage dress, the other in what appears to be booty shorts and a revealing low-cut shirt straight out of an Instagram ad for Fashion Nova. The man—let's call him Costner, an ode to Kevin Costner's titular role in the iconic 1992 Whitney Houston vehicle *The Bodyguard*—stands to the side, leering.

Bucky turns his head toward the water. "Shit on a buttered biscuit! We can't let them see me."

Patrick's face is suddenly possessed by a stupid grin. Now that there's evidence of actual women, his vibe seems to have flipped from just-as-concerned-as-me to straight-up giddy. This puzzles me for a moment before I realize that he's thinking with his dick. I guess if there were two hot dudes about to do a striptease, I'd also be mindlessly excited.

"Here's what we're gonna do," Patrick says. "I'll go up there, quickly accept my lap dances, and send them off. You guys can wait it out in the lighthouse. I'll come back down when they're gone."

"Both of us?" I ask.

I'm not sure what's more frightening: the thought of getting breasts shoved in my face while an armed chaperone looks on, or the thought of being trapped in a small, dark space with Bucky Graham for an hour.

Hmm.

Turns out it's the latter. At least the private lap dance would be a life experience, you know? Something to check off the bucket list. "Maybe I should go up there, too."

"But Bucky—" Patrick starts.

"I'll be fine," Bucky insists. "I can just scroll through my ph—oh. Dangit. I left my phone in the house."

"Dom will go inside and bring it back down for you." Patrick is clearly eager to get off the beach and go up to Breastville. And also to get rid of me. "Won't you, Dom?"

11

Ladies! Meet the groom, Patrick." Wilson has one woman on each arm as Patrick and I approach the bar. "And his gay best man...Diva Dom."

Greeny's eyes narrow at us. "Where's Bu—"

"Zz," I finish. Look at me! Thinking on my toes. "*Buzz* had to go." I tilt my head and scrunch my face to indicate that they need to follow me on this journey. "He's got an early day tomorrow."

"Is Dom wasted?" Wilson asks everyone and no one. "What is he talking about?"

"Don't worry about Buzz," Patrick says. He touches the hand of the woman in the bandage dress, which she takes as a cue to wrap herself around his torso. "What's your name, gorgeous?"

Why is he doing this? And why do I get the sense that he's definitely done it before?

"Lexus," she answers through a giggle. "You know, like the car."

I have to hand it to her; she's hot. Her eye makeup is flawless—even Kate would approve—and she's got this bouncy red hair that goes halfway down her back, like Ariel from *The Little Mermaid*.

"You like?" Wilson asks Patrick. "We splurged on the diamond package for you, bro."

"And we specifically requested no blondes," Greeny adds.

"You get enough of that at home. Thought we'd give you a taste of something different on your last weekend of freedom."

A *taste*? There will be no tasting! There will be innocent lap dances only. Surely Costner will see to that. Why else would he be here?

"I'm Kitty," the other woman says. And then before I know it, Kitty slinks her arms around *my* waist. She smells like Victoria's Secret Dream Angel perfume—a scent I'll always remember because it was a favorite of my high school girlfriend—and baby powder. "Are you actually gay? Or are your friends just giving you shit?"

For some reason this question makes my throat go dry.

"Pretty much." I say it through an awkward cough, aware that my answer is vague enough to be interpreted as either confirmation that I am gay *or* confirmation that they're just giving me shit. I have a dark instinct to pass as straight right now, because what if this Costner guy is homophobic, you know?

"He's gayer than a box of jockstraps," Wilson says, instantly bursting my bubble. Here's hoping I don't get hate-crimed. "And proud. Right, Dom?"

Patrick bursts into laughter at this.

"I love it," Kitty says. And then grabs my ass. "You and I are going to have so much fun together."

Something tells me that Kitty and I would be great friends in real life. I like her spunk! If Lexus is an Ariel, Kitty is a total Belle. And *Beauty and the Beast* was my favorite Disney movie growing up, so. (Sidenote: Did those Disney animators realize at the time that they were establishing the beauty standards for an entire generation of sex workers and their clientele? I wonder.)

"We should go inside," Patrick suggests. He shoots me a look and then subtly gestures toward the lighthouse shed. Oh! Right. Bucky's phone. "We all need fresh drinks, don't we?"

"The girls are gonna require a private room to freshen up in," Costner says. His voice is Darth Vader-ish. Terrifying. "Then you've got 'em for two hours."

That...sounds like a long time. These women probably only have like five items of clothing to remove between the two of them; how long can you bounce around naked before everything starts to feel a bit redundant?

Patrick sends the dancers into his first floor master suite. Darth Costner stands guard outside the door as the rest of us regroup in the kitchen. Greeny pops open the fridge and randomly takes out a leftover lobster roll. I'm tempted to do the same, but I'm afraid I might just puke it back up. Every organ in my body continues to churn with dread about the precariousness of this situation.

"You didn't leave anything valuable in your room, did you?" I whisper to Patrick. "They could be robbing us right now."

"They already have, bro." Wilson throws us all beers. "You don't wanna know what we paid for this extravagance."

"Worth it, though." Greeny grimaces at me. "You'll see."

"Dom's not staying for the show," Patrick says—a little too quickly, like he's eagerly awaiting my exit. "He's gotta bring Bucky his phone."

"Yo! I forgot Graham Cracker was even here," Wilson says. "Where is he?"

"Hiding out in the shed by the beach," I say. "Doesn't wanna risk bad press. In case the girls recognize him."

Greeny's face falls. "I didn't even think of that. Now I feel kinda bad."

"It's fine," Patrick says. "Bucky probably gets enough groupie ass on tour. He's not missing anything."

"Groupie ass? But what about Trista?" I ask. "She seems so nice."

Wilson shoots Patrick a look. "Okay, yeah. Diva Dom is definitely gonna have to stay locked up in the shed for this."

As worried as I am about all the things that could go wrong, I still don't want to leave. What the hell would I even do in the shed with Bucky?

Plus I'd love to hang out with Kitty and Lexus some more. After a day of being surrounded by dudes, the feminine energy is refreshing. I don't know if it's because of the cliché that being a gay man means having an affinity for hyperfeminine divas, but something inside of me is just so drawn to them. They're feisty, hot, and totally in control of their sexuality. It's all very Christina Aguilera circa her infamous "Dirrty" era—which I suppose makes perfect sense, given that the song "Dirrty" literally appeared on an album called *Stripped*.

"I'm staying!" I blurt.

"Nah." Patrick grabs my shoulders in that way of his. "I don't think you can handle it."

"It might be kinda funny," Greeny offers. "I vote that Dom stays."

"Easy for you to say," Wilson quips. "You don't have a wife to worry about."

"Dude," I huff. "I already promised Patrick I wouldn't say anything."

"Fine, man." Patrick shrugs. Greeny and Wilson follow suit. "Whatever you wanna do. But you still gotta bring Bucky his phone."

Adorable that Patrick is so concerned about Bucky's comfort. I can't help but wonder if he'd do the same for me if I were the one stranded out there.

"There we go!" Greeny says. "Let's do a round of shots."

He lines up four little glasses and fills each with two ounces of eighteen-year-aged Jameson. It's supposed to be smoother than normal whiskey, but it still burns going down. I chase it with the rest of my beer and then grab a new one from the fridge.

I head over to the living room to retrieve Bucky's phone, but I'm interrupted by Darth Costner in the hallway.

"One minute." He gestures around at the living room. "The girls will perform right here."

And then I hear the master suite door swing open down the hall, followed by the sound of Lexus and Kitty hooting and hollering.

"Yoo hoo!" one of them yells. It's unclear which. "We're gonna need the groom and the best man. Pronto!"

Well, damn. Looks like Bucky will just have to deal with being offline.

12

~

I've never seen this living room in anything less than pristine condition. I remember one time in middle school, I accidentally let my gum fall out of my mouth, and it somehow got stuck on one of the linen love seats. Mrs. Cooper was very nice about it, but she had the entire thing reupholstered literally the next day. Just like that. She said she'd been meaning to anyway, but still. I knew it was because she just couldn't stand to think there was a single blemish within the summer oasis she'd spent so much time perfecting.

Which is why this scenario feels so wrong.

If Mrs. Cooper freaked out over a gum stain, imagine how she'd feel about the fact that Lexus and Kitty scratched her hardwood floors dragging two of her precious taupe Crate & Barrel accent chairs into the middle of the room for back-to-back lap dances. Which Patrick and I are currently receiving, soundtracked by the pulsing bass of "Pour It Up" by Rihanna. It's wrong! Wrong, wrong, wrong, wrong, wrong.

But at least the piano is safe in the other room.

And I will say I'm quite glad I got Kitty (a.k.a. Belle), whose knees are currently pressed into my hips as she straddles me. She's the fun one! Lexus has been a bit quieter and more subdued since she came back from the bedroom.

"I love your energy," I tell Kitty as she removes her top and throws it to the side. It hits Wilson in the face, and he cheers. "Are you from Mystic?"

"My energy? Don't think I've ever heard that one before." She laughs and pours her long brown hair all over my face. It smells amazing, like lavender and tea tree oil. "You're adorable."

She throws her head back and unclasps her bra.

This is escalating quickly.

I have no idea what to do. I wish I could actually see Patrick right now so I could follow his lead, like I've always done in scenarios that call for hypermasculinity over the years. But his back is to mine.

I tune my ears behind me and detect that he and Lexus are in a groove. She keeps saying things like "you like that?" and he keeps saying "yeah, baby." But there's no way I could say something like "yeah, baby" with a straight face, so instead I just take a swig of my Coors Light and cheer as Kitty caresses herself.

Of course, my cheer is drowned out by those of the two groomsmen on the sidelines. Did I mention they've been throwing dollar bills at us this whole time? Weird because I thought they'd already paid.

"This lucky prick doesn't appreciate your jugs!" Wilson yells at Kitty. "Hey Dom, we're trading spots."

"Not so fast," Kitty protests. "He's gotta get the official best man treatment." She thrusts herself into my face until my nose is fully swallowed by cleavage. There's that Dream Angel baby powder scent again. I gotta say: I never realized lap dances had such an element of aromatherapy to them. "It's tradition."

Kitty jumps off of me and drops her booty shorts to the ground, revealing a lacy black thong. She skips over to Wilson for a hot second and twerks on him—he shoves a single into her G-string—before heading back over to me.

After a few slinky dance moves, she positions herself directly in front of me so we're basically ass-to-face. This makes things feel *very* porn-y—and I suddenly feel the hot breath of Wilson and Greeny on my neck, gawking.

Greeny grabs my arm. "This right here is the best view ever. You have no idea."

Kitty flips her head forward and looks at me with lascivious eyes. She gets up and starts straddling me again, then grabs my beer out of my hand and gives it to one of the guys. Some of the beer spills out onto Mrs. Cooper's new Restoration Hardware hand-sheared area rug in the process, but I can barely even clock the damage before Kitty takes both my hands and guides them all over her body.

"Come on," she says. "Squeeze!"

My chest tightens as I think about Darth Costner looking on from the fireplace in the corner. What if touching isn't allowed and he shoots me? Oh my God! But then again, she is the one forcing me to do it. So this must be acceptable.

I do as instructed, taking a chunk of her silky flesh in my grip. She giggles in delight. "That's more like it!"

Kitty does a few more moves and buries my face in her breasts again. While my hands remain in the general vicinity of her butt, hers are wandering all over me. I feel…violated? Especially since she's now under my shirt and I have to actively suck in my stomach, which is making it difficult to breathe.

Her left hand slowly travels south until it reaches my—oh. Okay then. So that's a thing that's happening. A stripper's hand is currently wrapped around my penis, which happens to be floppier than the movie *Gigli* starring Jennifer Lopez and Ben Affleck. (Remember *Gigli*?)

"Wow." Kitty sounds disappointed. "You really *are* gay."

Instead of accepting this statement as fact, though, she gives a last-ditch effort and somehow manages to stand on the chair—balancing herself like a gymnast directly over my face. And can I just say? Props to whoever does her waxing. Her bikini line is smoother than a Kenny G sax interlude.

At this point my arms are back to flailing on either side of me. I'm afraid to move my head even a millimeter forward—lest I accidentally make facial contact with her vagina, which, even though she just touched my limp fettucine, feels like it would really be crossing the line. So instead I recline as far back as possible, and then—

Clack! I just hit the back of my head against the back of Patrick's head, whom I forgot was behind me this entire time. The timing is quite poetic, as the music stops pretty much at that exact moment. Which really kills all the momentum that's been building up in here like a pressure cooker.

"Ouch, man. That hurt." Patrick turns to me and laughs as Lexus and Kitty jump off of us and go to fix the music. "You enjoying this? It's awesome, right?"

"It's…" I'm not sure if I'm glad I chose to stay here or if I should've just powered through the awkwardness with Bucky and avoided this hetero trauma altogether. "It's an experience, that's for sure."

"These chicks are wild," Greeny says from the couch across from us. He has a very visible bulge in his khaki shorts. Oh my God. *Don't look.* "Dom. You're hating this, aren't you?"

Pretty much. "Not at all."

Wilson laughs. "All I know is that when they get back in here, it's *our* turn."

The music starts back up again. Now it's "Partition" by Beyoncé, which makes me think about all the times I've run to this song at the gym.

The girls reenter from the hallway, this time wearing nothing but a few mounds of strategically placed whipped cream.

"We're next!" Wilson exclaims, gesturing between himself and Greeny. "They've had enough."

"We'll get to you," Kitty says. "But first we have one last ritual for the groom and best man."

"Can I just say that I loved Ali Larter in *Varsity Blues*," I offer in an effort to make this entire scenario feel a little more casual. "I really appreciate the homage you're paying her with these whipped cream bikinis."

The girls laugh. And then they move the chairs off the rug—*drag, drag, dragging* their sharp legs onto the hardwood—and lie down side-by-side in the center.

"You guys ready to race?" Kitty asks. "The first to lick one of us completely clean, wins."

I gulp. There are two naked bodies on Mrs. Cooper's beloved Restoration Hardware rug right now. With its sophisticated blend of hand-spun silk and wool and intricate custom weave pattern. Some people probably wouldn't look twice at it, but I've flip-flopped between the worlds of rich and poor enough in my life to recognize high end décor when I see it. Judging from the texture and material, this one probably cost the Coopers a clean ten grand. And Kitty and Lexus are just *laying* their bare asses on it.

"Wait." I refocus my attention on Kitty after processing her last statement. "What do you mean when you say *licked clean*? Like...with our mouths?"

The guys all boo me.

"Oh, baby." Kitty looks up at me and then at everyone else in the room. "You really are so precious. Yes, with your mouths! Now hurry up."

A series of panicked thoughts races through my head.

Is Patrick really going to do this? What about Kate? Is this safe? Can I put a condom on my tongue?

But most of all:

I need to move fast so that no whipped cream drips onto the rug.

Patrick shakes his head and lets out a sloppy laugh. His ears are bright red, a clear sign that he's completely smashed. We both get down on our knees on the rug—him in front of Lexus, me in front of Kitty.

Greeny gives a quick *ready, set, go.*

I think back to that old gum stain on Mrs. Cooper's couch, which fuels me with the motivation to go to *town*—lapping up the whipped cream faster than a ravenous puppy. The integrity of the rug depends on it. I catch an errant drip that's steadily making its way down Kitty's rib cage—close call—and continue until there's nothing left.

"Done!" I shout through a mouthful of dairy. Meanwhile, Patrick is barely even halfway through with Lexus. "I win!"

Kitty has the smile of a proud parent as she confirms my victory. "I clearly underestimated you."

I stand up and take a wobbly bow.

"Time for a smoke break!" Kitty tells the group.

"What about us?" Wilson barks with his hands out. He sounds serious, like he's getting impatient to receive what he's paid for. "What the hell?"

"Relax," Kitty says. "We'll be back in fifteen"—she tugs at his Vineyard Vines polo—"and then it's *all* about you."

The girls (plus Costner) disappear into the bedroom, at which point my head stops spinning for just long enough to assess the state of the living room. It's not great. While the rug has proven itself to be surprisingly resilient, the overall scene is pure chaos. Somehow one of the accent chairs has been flipped over. The end tables and credenzas are all littered with empty beer bottles. And there's a Rorschach splattering of mysterious moisture on the hickory hardwood floor, just begging to be mopped.

"How you feeling, buddy?" Patrick asks before I can verbalize my desire to send the girls home immediately so I can start the cleanup process before bed. It's almost midnight, after all.

"Fine," I tell him. "Still processing everything that just happened—"

"Don't process," he slurs. "Just forget."

This advice reminds me of the groomsman we left stranded without a phone.

"Speaking of forgetting things." I gesture outside toward the beach. "Bucky."

Patrick's face tightens—like I've just mildly sobered him up with the reminder. "Oh, yeah. We gotta go get him."

"Don't worry about it," I offer. Looking at the disarrayed state of the living room has me realizing that I've already hit my partying threshold for the night. "I'll go check on him."

"Catch." Wilson eagerly tosses me Bucky's phone. "We'll text ya when the girls leave."

I can tell he's been waiting all night for this moment.

And you know what? Same.

13

The second I step outside, I'm surrounded by a cloud of smoke. Kitty's taking her cig break on the wraparound front porch while Costner sits off to the side, lost in his phone. Damnit. The whole reason I went out the front was to avoid the possibility that they were taking their break out back.

"Sorry to interrupt," I whisper. "I'll just—"

"Don't be silly!" Kitty smiles at me. She's clothed again: booty shorts and a little black bra. "Stay. Have a smoke."

"I'm good." I shift my gaze to Darth and shoot her a look, like, *Is this even allowed or will I get murdered for speaking to you off the clock?* "Thanks."

"Don't worry about Jimbo," Kitty says, uncovering the mystery of his actual name. "He's just here to protect us from potential creeps. Obviously that's not an issue with this crew. You guys are very tame compared to some of our other clientele."

"Well, you know," I start, totally unsure how to respond, "we're from Connecticut."

Kitty furrows her expertly tweezed brow at me and chuckles. "Right."

"Anyway," I continue, "where's your friend?"

"Lexus? Probably inside taking a boiling hot shower before

Act Two." She rolls her eyes. "I don't know why that girl bothers coming out on these jobs. She hates being naked. But I guess I can't blame a bitch for needing the cash."

"That's so sad." I lean against the white railing and think about how unfortunate it is that not only did Patrick betray Kate a few moments ago, but he did so by licking the breasts of someone who didn't even enjoy it. "What about you?"

"I love what I do," Kitty says. "So many people give me shit for it, but I couldn't care less. I love being naked, and I love dancing on guys. The money is just the icing on the cake." She blows out a little more smoke. "But you know. It's not for everyone."

A wave of envy washes over me. I'm a lawyer, and I *hate* what I do. I barely even recognize myself when I'm in the office— everything from the way I dress, to the way I talk, to the way I write my emails is an elaborate performance of fake professionalism. Just thinking about my typical weekday routine makes me want to vomit.

When did I decide that was an acceptable price to pay in exchange for society's approval? At least Kitty is enjoying herself while she makes her money.

"You really don't care if people judge you?" I ask.

"Hell no," she says. "Why should I lose sleep over other people projecting their stupid insecurities on me? I can't imagine being some cookie-cutter bitch with a normal job and a boring-ass Stepford husband. *No, thank you.*"

"Fair enough." I think about how being a cookie-cutter bitch with a normal job and a boring-ass Stepford husband is literally all I've ever wanted in life. "I gotta say, I wish I had your confidence."

She looks at me like I'm a sick dog and then smiles. "You sure had a lot of confidence during that whipped cream challenge. I almost thought you were into me for a second there."

My cheeks burn with embarrassment. "I was worried about getting whipped cream on the rug. It's Restoration Hardware, you know."

"Oh my God, shut up." She blows a puff of smoke out the side of her mouth and laughs as if I just told a joke. "You are truly something else. I'm so glad I took this job tonight."

"You know what? I'm glad you took it, too. Granted—I wish they didn't place an order for strippers in the first place." The honesty surprises even myself. I thought I had been doing a good job at embracing the debauchery, but clearly that's not the case. "Since I'm good friends with the bride, too, and I'm gonna be at *her* bachelorette party next month. So now I have this huge secret on my shoulders—"

"Give me a break," she says. "All your friend did was lick some whipped cream off Lexus's tits! It's not like he engaged in our *other* services." She takes another drag and puts her cigarette out in one of Mrs. Cooper's nearby begonia planters, which I make a mental note to clean up in the morning. "Although your friends did prepay for them, so…"

Panic floods my chest. "Are you serious?"

"Aww." She gives me that look again. "You are cute as a button."

"Patrick would never do that," I say—struggling to believe myself. "Not to Kate."

"That's what they all say, baby." She pats me on the ass before heading back toward the front door. "Word of advice? What *Kate* doesn't know won't hurt her."

14

‿

My head spins as I stumble down the hill toward the light-house shed. I should have just stayed down here with Bucky the whole night. A couple hours of awkward conversation would have been nothing compared to the bomb Kitty just dropped.

This isn't fair.

It's not fair that *Patrick's* infidelity is going to be *my* problem. It's not fair that Kate is going to get pissed at *me* if she finds out, as if somehow I—or anyone but Patrick himself—could be responsible for the choices that *he* makes.

And it's especially not fair that somehow *I'm* the one who got dumped by my fiancé this summer. I've never lied to Ted about anything! And I sure as hell never licked dairy off another guy's crotch while we were together. Meanwhile, Patrick has no qualms about doing either of those things to Kate—and God knows what else—and he's the one who gets to end up with the picture-perfect American marriage.

But then again, why wouldn't he? He's entitled to it. Just like he's always been entitled to everything else I've ever wanted.

It's so typical. I work my ass off to get the things I want—holding onto them as tightly as I can—and still somehow lose them. And then Patrick is just handed those very same things—never acknowledging how lucky he is, barely applying his grip to them—and never has to worry about them slipping away.

My rage hits a boiling point by the time I approach the light-house door.

"…Hello?" I ask as I step inside.

But it's empty.

The scent of old pine emanates from the walls. It would be pitch-black in here if not for a single beam of moonlight slic-ing through from the narrow ceiling windows above my head. I reach around to the light switch and flick it on, which illumi-nates the top of the structure (mimicking an actual lighthouse) along with a few built-in night-lights dotted around the wooden plank walls.

This was always more of a playhouse for Patrick and me than an actual shed, but I'm surprised the Coopers haven't loaded it up with random crap in the decades since we've grown up. Our old L.L.Bean sleeping bags are still tucked into a nook in the corner, where they've been stored since we were teenagers.

The sight of them floods me with that one memory from tenth grade. The last time Patrick and I had one of our sleepovers out here. When—no.

I'm not gonna think about—actually? Fuck it. Let's go there. If I'm gonna slip into a drunken Patrick-hate spiral tonight, I might as well make it count.

I've never talked to anyone about that night. Not even Patrick, not even as it was happening. And yet every detail has been per-manently etched into my mind; I thought about it obsessively in the weeks that followed, replaying every second over and over on a loop until I had it memorized.

It was our first Mystic weekend of the year. School hadn't even let out yet. We were eager to kick off the summer—both of us had learner's permits and were giddy about the prospect of reinventing ourselves as licensed drivers in the coming months.

We spent Saturday taking turns driving Mr. Cooper's car—a brand new Beamer—around the quiet streets of Mystic, right along the river. At first I was terrified of veering into the guardrail and driving us all into the water, but Patrick and his dad had this way of keeping the mood calm. It was nothing like the sessions I had driving around with my dad, who barked frantic orders at me to brake, signal, stop, turn, slow down, speed up—as if I was incapable of making even the most basic judgment call on my own.

Mrs. Cooper had lobster rolls waiting for us when we got home for dinner that evening—she knew I how much I loved them—and by nine o'clock Patrick and I were camped out in the shed for the night.

By this time in our friendship, I was already three years into my crush on him. Or at least I thought that's what it was at the time. In retrospect, it was more curiosity than anything else. When puberty hit in sixth grade and I realized I liked guys, I just gravitated toward Patrick as a matter of default. We knew each other so well, and we already shared everything together—so why not our bodies? You know how hormones are. And Patrick was *right there*—the only boy with whom I was close enough to even think about initiating something with.

Plus he's always been so damn handsome.

But of course, middle school came and went without my making a move. Patrick was quite obviously straight. We talked about sex and masturbation pretty much all the time, but he always led the discussions, and they always revolved around girls. I played along as best I could, begrudgingly accepting the fact that I was alone in my secret homosexuality.

Sometimes I wondered if he suspected anything of me. We

never got naked in front of each other, even when sharing a bed-room and changing during beach days. I worried if it was because he knew I was in fact *dying* to see him naked, so I always went out of my way to feign disgust at even the thought of male nudity. And it was tragically easy to do. I mean, this was during a period of time when Eminem was the biggest thing in music and "faggot" was the go-to insult among boys of our age group. "No homo" was a phrase we uttered—without irony—on a daily basis.

You can imagine how shocked I was, then, on that tenth-grade night when Patrick climbed out of his sleeping bag, tapped me on the shoulder, and quietly asked if I wanted to get naked and fool around.

Just like that! This question that had been torturing me for years—this desire to be sexual with him that I could never bring myself to acknowledge out loud—rolled off his tongue as casually as if he were suggesting waffles for breakfast.

I cleared my throat and said, *yeah, sure, let's do it,* instinctively trying to match his nonchalance, despite the fact that my heart was pounding with excitement.

And so we did it.

My first sexual experience, and it was with the Golden Boy of our high school. He was a track star by then. His girlfriend Mandy was a popular cheerleader. But that night, he was mine.

After we both finished up, he just said, "Huh."

Followed by, "Night, bud."

It wasn't exactly the revelatory discussion of our shared sex-uality that I was hoping we'd have, but I figured he was just tired from a long day.

As he passed out in the sleeping bag beside me, my mind raced with plans for our future. Not only would we come back to school junior year as licensed drivers—we'd come back as openly gay guys. Coming out of the closet had never even crossed my mind at that point, but now I felt like maybe I wasn't such an abomination after all. *If Patrick's gay, then it must be okay.* And I figured we'd have to come out in order to become boyfriends. Something about the closeness of what we'd just done made me yearn for a label beyond the basic, run-of-the-mill "best friend."

Jesus. Just thinking about how delusional I was that night makes me want to crawl into a sewer and live out the rest of my days in filthy seclusion à la Danny DeVito's hideous Penguin character in *Batman Returns*.

Because—predictably—Patrick and I woke up the next morning, and nothing about our friendship had changed. Over cereal, he talked about how much he loved doing "everything but" with Mandy and couldn't wait until he had a car of his own so they could go all the way in the back seat. I couldn't decide if he was trying to act like the previous night had never happened at all, or if he was trying to act like we had done it a million times and it was therefore not even worth mentioning.

Every time we hung out in the months that followed, I eagerly anticipated a repeat episode. But it never happened. He never made another move. He didn't even seem like it had crossed his mind. And since I always took my cues from him, our friendship just carried on as if there was zero sexual tension or suppressed desire to speak of. I buried it all deep inside me. The only thing that changed was that I couldn't even bear to look at a lighthouse—not even on a bag of Cape Cod potato chips—without my stomach turning.

We never had a sleepover out there again.

Over the years, I've come to accept that night for what it was. An experimental adolescent experience in which Patrick was either curious or horny or both, and just gave it a whirl before realizing it wasn't for him. I know he's not gay—his heterosexuality isn't a question at this point—and I'm glad I never actually expressed any of the desires that invaded my mind afterward. But still. It would've been nice for him to at least acknowledge it. Even if he had just said, "Listen, you're not a defective freak for having enjoyed that."

And shit. Now I'm crying.

I squeeze my eyes shut and wipe the tears with my wrist. And then I pick up one of the sleeping bags, brush fifteen years of dust off its polyester shell, and start to unfurl it. I might as well try to get somewhat comfortable while I descend into a haze of repressed anger. Maybe I'll even get lucky and fall asleep.

I collapse onto the lumpy relic and close my eyes, but they're immediately jolted back open by the sound of footsteps approaching right outside.

15
~

Bucky lets himself in.

"You alright?" he asks. "You look like you just got back from a funeral or somethin'…"

"Oh." I stand up and force an awkward laugh. "Hey." I wipe my eyes—hard, so as to shock myself into numbness—and throw him his phone. "I'm fine. Sorry. I was looking for you. Thought you might've left."

"Without this?" He waves the phone in his hand. "Nah. I was just outside fiddlin' around on my swing." He chuckles to himself. "In the dark. By the water. Without any balls."

I had barely even registered the golf club in his hand. He's always holding one on TV and in photo shoots (even whilst naked in the Body Issue); it kind of just seems like a natural extension of his arm at this point.

"I was goin' stir crazy in here." He places the club against the wall and lets out a deep sigh that sounds like it belongs to the leading man of a Hallmark rom-com set in small-town Alabama. "Too much quiet time makes me jumpier than a cockroach in a fryin' pan."

I can't help but laugh at his choice of words. I'd almost forgotten about his tendency to speak exclusively in weird Southern idioms. "I apologize. I was gonna bring your phone down sooner, but things went off the rails up at the house."

"I don't wanna know," he says. "Do I?"

"It's probably for the best that you sat out."

"I reckon that's true." He leans against the wall opposite the one I'm leaning against, directly under a dim ceiling light. I'm afraid to make too much eye contact, so I cast my gaze downward. Bucky's torso looks as chiseled as ever beneath his white athletic polo. "This week has been bad enough for my career. No need to add more fuel to a burnin' fire."

"It sucks you had to drop out of the tournament, but I know Patrick is happy you were able to be here." I'm trying to speak in a tone that conveys a general sense of *I'm definitely not picturing you naked right now* and *of course I've never masturbated to your Body Issue pics.* "How is your back feeling, anyway?"

He tenses up like I've just caught him in a lie—which I suppose I have. Why would he go outside to swing a golf club if he was told by doctors to not do that exact thing?

"Better, thanks." He scratches his neck. "It was more of a precaution than anything. Just to make sure I'm good and ready for the British Open a month out."

"So you're not playing with the guys tomorrow? Patrick booked a last-minute tee time for eleven."

"I didn't know that. But nah. I can't be caught dead showin' my mug on a golf course this weekend."

What a stupid question. "Oh. Right."

"What about you?" he asks. "You play?"

"Not really. I'll probably just hang back here and recuperate."

His lips curl into a half-open smile, revealing a hint of perfect white teeth and a dimple in his left cheek. "So I guess we'd better get used to each other's company then."

"What do you mean?" I ask.

He gives me a puzzled look. "Tomorrow. When everyone's out at the course."

"Ah. Right."

We both go silent for a moment, our voices replaced by the sound of the water. I'm stunned that Bucky just talked about tomorrow as though he's gonna stay at the house and not go off to do his own thing. Why would he choose to stick around?

Then I remember last night, when Patrick said he wanted Bucky and me to get to know each other better ahead of the wedding. Maybe he said the same thing to Bucky. Maybe Bucky agreed to keep me company as a favor to Patrick, and that's why he's being so nice. It would certainly track with the recent trend of *me being a charity case to all the men in my life.*

"I'm sorry about what happened with your fiancé," Bucky says out of nowhere. "Coop told me. I reckon that's why you were cryin' when I came in?"

"Well..." I don't know if it's the alcohol in my system or the effect of Bucky's casual Southern charm—but for a moment I consider telling him the truth. Just full-on confiding in him that I once hooked up with our mutual best friend and it basically gave me a lifelong complex. But then I come to my senses. "Yeah. It's been rough. We were together a long time."

"I've been there, man." He pats my arm. "Well. Except for the whole 'long time' thing."

Right. Bucky had cycled through at least four or five starlets and swimsuit models in the time I was with Ted.

"But I know how hard relationships can be," he continues. "All Trista and I ever do is fight. Pretty dumb on my part, since arguin' with *her* is like a bug arguin' with a chicken. You ain't never gonna win."

"My ex, Ted, would probably say the same about me," I confess. "Even though it would be entirely unwarranted. I let him win far more times than not. He just chose to focus on the times I didn't. He had it made up in his mind that I was difficult, and so that's what I was."

Bucky looks at me like I just accused him of being the problem in his relationship.

"Not that I'm saying you're like that," I quickly clarify.

He smirks. "We're all a little bit like that, though, ain't we?"

I think about this for a moment and nod in agreement.

He steps away from the wall and swipes the other sleeping bag from the corner. "Mind if I get more comfortable? Somethin' tells me they're gonna be a while up there."

Within moments we're lying side by side, staring up at the tiny circular ceiling. The fact that we don't have to look at each other helps make it less uncomfortable than I'm sure it would be if we were sitting across from each other in daylight. Makes the air between us feel more breathable or something. I close my eyes and remember being in this exact position with Patrick all those years ago. It feels like a lifetime—and no time—has passed since then.

"So…" I search for something to fill the quiet. "How's your back?"

Bucky turns toward me for a moment, breaking the no eye-contact rule; his eyes are incredibly blue. "You asked me that already."

My cheeks flush. "Ah. Right."

He cracks the slightest smile and then returns to lying flat beside me. "Ask me a real question." His voice takes on a playful, truth or dare-ish quality—yet another reminder of those old nights with Patrick. "Somethin' good. Personal. Anything."

My cheeks flush even more. "Why would I do that?"

"Because we're trapped together in this little ol' shed and small talk is boring."

I have no idea how to tread here. My entire operating code around guys like Bucky has always revolved *exclusively* around small talk.

"Come on," he continues. "I've been all isolated out on tour all year. Haven't had a deep conversation in months."

This confuses me. "Isolated?"

"Yeah," he says. "Some of the other players on tour are my best buddies, sure. But we don't talk about nothin' but golf."

Is Bucky Graham trying to tell me that he—of all people in the world—gets lonely? The idea that he could suffer from such an embarrassing human emotion goes entirely against his reputation as a carefree sports star who can have anything (and anyone) he wants.

"Do you love her?" I finally ask. Might as well start with the girlfriend. "Trista?"

"Huh." Bucky clicks his tongue. "She looks damn good, I'll tell ya that. And we look good together, which probably means more to her than anything. With her career and her image—I know she just loves the idea of being with a pro athlete."

Damn. This also feels like something Ted might say about how I approached our relationship—more consumed with its presentation than its truth.

"But I'm a big ol' hypocrite," Bucky continues. "Because I just love the idea of being with a model. And then people see us together and we look happy. And we both spend so much time seein' ourselves through other people's eyes—so on some artificial level, we *are* happy."

"But you don't love her?" I ask. At this point I'm invested in the answer—as if whatever he says about Trista will be exactly what Ted would say about me if he were asked the same question.

Bucky pretends he didn't hear me. "Good lord," he says. "You got me over here flappin' my lips like I'm in therapy or something."

"You quite literally asked for it," I crack.

"My turn." He props himself up on his elbows and looks down at me again. The rugged lines of his face are balanced by a softness that I've never seen before. There's no trace of the cockiness he tends to give off on television interviews and in larger groups. "Why are you so...tense?"

"Tense?" I ask. Tensing up. "I'm not tense."

He laughs. "You've got somethin' on your mind. I could tell ever since I ran into you at the pisser earlier. Is it that ex-fiancé of yours?"

I'm tempted to deflect and pivot the conversation back to him and Trista, but then I catch a glimpse of those eyes again. They're open and kind and seem genuinely interested in hearing what I have to say. So maybe I can let my guard down. At least a little.

"It's partially that," I confirm as Bucky plops back down, which helps me relax even more. "But really it's Patrick. I promised Kate I'd keep him in line this weekend, and I'm pretty sure he's cheating on her with a sex worker right now."

Bucky coughs. "You really think Coop is—"

"That's what one of the women said he'd be doing," I explain. "I mean, I hope he wouldn't. Do you think he would do that?"

"I sure don't. But you're the one who's been best friends with him since y'all were knee-high. Why are you asking me?"

"It's complicated with us."

"How so?"

I close my eyes and search for words. "Well. There was that whole three years in college when we didn't talk. After I came out. I honestly thought our friendship was over forever." I pause. "By the time we reconnected in law school, it was like we were two different people."

"I never understood why y'all stopped talkin' like that in the first place," Bucky says. "I know Coop didn't have a problem with you bein' gay."

"He *said* he didn't." I take a moment to sort through my feelings on the matter. "But something changed between us after I came out. Our friendship became less intimate, I guess you could say, because now there was this fundamental difference between us. Almost like a language barrier. And then he joined the frat, I moved in with my boyfriend, and I don't know. Eventually we stopped talking altogether. Which killed me, because that was exactly why I had stayed in the closet so long to begin with. I didn't wanna lose my best friend."

"Dang," Bucky says softly. "You almost sound like you regret comin' out."

"Oh, no. Trust me—I *needed* to come out. I couldn't torture myself any longer than I already had."

"Torture? How's that?"

This is a tough one. How can I explain to someone like Bucky Graham what it's like to be in the closet? The idea of having to keep his true self hidden from others is probably so foreign to him as to be incomprehensible.

But I give it a shot. "You know how some dogs have to wear those big cone-collars so they don't scratch at their itches? I felt like I had one of those around my head all my life. I had the most intense itch ever, but I wasn't allowed to scratch it. Coming out was like finally getting that damn cone off my head."

Bucky considers this a moment. Then he clears his throat and taps my shoulder. "Aren't those cones for makin' sure dogs don't lick their nuts after gettin' snipped?"

"Oh. Right." I wince at my poor choice of words. "They are also for that. I suppose it wasn't a very elegant metaphor..."

"I understood what you were gettin' at." He sounds like he's smiling for a second before his voice goes soft and low again. "So are you sayin' you never...scratched your itch...while you were *in* the closet?"

"Once—kinda." I intentionally omit the fact that it was with our mutual best friend. "But not really, no. I didn't have the energy or organizational skills to attempt a full-on double life."

"Ha." Bucky's laugh sounds sad on my behalf, and I'm suddenly hyperaware that I've just allowed myself to be way more vulnerable than I'd intended to. He must think I'm pathetic.

"You lived with Patrick during those three years," I say in an effort to steer the conversation away from myself. "So in a way you probably know him better."

"I might know him different, but I don't know him better. When you grow up with someone the way y'all did, that's special." He pauses. "How'd you become friends to start with, anyway?"

"School."

"That's all you're gonna give me? Really?"

His tone is so disarming, I can't help but smile. Good thing he can't see my face.

"I guess it was third grade," I begin. "We were both stuck outside after missing the bus, and we just started cracking jokes about our teachers." I try to dig deeper for some other detail to explain why such a random encounter would evolve into a lifelong friendship. "His mom ended up giving me a ride home that day, because I actually didn't have anyone to pick me up at all— my dad worked several low-paying jobs, around the clock, and all that. I think Patrick and his mom took pity on me when they dropped me off and saw me take out my key to let myself into our crappy little house all alone. The next day at school, Patrick insisted I come over and play N64 with him after school...and then we were just inseparable ever since."

"See what I mean?" Bucky says. "Coop and I met as nineteen-year-olds rushing a frat. We don't go nearly that far back." He thinks for a moment and then chuckles. "Though some of the stuff we went through as pledges should probably count as dog years."

"Like what?"

"One time we had to chug eight beers each—while wearing nothin' but a couple of adult diapers—and then got locked in a dark room with a strobe light and a two-hundred-piece puzzle. Our big brothers wouldn't let us out until that stupid puzzle was finished, not even to take a leak. Hence the diapers." He shivers. "I still have nightmares."

This (horrifying) anecdote has the exact opposite effect than the one I assume he intended.

"You just proved my point," I tell him. "I wasn't there for any of that. Ever since we became friends again in law school, he's kept me in a different category from the rest of his guy friends. Almost like he censors himself in front of me." I pause for a moment and realize it's probably not quite so one-sided. "And sometimes it's hard for me to be myself around him. Which I know sounds ridic- ulous, because we do have so much history. But, again, I think it all comes back to me being—"

"Gay."

"Well…" I think about it some more. "Yeah. I'm not just the best friend. I'm the gay best friend. There's a difference."

Bucky takes a breath, like he's about to say something, but then doesn't. The air goes quiet. It occurs to me that I might've killed the conversation by opening up just a bit too much. Why did I think a macho pro golfer from the South would be a good audience for all my buried gay grievances? He's probably trying to determine the fastest way out of this shed right now—weighing the pros and cons of risking the bad PR and running directly into the arms of one of the strippers up the hill.

I consider making an abrupt subject change—something light and funny and shallow—but can't muster the will to try so hard. If he wants to leave, he can leave.

I close my eyes and soak in the distant sound of waves crashing against rocks.

By the time I open them back up again, Bucky's on his side.

Facing me.

We silently lock eyes for a moment before each rolling back to our respective supine positions. I'm not quite sure what just happened, but it felt strangely comfortable. Like we just spoke without speaking.

"I'll be honest," Bucky says. Out loud this time. "Frat culture could be homophobic as hell. At least when we were all in school. I'm 'bout as open-minded as they come—now that I've lived some life and all—but back then? I was so ignorant, you coulda put my brain in a matchbox, and it'd have rolled around like a marble in a coffee can."

"I knew Patrick wasn't as cool with it as he claimed—"

"Let me finish," he continues. "I think you got the story wrong. From what I remember, Coop always thought you stopped talking to *him*. Because you didn't feel safe around us or something. But I know he missed you, man. He talked about missin' you. And whenever one of the brothers would say some homophobic crap, he'd always challenge it."

It's contrary to every assumption I've ever made, but Bucky has no reason to lie. And I guess it does make sense. Prior to my coming out, Patrick was a zealot about defending me from bullies. Why did I believe he had it in him to flip so easily?

"Y'all have seriously never talked about any of this?" Bucky asks. "I'd have thought this would be a dead horse after all these years."

"That's the thing," I say. "When we talk, we never get past the surface."

"Maybe he's scared to say the wrong thing to you," Bucky suggests.

"Patrick?" I ask. "He's never been scared of anything."

"Fair—I've been cliff divin' with him in Cabo." He laughs. "Well. If it's any consolation, I don't get all that deep with Coop, either. I always just figured it was a Yankee thing. Or maybe a WASP thing. They got all those walls up. They like to keep things nice and neat."

I think about how what Patrick is doing up at the house right now is anything *but* nice and neat. But Bucky's right. Because I also know that once the girls leave and the mess is all cleaned up, he'll act as if tonight never happened. Nice and neat. And he'll expect me to do the same. Only I'm not so sure I have it in me anymore.

"Thanks for this chat," I tell Bucky—just now starting to process the fact that this conversation is a real thing that has actually happened. "I didn't realize how much I needed to get off my chest."

"Sure thing." His hand finds my shoulder in the dark and gives it a pat. "Can't wait to do it again tomorrow."

16

'm nudged into consciousness by the creak of the shed door opening and the sight of Bucky's multimillion-dollar ass creeping out of it. A flood of bright summer light pours in, forcing me to re-close my eyes. I keep them shut until the sound of Bucky's footsteps fades.

I dig into my pocket for my phone, but it's dead. It's either six in the morning or...noon. How long were we asleep?

The act of peeling myself off my sleeping bag triggers a pounding headache. Along with a bitch of a backache. The fact that Bucky also subjected himself to such an uncomfortable sleeping arrangement—and wasn't straight up hobbling out of the shed when I peeked at him just now—confirms my belief that he's totally faking this back injury. But why?

This question is drowned out by several others on my walk up to the house. When did the strippers leave? What did Patrick and the other guys *do* with them? Is the house going to be completely trashed when I walk in? Are they even gonna be there or did they already head to the golf course?

I sneak into the kitchen to find Patrick sitting at the island, phone in one hand and coffee mug in the other. He's in head-to-toe Under Armour golf attire—synthetic polo shirt and tan shorts hugging toned biceps and tight thighs. He almost wears the look as well as his professional best friend does.

"Hey, man," I croak. "Have fun last night?"

He just laughs in response. "Thank God for 5-hour ENERGY. Me and the boys were out here until 3:00 a.m. cleaning up." He gestures around at the glistening kitchen, which impresses even me. But the living room will be the real test. "We did a pretty good job for a pack of drunk fools, wouldn't you say?"

I grab the pot of coffee and pour a mug for myself. "Thanks for that. I was worried I'd have to pick up after you guys all morning."

"No sweat. We were all hyped up from adrenaline anyway. Those girls..." He trails off, probably because he realizes he's about to incriminate himself. "Bucky came in a second ago. He said you guys fell asleep out there? How did *that* go?"

"Fine." I say it quickly, like I'm trying to hide something. But what? All we did was engage in some deep conversation. Then again, the conversation was pretty much all about Patrick. "We just passed out."

"Have you talked to Kate?" Patrick asks.

The mention of her name triggers a mental replay of her cruel voicemail to me yesterday. I'm so not in the mood to be grilled by him now, too.

"When would I have had a chance to talk to Kate?" I ask. "I already told you I wasn't gonna say anything to her. Get off my dick about it."

His eyes widen at my random outburst. "Whoa, whoa, whoa. I wasn't trying to say that, dude. Calm down. I was just talking with her, and she asked me what your deal was. She's been texting you with a question about the bachelorette party."

"Oh." I press my weight against the counter. "Gotcha. Sorry."

Patrick straightens his posture. "Are you pissed at me or something?"

"I'm not pissed," I say. Pissily.

"You're not? Because it sounds like—"

"What did you do up here after I left last night?"

Patrick chokes on his coffee. "Do you really want me to answer that?"

A part of me wants to say *no, I don't*, because hearing him say it out loud will officially destroy any chance I might have at convincing myself of his innocence. But the other part of me wants to punish him. Force him to acknowledge his crime in the light of day. Maybe then he'll be able to grasp just how unfair of a position he's putting me in.

"Yes." I clear my throat. "Tell me."

Patrick's shoulders tense up with what I can only imagine is an extreme sensation of guilt. "I think it's probably better if I don't." He releases a long sigh. "Dom, are you—"

"Am I shocked that you'd sleep with a random stranger behind Kate's back?" I finally snap. "Yes! I am! I thought you were better than that, man. Licking whipped cream off a stripper's breasts is one thing, but to actually cheat—" I cut myself off as Patrick's face morphs into disgust. Probably at his assumption that I'm now a ticking time bomb, liable to tell Kate the truth in the coming days, destroying his marriage before it begins. "Don't worry. I promised you I wouldn't tell Kate anything, so I won't. I'll just pretend this never happened and everything is peachy fucking keen."

"Dude," he says. "You've got to—"

"Coop!" Wilson shouts from the foyer. "We're gonna miss our tee time!"

Greeny's voice joins in over the sound of footsteps barreling down stairs. "Let's goooo!"

"Shit." Patrick's eyes narrow to a desperate squint. "Let's talk about this later."

I shake my head and yawn performatively. "No need. Have fun at golf."

17

~

'm on my hands and knees, meticulously scanning every inch of Mrs. Cooper's prized Restoration Hardware rug. And I gotta hand it to the guys. There's not a single remnant of whipped cream or beer or any of the other substances that may or may not have been flung around last night after I left.

The rest of the living room looks good, too. Even the accent chairs have been freshly vacuumed. The windows are open, and the air smells of sunshine and fresh beach.

Aside from the breeze outside, it's totally quiet. Just empty and peaceful enough for me to decompress from the past twenty-four hours.

At least until my phone picks up enough charge to load all the texts I've missed.

I hover over the outlet in the corner and assess the barrage. They're pretty much all from Kate. Lots of hello??? and where the hell are you? and call me ASAP.

I take a deep breath and grant her request. Might as well rip the Band-Aid off so I don't have to deal with more of this all day.

"Finally!" She picks up on the first ring and launches right into her interrogation—but it's not the one I was expecting. "Listen, Dom, we have a situation. What did you say to Bucky last night?"

"What did I... Who? I'm not following."

"He just broke up with Trista," she says. "And now Trista is a wreck. She's refusing to come to the bachelorette party. She thinks it's all your fault, but of course she barely knows you, so she's taking it all out on *me*."

"Why would *Trista Harlow* blame me for her breakup? I'm a nobody lawyer who minds my own business."

"Because you told him to do it!"

"That's absurd!" I can't recall exactly what I said last night after Bucky confessed his lack of love for Trista, but I'm certain I didn't respond with *dump her ass*. "She must have misunderstood something."

"He said he had some kind of talk with you last night, and then he woke up with an epiphany..." She pauses. "And then *boom*."

Unbelievable. I now have to add golf/modeling power-couple Bucky Graham and Trista Harlow to the list of messy straights who think I only exist as a scapegoat/pawn/token for their endless relationship drama.

"So things between them were perfect until he talked to me?" I counter. "Come on. Clearly they were already having issues. And also, I hate to say this, but Trista sounds like a real asshole. If she's gonna bail on your bachelorette party just because of—"

"And on a *separate* note," Kate interrupts. "Where were Patrick and the other guys while you and Bucky were off having your little Trista-bashing session?"

"Calm down."

Why did I call her again?

"I am calm, babe." Her voice has a dragon-like quality that makes the statement sound like a threat. This is by far the tensest exchange we've ever had. "Let me guess: you were keeping Bucky company while he avoided the bad PR of being seen with a house full of hookers—"

"I'm not doing this," I mutter. If she already knows what happened last night, this is a no-win situation for me. Confirm or deny, I'm screwed either way. "I gotta go."

I slam my phone down and stomp out of the living room—already exhausted from today's serving of other peoples' problems. Everyone seems to have forgotten that I have enough of my own crap to deal with right now.

My feet drag themselves out to the great room as if controlled by an external force. And then—barely aware that I'm doing it—I finally allow myself to sit down at the piano.

The shine of the keys takes me right back to college, the last time I can remember feeling any sense of excitement about the possibilities of life. My thirties felt so far away all those years ago, so *I'll-definitely-be-living-my-best-life-by-then*. And now here I am—thirty and alone and living what is quite possibly my worst life. How did I let this happen? I know it can't all be Ted's fault—my unhappiness had been festering for years before he left me.

I play a single note.

A long-lost memory surfaces. This quirky psychic I visited once during the summer before I entered law school. It was my New Age phase and I felt generally lost in life—chronically insecure and anxious about the future. Law school was supposed to represent the promise of a bright one, but it also entailed a quiet sense of dread that I couldn't quite keep buried.

"I see you sitting down at a piano," the psychic had said. She touched my hands and closed her eyes. "And it's so meditative for you, it's pure *flow*. Like therapy."

She then looked directly at me. "Follow that feeling!"

I'm not sure if she was truly having a clairvoyant vision or if she had just looked me up on social media ahead of time, but I was crushed. I had come to her seeking confirmation that I was making the right decision about law school in spite of my cold feet—not confirmation that I was making a six-figure mistake. Loans had already been disbursed. Classes had been registered for. Textbooks had been purchased.

And so I ignored her advice, allowing my musical aspirations to die in favor of a more lucrative and secure career path. The fact that I ended up working at a music streaming company is just the sick joke on top of the shattered dream.

I shake the memory out of my head and allow myself to play another note.

It's not long before I'm several bars deep into Chopin's famous "Nocturne in C-sharp Minor." Even after years of not playing, this one comes easily to me. I taught it to myself when I was fourteen. Once I had it memorized, I played it daily for years afterward—vacillating between my shitty Casio keyboard at home and the upright practice room piano at school.

But it has always sounded the most beautiful at this house, on this piano. The low notes feel richer, the highs purer. It helps that the acoustics in this room—with its vaulted ceiling and wide walls—are a melodic dream.

I close my eyes and hum while playing, letting the music penetrate every molecule of my being.

It's not until I reach the last few measures that I return to the present moment, mortified to discover that Bucky is standing across the room.

"Please don't stop," he says. "That was freakin' beautiful, man."

I stand up. "What are you doing here?"

"Didn't mean to interrupt. I was really enjoying that." He's wearing another standard khakis-and-polo combo, but this time the polo's a light pink that really accentuates his golden tan. His eyes are bloodshot—tired and sad—but his demeanor is cheery. It's a strange combination, like when you see someone at a funeral laugh two seconds after they were just crying. "I told you last night I'd be sticking around today—remember? We said we were gonna shoot the shit again."

"Right." Everything in me wants to confront him about throwing me under the bus with Trista, but I don't have the balls to be so direct. It's the light of day and he *is* Bucky Graham. "I guess I forgot."

His face falls. "Really? I made up a whole list of things for us to get into..."

"No, you didn't."

"Sure did. Even swiped the keys to the pontoon out back. I thought we could take it out and do some fishin' and cook something up just like I used to do back home." He pauses. "But I'd be just as happy to listen to you play all day. I haven't heard Chopin in forever."

My jaw drops to the floor. He even pronounced the name right. "You haven't heard... What? How do you know Chopin?"

He laughs. "What? Just 'cause I'm an ol' Texas boy you think I don't know any classical music?"

"That's exactly what I think," I blurt. "No offense."

He smiles. "My granny was a part-time piano teacher. She raised me. Played that tune damn near every night on her crappy ol' upright in the kitchen..." He places a hand on his heart. "It's a masterpiece, if you ask me. Haunting, but hopeful."

"Huh." Who even is this guy? "Those are the exact two adjectives I'd use to describe it myself."

He nods in satisfaction, as if I've just named him Music Critic of the Year.

"Wait," I add. "Why was your piano in the kitchen?"

"Oh." He picks at his shirt. "We didn't have much. My granny worked 'til she was in her seventies, but she was still broker than dirt half the time."

This anecdote stuns me. I thought I was the only person at this party who knew what it's like to grow up with a working-class single parent. "You really didn't come from money? I've always just assumed—"

"I'm different from most golfers," Bucky says. "People don't realize my first set of clubs were just some ol' hand-me-downs from my buddy's dad. Same buddy's dad who let me play at his course in exchange for workin' the clubhouse kitchen."

Huh. "Why don't you ever talk about this on TV?"

He brushes the suggestion aside with a half-smile. "Ruins the image."

"Ah." This strikes me as sad. Surely there are golf fans out there who'd love a rags-to-riches story like his. Why not own it? But I guess I'm not one to talk. The way I try to distance myself from my own upbringing and all. "I get it."

"So what do you say?" he asks. "Pontoon?"

There's an eager quality to his voice that I can't help but feel touched by. Perhaps I could see myself being comfortable—or even having fun—on a boat with him. Maybe I'll even be able to muster the courage to confront him about the whole Trista thing. Once the confessions start flowing again.

"You know what?" I say. "Alright. Let's go catch some fish."

He slaps my arm. "'Atta boy! I'll go get everything set up. Meet me at the dock in twenty."

18

I spend my twenty minutes freshening up, making a pitcher of spicy Bloody Marys, and packing a Yeti with beer. Hair of the dog and all that. Plus if I'm gonna start a dialogue with Bucky about all the shit he stirred this morning, I'll need several ounces of liquid courage.

"You fixin' to get skunk-drunk out there with that big ol' cooler?" he asks as I jump onto the boat—basically a giant tricked-out raft on floaties. He smiles devilishly. "'Cause I sure am."

"Are skunks supposed to be known alcoholics?" I tease.

Bucky laughs. "Well, they're always creepin' around at night and walkin' all crooked…"

It occurs to me as I board *Mystic Miranda*—lovingly named after Mrs. Cooper—that I haven't stepped foot on this thing in well over a decade. Patrick and I used to go fishing with his dad at least a couple times a summer, before our college friendship hiatus. But after we reunited, the boat trips stopped happening. At this point I assumed it just reappeared at the dock every summer for show.

"You sure this thing is safe?" I ask Bucky. "It runs and has gas and everything?"

"Full tank." Bucky cocks his head from behind the steering wheel. "And she rides like a dream."

Soon enough we're careening out of the harbor toward Mystic River and the Long Island Sound. Bucky steers as I recline on a shiny built-in seat, sipping my Bloody Mary like it's an essential medicine. Which I suppose it is. "Sweet Home Alabama" by Lynyrd Skynyrd blares through the speakers. Bucky crashes up against a wave, causing a cloud of mist to hit my face. I close my eyes and let it spray me.

When I open them, we're cruising past Mystic Seaport—a large waterfront museum of old-timey sailboats and maritime history. Actors and staff shuffle around on the docks in full nineteenth-century garb, creating a blur of bonnets and burlap.

The scene induces a memory from fifth grade, when our class went there on a field trip. For some reason Patrick stayed home that day, so I basically hung out with our Social Studies teacher the whole time. At one point I told her all about how I came to Mystic frequently during the summers. When she asked why, I told her it was because *my* family had a house on the water. She had to know I was lying—just one parent-teacher meeting could confirm that my father was not of the vacation home set—but she humored me nonetheless. Even all these years later, the memory makes me cringe so hard that I have no choice but to guzzle the remaining contents of my drink. The Tabasco burns like a flame down my esophagus.

"You alright there?" Bucky asks upon noticing that I'm actively choking. He rounds a corner past a lighthouse and leaves Mystic Seaport behind.

I clear my throat and give him a thumbs up as I set my thermos in a cup holder and switch to beer. He keeps steering the boat forward, as if he has a specific destination in mind. We pass about five more lighthouses before finally stopping in a secluded cove.

Bucky grabs a beer and plops down next to me.

"Cheers." His cheeks dimple as he says it. The sadness in his eyes from earlier is gone. Like all his worries were left back on land. "Now this is the life, ain't it?"

"Have you boated out here before?" I ask. "You seem like you know your way around."

He shoots me a funny look. "I'm friends with Coop, ain't I? You know that boy loves to fish. Especially for a Yankee."

Right. So I'll have to add "fishing" to the list of activities I didn't realize Patrick has been excluding me from ever since I came out. It's almost like Bucky and I are friends with two different Patrick Coopers.

I chug my beer and hope for that liquid courage to kick in any minute now.

"So how's Trista?" I ask. It's a different kind of fishing than what we came out here for, but it's a start. "You talk to her since last night?"

"Nah," he says. "I'm sure she's fine, though."

"That's weird." My chest tightens and then goes hollow. How the hell do other people initiate confrontation like it's nothing? I'm over here just trying to passive-aggressively call him out on a lie, and I swear to God it's like jumping off a cliff. "I heard you broke up with her this morning."

Bucky sighs. "Kate told you?"

He takes his Ray-Bans off and throws his head back to let the sun hit his face. He seems to have absolutely no shame about being caught in a lie. This confidence he has is so foreign to me. I mean, my default state is one of shame. I get awkward if I even *think* that someone *thinks* that I have *thought* about lying.

"It's not worth gettin' into," he says conclusively. "It's complicated and whatnot."

I could press him for more details, ask him why he dragged

my name into it. I could pivot to admonishing him for breaking
Bro Code and telling Trista about the strippers. Or I could let his
nonchalance rub off on me and restore the air of fake politeness
we had going before I brought up the subject of Trista and made
myself look like a crazy person for thinking any of this is a big
deal. I naturally opt for that last one.

"Right," I say through clenched teeth. "Got it."

He throws his shades back on and faces me. "Trista Harlow is
the least of my problems right now, man."

"You mean your back? How is it today? Think you'll be able
to play again soon?"

He gets quiet, leans forward, cracks open another beer. There's
a subtle change in his demeanor—shoulders less relaxed, face less
carefree. I think there might even be a worry line or two on his
forehead, a nervous quiver to his lip, and—you know what? I need
to stop staring at him.

I lower my no-name drugstore sunglasses and refocus my gaze
on the shore. Nothing but woods, rocks, sand. Bucky managed to
find the only bay in Mystic that's not dotted with waterfront estates.
The privacy nearly reminds me of the seclusion we enjoyed in the
lighthouse last night. Like we can say anything and it won't count.

"You know damn well my back is fine," Bucky finally says.
He must feel the same way I do about our clandestine location.
"It's dead obvious, ain't it?"

I hesitate, looking out at the water. "Yeah." I scratch the rim
of my nose. "So what's really going on, then?"

He takes a long sip of booze. Then he exhales, slowly and
loudly. Like he's sizing up a huge, intimidating mess that he has
no idea how to clean.

"I did somethin' stupid," he says. "And now I'm in a bad row
of stumps."

Despite his obvious misery, I can't help but crack a smile at his usage of another expression I've never heard.

"What...stumps...are you in?"

He half-smiles for a quick second before his face assumes a gloomy expression. The sad eyes have returned, and I now understand they had nothing to do with Trista at all.

"You promise you ain't gonna say anything to anyone, right? Especially Cooper. And the press. The only person who knows right now is my manager and my agent and..." He trails off. "I know I can trust you, man. I feel like we connected last night."

The last thing I need is yet another straight person's dirty secret to carry around, but also, the thought of having a piece of Bucky that Patrick doesn't have is intoxicating.

"Of course," I assure him. "My lips are sealed."

"The goddamn PGA suspended me," he confesses. His voice takes on an almost violent tone when he says this. If we weren't on a boat, I'm positive he would've just punched a hole in the nearest wall. "It happened Wednesday."

This sounds like a big deal. Patrick himself said that missing just one tournament is missing out on big money. And didn't he also say something about players losing their tour card if they don't participate in enough events? I'd imagine it's difficult to participate in enough events if you're literally prohibited from doing so.

"This game is my life," Bucky continues. "You know how I was gonna miss the party this weekend? I was fine with that. It's my reality. I'm always missin' holidays, weddings, funerals... Hell, I didn't even get to meet my nephew until he was ten months old. Now he's four and mostly just knows me as some guy on the Golf Channel."

He takes a moment to rub a bead of sweat out of his eyes. "I'm always training. Or on tour. I've devoted my entire life to this sport.

And that's fine by me, because I sure as shit love everything about it. And I care more about being the best golfer I can be than I do about havin' a personal life." He catches his breath. "But now it's like they're rippin' my life away from me because of one bad decision."

I lean forward. "What was the bad decision?"

"Doping." He shakes his head. "Failed a surprise drug test."

"Drugs?" I ask through a dropped jaw. "Like steroids? Or—"

"Yeah." He lowers his head—in shame. That emotion I previously thought he was immune to. "I just tried 'em a few times. It's not something I do on a regular basis. I know guys who dope, and that's not me. I got mixed up with this new trainer who promised the 'supplements' he was slippin' me were legit. I had my doubts, but I took 'em anyway..." He swallows. "I don't know, man. I just need a boost sometimes. You drink coffee at your job, right?"

Something tells me a disillusioned lawyer guzzling a venti cold brew is not the same thing as an elite professional athlete shooting up performance-enhancing drugs, but I keep this thought to myself. Bucky seems weak—despite his superhuman biceps—which I now know are *literally* superhuman—and my only instinct is to comfort him like he comforted me last night.

I put my hands up. "No judgment here. I'm sorry that happened. So what now?"

"I gotta pass the next test," he says. "Until then, jury's out if I'll be allowed to play next week's tournament. Or the tournament after that. If this gets out to the public—if I can't play in any more events this year—I'll just die." He sighs. "I find out the official terms of my suspension on Monday."

I consider moving closer to him and offering some form of physical comfort but decide against it. "That sucks, man."

"Thanks, buddy." He throws his arm over the side of the boat. It's not exactly around me, but it's behind me. Something about it feels like the exact type of intimacy I just decided against displaying myself.

"Are you really not gonna tell Patrick?" I ask. Not to be a jerk, but because I'd imagine Patrick could do a lot more to help in a situation like this than simply offering a *that sucks, man*.

Bucky sighs. "Can't bring myself to do it. Coop might be my lawyer, but he still looks up to me like he did back at the OKB house…"

This statement makes me wonder how many mistakes and shortcomings Patrick has kept from me over the years, purely because he knows *I* look up to *him*.

"Please don't tell him," Bucky continues. "Or any of the other guys. You know they all have me up on a pedestal. I really don't wanna let them down."

I give him my word and file the information away.

Another secret for the list.

19

As it turns out, I suck at fishing. This isn't to say I haven't always sucked at fishing, but at least fifteen years ago I could blame it on my youth. It takes me five attempts at casting my line before Bucky—laughing at me like a sadistic Southern menace—takes my rod and does it for me, his carefree confidence snapping back into place after a few beers. I chug along and follow his lead as he instructs me to wait until a fish takes a bite.

"How will I know?" I ask, channeling my inner Whitney.

"You'll know," he replies coolly.

But my line never moves. It's like the fish are actively *repelled* by my bait. And then for some reason it all turns into a big metaphor about how now that I'm single again, no one's gonna want me. Fishing hook, Tinder profile. *Tomato, tomahto.* Better get used to this.

Meanwhile, Bucky somehow manages to catch two bluefish right off the bat. He initially wants to take them home and fry them up, but then we see a fish advisory sign warning of contamination.

A quick boat trip later and we're back at the house.

We order a pizza and head to separate bathrooms for our respective post-fishing showers. The other guys are still out on the golf course. Assuming they have a few rounds of beers after the eighteenth hole—which Patrick always does—they won't be back for at least another hour or so.

Before starting the water, I nakedly scroll through my phone in front of the bathroom mirror. There are a few missed calls and texts from Kate, but it looks like she finally gave up on trying to reach me sometime around noon. With any luck, I can make it two more nights to the end of this party and *then* figure out how I'm going to deal with her.

My thoughts wander to Bucky as I look up and take in the reflection of my body. It's lean on account of the several shame-fueled miles I run each week, but still fleshy in places where Bucky's is muscled. I close out of Kate's texts and—barely conscious of what I'm doing—pull up his Body Issue photos. Was *this* secretly the reason for the steroids? Because he wanted to look buff for the cameras? Because, I mean, I've golfed before. Retired grandmothers in central Florida golf. It is not a sport that requires herculean strength.

Just one look at Bucky's pictures sends a rush of blood below my waist. I can't resist touching myself.

This is so twisted. It was one thing to get off on these pictures when I was just vaguely acquainted with him through Patrick. But now I know him. As a person. We have a budding friendship of our own.

I swipe to the next picture. In this one, he's leaning over a golf ball by a "Par 4" sign, preparing to tee off, his bare body angled so that you can see his ass but not his junk. The suggestion of it alone is always enough to get me hot, though.

I increase my speed. Let's just get this over with and pretend it never happened.

Right as I'm about to finish, my phone starts buzzing with a call. From *Ted*.

Christ! It's as if this is five months ago, back in our apartment, me locked in the bathroom with the water running, rubbing one out to pictures of Bucky, Ted sulking on the couch over whatever our most recent argument was about...and then Ted knocking on the door *right* at the worst possible moment. How did he always know? How does he know *now*? We haven't talked in weeks.

Which means this must be important.

"Yes?" I answer.

"Hi." His voice is short, like this phone call was a last resort solution for whatever his problem is. "Are you okay?"

"What do you mean? I'm fine."

"I figured. Listen, you need to call Kate. She's been texting me. She can't get a hold of you and she's worried."

He figured? What a prick. For all he knows, I could have actually been in peril.

"Just ignore her." Despite the time that's passed, it feels as familiar as ever to be talking to him. "It's Patrick's bachelor weekend and she's been trying to get me to dish about what's going on here, and also she's blaming me for Trista's breakup, and so I've been ignoring her all day, but—"

"I see nothing's changed." His voice is judgy and assholish. Basically the exact opposite of Bucky's warm drawl. "Still desperate to please all your rich, straight friends."

"I'm literally ignoring her," I snap. "That's the opposite of people-pleasing."

"You're only ignoring her because it's the easiest way to avoid conflict right now. Once the party's over, you'll run back and apologize and figure out some way to make it up to her without ever actually addressing how messed up it was to expect you to spy for her in the first place." He takes a breath. "Just a hunch. I don't know all the details of this particular situation."

"First of all, go fuck yourself." If there's anyone I'm *not* afraid of initiating conflict with, it's Ted. Along with every other ex I've ever had. Relationships have always been my safe space for expressing my true feelings without overthinking everything. "You're wrong. And even if you weren't, you don't get to psycho-analyze me anymore. You lost that privilege when you broke up with me five months before our wedding day. Remember?"

"Fair enough," he says—sounding unbothered, which is even more infuriating than how he sounded when he was reading me for filth. "Bye."

"Asshole!" I shout into the phone.

But he's already hung up.

20

~

I arrive downstairs to the sight of Bucky rummaging through the fridge, wearing nothing but a towel around his tight yet beefy waist.

That famous body—from phone to flesh in a matter of minutes.

Why did Ted have to interrupt? The fact that I didn't get to finish off is making this situation ten times more unbearable than it should be right now. I wish I had steroids of my own to gather the strength needed not to get unwillingly excited by the sight of Bucky's bare skin.

I try my best to focus my gaze on the sparkle of the stainless-steel appliances, the grain of the kitchen cabinets, the blue of the water outside the window. I throw in a mental image of old Rose from *Titanic* for good boner-killing measure. (Which is tragically fitting, as *it's been 84 years* since I've gotten laid.)

"Hey, man." He picks his head up out of the deli drawer. "This pizza's takin' 'bout near forever." He looks at me and seems to register that his nakedness is distracting. "Sorry, I shoulda put some clothes on before I stalked out here. I'm just so hungry I could eat the north end of a southbound goat."

"No worries," I say in what I hope is a tone that conveys total indifference to the fact that there is but a thin layer of organic cotton between the air and his junk. The junk that *ESPN Magazine* photographers so expertly left shrouded in mystery amid pages and pages of nude photos. "I'm hungry, too."

For your body.

Oh my God! Stop. I really need to not be a thirsty horndog right now. This is exactly why homophobes get all weird around gay guys—they think we objectify them the same way they objectify women. Which is total bullshit. Especially because the straight men who are worried about stuff like that are generally the *last* ones you'd ever want to see naked anyway.

But how can I look away right now? Literally any man-loving person with a pulse would get flustered by the sight of Bucky Graham in a towel. He has to know that.

"Maybe another couple beers will help hold us over," Bucky suggests. One hand is on his towel, and with the other he grabs two Sam Adams Summer Ales from the fridge. "Here you go."

I accept one of the bottles and attempt to twist off the cap but soon realize it's not a twist-off. We've clearly been drinking too much Coors Light today.

Bucky appears to have made the same error as me.

"Did we bring that bottle opener back inside or leave it on the boat?" I ask, leaning against the kitchen island across from him. "Or actually, wait, they probably have another one in a drawer somewhere."

"I can just crack it against the counter here," Bucky responds. "Watch this."

He takes the bottle and places it under the ledge of the quartz countertop, and then takes his other hand off his towel and—

"Ah," he exclaims, "shit."

The towel falls to the floor in one swift drop and—

HOUSTON, WE HAVE A PENIS.

A *famous* penis.

And with it, a somewhat surprising revelation: *Bucky Graham is uncircumcised*. Not something I've ever been particularly into, but I am now. Because Bucky's dick is unquestionably in the ninety-ninth percentile of dicks I've ever seen. Well-proportioned, unfussy, with clean lines and strong definition. Clearly reliable, durable. And begging to be sat on. Wait—am I still talking about a penis right now? Or a sectional sofa?

Stop looking!

I need to *stop looking*.

But also...why hasn't he picked that damn towel back up yet? It's just pooled around his feet, like a discarded robe in a cheap seventies porn flick.

Stop looking! Stop looking! Stop look—is he purposefully trying to torture me right now?—*ing!*

He turns the other way—his familiar ass now facing me—and finishes cracking open both of our beers on the opposite counter. Then he turns back around, giving me another full-frontal view, and takes a sip.

Still fully nude! Is this normal? Is this the kind of thing that straight adult men do around each other? I must admit I've always wondered if Patrick and the other guys of Omega Kappa Beta were all walking around that house with their schlongs swinging about in the wind every day. There's nothing straighter than the concept of a fraternity—but there's also nothing gayer than the concept of a fraternity.

It feels like an eternity passes before Bucky finally places his beer down and picks the towel up and wraps it back around his waist.

My face and ears are so hot, they must look volcanic.

"That was my bad," he says. "I forgot it takes two hands."

"No worries," I stammer. "Thanks for that."

"For showing you my willy?" he says with a mischievous grin.

Okay. This is definitely not an exchange two straight men would have with each other. Right? Right? Righ—

"For opening my beer," I say in an attempt to stop the spiraling in my head. I need to sound calm, cool, collected, like there is absolutely nothing weird about anything that has just happened. "But I mean, yeah, that too."

What did I just say? Why did I let myself say that?!

"You got it." Bucky laughs. "Anytime."

21

We split a large pepperoni—with a side of fully clothed conversation—on the back patio. The sexual tension from the kitchen has fully evaporated with the steam from the pizza box.

Maybe it was just imagined on my part.

"You promise you're not gonna say anything, right?" Bucky asks after a short period of silence. I get the sense that this question is an extension of a much longer dialogue he's been having in his head for the past several minutes. "I really shouldn't have done that."

"Oh, yeah, no." I wipe a glob of grease off my face. "Please. No big deal. I've seen a million dicks in my life." Well. That came out weird and slutty. "I mean, you know—"

"I wasn't talkin' about that." He smiles and shakes his head in what seems like an odd mixture of amusement and fear. "I mean, what I told you out on the boat. My back injury."

Alrighty then! Our heads are in completely different places right now.

"Of course," I promise. "Forgot about it already."

His arms relax the tiniest bit. "Thanks. It's been crazy, these past couple days. Normally my summer is nonstop. I'm either playin' an event or travelin' to the next one or trainin' for the next one or recoverin' from the *last* one…"

Now he sounds like he might cry. "I miss all of it. I've been dyin' inside since that stuff went down with the suspension. Talkin' to you last night was the first time I was able to forget about it a little. Which I reckon is why I was so hell-bent on spending more time with you today. Some socialization to keep my mind off of it, you know? But still. It doesn't change the fact that my career is hangin' in the balance here, man. So I appreciate you keeping it quiet while this whole thing plays out."

I can tell there's a lot he's not saying, probably because he figures I wouldn't understand everything that's at stake for him. And maybe I don't get all the details that go into it, but I get the overall picture. Golf is his life. His life is in jeopardy. It would be like if I had somehow managed to achieve my dream of being a professional pianist and then...I don't know...broke a finger or something. Then again, I suppose the fact that I gave up on it alto-gether means I already willingly broke them all myself years ago.

"I'm sure it'll all be alright," I finally tell Bucky.

He raises his bottle and cheerses the air. "So I've been flappin' away about my problems all day. What about you? What's goin' on in your life? When are you gonna play me another song on that piano?"

My face burns with embarrassment. "The answer to that last one is *never*. I was just messing around this morning. I don't play anymore."

"Are you kidding? But you're so dang good!"

"I'm not that good." I shift in my seat. "There's no room in my apartment...or my life...for piano. It's fine."

Bucky furrows his brow. "I watched you play for that whole song. You were in the zone—just like I get on the golf course—"

"It's not the same," I interrupt. "Golf is a lucrative career skill."

Bucky laughs. "Not for ninety-nine percent of the people who play it, it isn't."

"You know what I mean," I say. "For you, it is."

"Even if it wasn't, I'd still go out there and play whenever I could."

"Can we drop the subject?" I snap.

"Yeah, man. It's dropped." Bucky puts his hands up in defeat. The air goes stale for a few moments of silence before he finally perks back up and says, "So what else is goin' on with you, then?"

I take a gulp of beer and huff for a moment before giving him the satisfaction of an answer. "I guess my biggest thing right now is the wedding. And this party. Yesterday really screwed with my plans. This was supposed to be a PG-13 weekend. And now Kate knows about the girls last night, and she won't stop hounding me about it."

"Kate?" he asks. "How'd she find out?"

And then it just comes out. "I'm guessing Trista told her after you told Trista."

"Whoa." Bucky straightens his posture. "I didn't say nothin' to Trista about the strippers. You kiddin' me? That would be a major violation of the Bro Code."

He sounds so serious I'm immediately convinced he's telling the truth. Still, I have to ask again. "You really didn't tell her?"

"You think I'd lie to you 'bout anything?" he asks. "With the amount of collateral you got on me right now?"

"But if it wasn't you, then how could she have found out?"

"Maybe it was just a lucky guess," he suggests. "What did she say, exactly?"

I flash back to our phone fight this morning and try to recall her exact words.

"She didn't say much," I admit. "She just told me that Trista told her about you and me having a conversation last night—and then she asked if you and I were left alone because you were trying to avoid the bad press of being caught with hookers. And then I hung up."

"I almost forgot." Bucky's voice veers into sincerity. "I should've apologized for this earlier: I did say your name to Trista this morning. I was tryin' to explain why I made this decision so suddenly and had to tell her over the phone, and then I thought about the talk we had and, well, it just came out. I'm sorry."

"What was it about our talk that made you want to leave her?"

"I'd been meanin' to do it. But after the suspension on Wednesday, and then hearing you talk about your ex-fiancé last night, I finally felt like I had the gumption to rip the Band-Aid off."

"It's fine," I say. "Whatever. I have bigger problems to worry about."

He cocks his head. "Do ya, really, though?"

"Well, yeah." I pause. "Let's say Kate's comment really was just a wild guess—"

"Not *that* wild," Bucky quips. "It's a bachelor party."

"But then how'd she know you were trying to avoid bad press?"

"I'm always tryin' to avoid bad press." He laughs. "She works in media, she gets it."

"Right." Damnit. This is all making too much sense. Kate really didn't know anything—she was just jumping to a conclusion. "But now my reaction to it has basically confirmed that her guess was right. Why else would I have freaked out the way I did? Ugh. I'm so stupid. This is gonna cause a huge blowout between them. And let's not even talk about the fact that Patrick went ahead and hooked up with—"

"Here's a question," Bucky interjects. "Why is any of this your problem?"

I've already asked myself this question enough times to know there's no reasonable answer. These things absolutely should not be my problem. But that doesn't change the fact that they are.

"Because I'm the gay best friend, remember? I have to play both sides. I don't have the luxury of *only* needing to follow Bro Code. I also have to follow…whatever the reverse of that is."

Bucky lets out a hearty laugh. "Can I tell you somethin' my granny told me once a long time ago?"

"Go for it."

He leans forward. "So it was back in my amateur days. I was bustin' my ass tryin' to qualify for the Houston Open. And I damn near drove myself crazy lookin' up all the stats on the other guys I knew from around my club, studyin' their swings, trying to size 'em up. I started addin' it up in my head—all the possible outcomes that could prevent me from making the cut. I couldn't think about anything else for days. So I finally asked my granny for advice. She told me, 'Son, worryin' only gives small things big shadows.' You can't control what everyone else does out there. So just get out on that course and do your thing."

I squint in his direction. "This feels…very much not the same."

"I think it is." Bucky smiles. "You can't control what Coop does, and you sure as shit can't control what Kate does. So stop worryin' about it."

22

~

The guys get back around five. Bucky stays outside with Wilson and Greeny, both of whom are eager to tell him all about their performance on the course while Patrick calls me into the first-floor master to touch base on the itinerary. Or so he says.

"Did you ever get back to Kate?" He takes his sweat-drenched polo off and paces across the room. "She seems pissed, man. Real pissed."

The fact that he feels like he has any right to be upset flicks a switch in me—makes me realize just how hurt I am on Kate's behalf. I'm ready to take her side entirely.

If I were in her position right now—sitting at home while my fiancé participates in three nights of partying with his bad-influence college buddies—I'd be just as anxious as she is.

And if Kate were somehow *there* for those three nights of partying, I'd fully expect her to dish for me. It wouldn't even be a question in my mind that I could count on her for the scoop. And if she didn't give it to me, I'd freak out. I'd spend the whole weekend stewing on the couch, imaging worst-case scenarios. Drinking wine. Spiraling to that point of revelation where whatever nightmare scenario I've concocted in my head feels like it has to be true, because all the random details I've arbitrarily connected and pieced together fit together too perfectly. This is what Kate's doing. And she's not crazy for doing it.

"Why shouldn't she be pissed?" I ask Patrick. "Given everything you did last night? I'd be pissed if I were her."

Patrick's face goes completely pale—or as pale as possible for someone who just spent his day traipsing around a sunny golf course. His eyebrows narrow in a bubbling rage.

"What did you tell her? You promised—"

"Nothing! I've been ignoring her all day so that I *don't* have to tell her anything. I'm just reminding you that she's not the asshole in this situation. You are." I lower my voice to a disappointed whisper. "You cheated on her last night."

He makes a face. "What are you talking about, man? Because I licked whipped cream off some girl's tits?"

"No," I say—even though it occurs to me that the whipped cream incident was a mild form of cheating in itself. "I'm talking about what happened after I went out to the lighthouse with Bucky."

"Dude, you weren't even here."

"You told me—by refusing to tell me—in the kitchen this morning!" I say. "And I talked to Kitty on her smoke break last night. She told me all about the 'other' services that the guys prepaid for. I know she and Lexus weren't just putting on some innocent strip show the whole time."

Patrick grabs me by the shoulders and sits me down next to him on the bed. "I did not have sex with a stripper last night. That's not even in the realm of..." He stammers. "Why would you think I would do that? Is your opinion of me really so low? I thought we were brothers, man."

"I was never in Omega Fucko Beta," I say. "Or whatever it's called."

Patrick almost manages a laugh. "You know what I mean. You *know* me. Better than all the other clowns here."

I consider going on a tangent here, explaining to him how skeptical I am of that statement. Surely he can't be oblivious to the wall he put up between us in college that has never fully come back down. Surely he knows there are parts of his personality that Bucky, Wilson, and Greeny have access to that I never will. Surely he remembers that he initially wanted Bucky to be his best man and not me. The only thing I have that the other guys don't is an extra decade of history that took place before our brains were even fully developed.

But I do know him enough to know that he doesn't sound like he's lying right now. He hasn't scratched his neck even once, which is his usual involuntary tell for when he's saying something he knows is full of shit.

"So then what did happen after I left?" I finally ask.

"Listen, it's still not something Kate can know." He squeezes my shoulder. "It sounds worse than it is."

"I'm not gonna tell her," I assure him. "At this point I just need to know for my own peace of mind."

"The girls put on a little...you know." He shrugs. "Sex show."

"Kitty and Lexus?" I ask with a gasp. "Together?"

"The fact that you remember their names..." He cracks and then stops himself from making a joke. "Yes. They gave us a performance. They seemed to really be into each other. It was totally innocent! On our parts, I mean." He gets grave for a moment. "But we do have a serious problem. I was trying to tell you when we talked this morning, before you got all short with me."

"What's the serious problem?"

"The girls used a...toy...in their act," he says. "It was this bright pink double-sided thing. And they left it here. We can't find it anywhere. That's the real reason we cleaned up so good last night."

"And you're sure it's here?"

"Yes! They told us to keep it as a wedding gift."

"I knew you were registered at Bed Bath and Beyond." I can't help myself. "But I had no idea that's what you meant by *beyond*."

"That's not funny!" Patrick says.

"It was too easy, sorry. So there's a mysterious sex toy just lurking somewhere in the house? Is it clean, at least?"

"They obviously used condoms." He says this as if it's common knowledge that that's the protocol with stripper sex shows. "Which is another thing. We only found one out of the two. So we need to find that, too."

"Maybe they hid it on purpose," I suggest. "As some kind of joke. Do you think we can call them and ask?"

"We already tried," Patrick says. "Their manager or whoever that guy was won't even let us talk to them unless we pay for another visit."

"That won't be happening," I say definitively.

Patrick laughs. "I know. So we need to get all the guys together and tear this place apart tonight. You know my mom is gonna do a sweep of this place after we leave and the last thing any of us need is her finding that thing."

"But tonight is poker night!" I say. "I even got a whole new set of Vegas-grade chips."

"First we find the rogue dildo," Patrick says. "Then we can play."

23

The five of us collapse in defeat sometime around nine. We have flipped this entire house inside out and haven't found a thing.

"This is for the birds," Greeny says. "One of us must've thrown it out last night and forgot about it. Let's just move on."

"I second that," Wilson says.

"Thirded," Bucky adds.

I know I should agree with them. We moved the furniture, raided the drawers and cabinets, triple-swept the floors. Checked the storage ottoman in the great room, the executive desk in the library, the umbrella holder by the front door. I even said several prayers to Saint Anthony—the go-to Italian strategy for the finding of lost possessions—and still nothing. (Am I the first person in the history of the world to pray to a Catholic saint for the recovery of a misplaced sex toy? Probably.)

But there is a gnawing fear inside of me that it's still here, hiding in the last place any of us would have thought to look. If someone had thrown it out already, wouldn't they remember doing so?

I consider voicing this concern but decide against it. I wasn't even here last night. Maybe Patrick is just being paranoid.

"Maybe I'm just being paranoid," Patrick says, right on cue. "Now that I think about it, those girls could be messing with our heads. Maybe they just told us they left it here because they knew we'd wind ourselves up looking for it."

"That would be a cruel prank," I say. "But also a good one."

"That settles it, then." Wilson pops up and reaches for the poker set I brought. "Who's ready for some Hold'em?"

I look over at Bucky and feel a tingle of discomfort (but also excitement) when I realize his eyes were already on me. How long has he been looking at me? He smirks in a way that feels private.

Greeny sets up the table—doling out the regulation amount of starting chips for each player—while the rest of us have a round of beers in the kitchen.

Wilson taps my shoulder with his bottle. "I bet you're glad we're having a low-key night tonight. I thought you were gonna have a heart attack yesterday when those girls showed up."

I squirm. "Please. I was chill."

The group erupts in laughter at my response.

"This is the best, though." Wilson takes a swig of beer and sighs wistfully. "Just the like old days at OKB. Man, I miss that creaky old frat house. No broads. No bullshit."

"Still going through that rough patch with Melanie?" Patrick asks.

"How'd you know that's what I call her crotch nowadays?" Wilson says. "The Rough Patch."

What a prick.

"You're wrong for that," Patrick says—laughing anyway.

"Just wait 'til you and Kate have kids," Wilson says. "You'll see."

I force a small chuckle in an effort to fit in, but honestly, what the fuck? This woman has created *life*—enduring nine months of sacrifices before ejecting a literal human from her body—and her husband is over here passing judgment on the state of her vagina! He of all people should be singing her praises.

I've never understood the casual misogyny of guys like Wilson. Isn't the whole point of being straight supposed to be that you *love* women? I love women—worship quite a few of them, to be honest (Drew Barrymore, Rihanna, Marisa Tomei, Mariah Carey...the list is endless)—and I'm gayer than a decorative sconce.

Patrick chuckles. "Good thing Kate doesn't want kids."

I laugh, thinking it's a joke.

"What?" Patrick asks. "She doesn't."

Except she does. Kate used to make a big thing about how she didn't want kids—to the point where it was basically a personality trait of hers—but that was back when we were in our early twenties and her aspirations to be a top beauty editor felt so far off that she couldn't possibly fathom fitting motherhood into a schedule that was solely focused on climbing the *Vogue* ladder. Now that she's reached the upper half of that ladder, though, she's been rethinking her stance altogether.

But of course she wouldn't tell Patrick that. He's only her future husband.

Wilson opens his mouth before I can respond. "I can't believe we're over here talking about Kate and Melanie"—he slaps Bucky on the back—"when *this one* over here is banging the latest *Sports Illustrated* swimsuit cover girl."

"How many models have you been through now?" Patrick says. "Seven...hundred?"

"Trista is the hottest yet," Wilson adds.

Bucky's face gets all pinched at the mention of her name. I imagine he's trying to figure out the best way to tell his friends that the relationship is over without fully killing the fun in the room.

"You know me." He clinks bottles with Wilson. "I got a taste for the finer things in life." He takes a swig of beer. "And that Trista Harlow sure is a fine thing."

Or that!

"What about you, Diva Dom?" Wilson asks. "How are things with your husband—"

"He was never my husband," I correct him. "Just my fiancé. And it's over."

"Oh," Wilson offers. "Sorry."

"It's alright," Patrick arrogantly says on my behalf. "Dom's better off without him." He puts his arm around me. "Right buddy?"

"Yep," I lie. Anything to move on from the subject of *me*. "Cheers to Patrick!"

Right after we all clink, Greeny pops back in to let us know the table is ready. We migrate to the den, where he's gone all-out in simulating a professional poker experience.

We each take a seat—I happen to be across from Bucky, which means I'll be staring directly at my chips for the duration of this game—and Greeny starts rattling off the standard rules and chip values. There's an empty ceramic vase off to the side, where we each throw in fifty dollars as a buy-in. I calculate in my head that the winner of this thing will walk away with two hundred and fifty bucks, which is money I could really use right now. I've been burning through my savings ever since I stopped splitting expenses with Ted.

After ten or so hands, Wilson is the first one out after going all-in on a pathetic bluff. He doesn't even have a single pair. The best part is that *I* win the hand, which I consider to be a symbolic victory for Melanie and her vagina.

We raise the blind bets, and several hands of rotating luck pass before we raise them again. Another several hands—Greeny and Bucky's stacks dwindling while Patrick's and mine continue to grow—and we raise them again.

Which is when shit gets real. Bucky and Greeny go head-to-head on a large pile of chips, which ultimately go to Bucky and his three queens. Another few hands pass—all of which are significantly unkind to Bucky and the newfound cockiness he picked up in that victory—until he goes all-in on three aces. Only to get owned by Patrick's full house.

And so Patrick and I are the last two players standing.

Groom and best man.

I can't help but think about how silly it would be for him—as wealthy as he is—to walk away with everyone's money. I also can't help but think about how I'm probably the only person at this table who's even thinking about the win in terms of money rather than just bragging rights.

Bucky assumes the role of designated dealer for our one-on-one face-off, which lasts a few hands of back-and-forth. I'm betting as conservatively as possible because I refuse to lose on a reckless whim, but eventually Greeny gets impatient and suggests that we double the blinds in order to speed things up.

"Whoa," I mindlessly gasp as I review my hand. Ace, king. Suited. Clubs. "I mean...ugh." I make awkward eye contact with Patrick for a second. "Or do I?"

"I can't tell if you suck at bluffing," Wilson quips. "Or if you're brilliant."

"That'd be the latter," Bucky chimes in. "I never know what to expect from this one."

Wilson cracks a laugh. "Dom is a low-key hustler."

"Enough with the small talk!" I say, high on the promise of my first two cards and eager to see how the hand is gonna shake out. "Let's see what the dealer's got."

"Well then, let's see 'em." Bucky turns over a jack and then a ten—both of clubs! I'm literally one card away from a royal flush. The best, most impossible hand in all of poker. He flips the last card. Jack of diamonds. Shit.

But I still have two chances left—the turn and the river.

Patrick looks around at everyone before finally settling on me. His mouth is bent ever so slightly into an entitled grin. Then he throws in two high-value chips, raising the bet to double the minimum. We both have giant stacks, so this is basically nothing. I check instantly.

Bucky and I playfully glare at each other from across the table as he prepares to flip the next card. An image of him naked in the kitchen flashes in my mind, which adds a twisted layer of sexual tension to this moment that I pray to God no one else at the table (especially Bucky himself) is picking up on. I remind myself that we've been drinking all night. None of us are all that perceptive right now.

He flips a two of hearts.

"All in," I hear myself say—because why the hell not. If the last card is a queen of clubs, I will literally have an unbeatable hand. But even if it's just *any* club, I'll still have a normal flush, which gives me great chances. And if it's a total dud, I already have two pairs with the aces and jacks. So overall this is a low-risk move. "Patrick?"

I have a very strong feeling that he's been bluffing—I saw him scratch his neck a moment ago—but alas he counts up his chips and throws them all into the center of the table with mine.

"Yeehaw!" Bucky slaps the table. "Winner takes all."

Bucky moves his hand in slow motion, gradually revealing the final card upon which this entire game hinges, and it's a...

Six of clubs.

Damnit.

Bucky rubs his hands together in excitement. "Let's see what y'all got. Dom?"

"Call me a toilet…" I start, trying to sound as cocky as these guys were before they floundered, like this is what I was going for the whole time. "…'cause I gotta *flush*."

This is met with exaggerated gasps and *ooh*s. From everyone except Patrick, who continues to smirk menacingly.

"Well, then, call me Danny Tanner." He lays his cards down—a jack of spades and two of diamonds. "'Cause this is a *full house*, brother!"

Everyone hoots and hollers at the upset.

Patrick wins. I lose.

How could I have ever expected otherwise?

24

I try to sleep but can't stop thinking about Bucky—analyzing all the time we've spent together so far this weekend. Replaying the image of his towel dropping to the floor over and over again on a mental loop like some kind of horny gay GIF.

At this time yesterday, he and I were in the shed. Now I'm up here alone—a loser, both at life and poker—as he sleeps downstairs in a shared bed with Patrick.

And I'm jealous.

I knew when Bucky came here that he'd just end up crashing in Patrick's room instead of a couch, but that was before we developed such an unexpected connection.

Or maybe this thing between us is all in my head.

I mean, sure, yeah, he's definitely been sending me signals of some kind—but his life is so upside down right now that he probably doesn't even realize he's doing it. He's probably just drawn to the distraction of *any* romantic attention. I've seen this happen before. Some straight guys love the feeling of being desired so much that they'll flirt with gay guys despite having zero interest in ever following through on the intimation of actual gay sex. I'm guilty of doing this myself with women. I can't even count how many girls I drunkenly made out with at straight bars in my early twenties—despite being a very active homosexual by then—purely high on the validation of knowing that someone in the room found me attractive.

But what if Bucky is bi (or at least bi-curious) and sending legitimate signals? Or what if he's gay, stuck in the closet due to the societal expectations placed on men in professional sports? There has never been an openly gay, active golfer on the PGA tour. Perhaps he's just waiting until the time is right to establish himself as the first.

I shake the thought out of my head before it progresses into a fantasy.

The most likely possibility is that there's absolutely nothing romantic about any of this. He just thinks he made a new friend, and I'm attaching all kinds of subtext to his friendliness purely because I saw his cock in the kitchen. (*Cock in the Kitchen.* That would be an excellent cookbook title.)

I squeeze my eyes shut and tell myself to stop thinking so much. Just go to sleep.

But then I hear something.

A quiet, tentative knock at my door.

I think?

And then there it is again.

I creep out of bed and reach for the knob, assuming it's Patrick. Although what he'd need to tell me at this hour—and why he wouldn't just text me from downstairs—is a mystery.

I softly crack the door open, and my heart rate doubles as Bucky whooshes into the room.

"Sorry to barge in like this," he whispers. There's a tipsy slur to his speech, but he clearly has his wits about him enough to have gotten up here so stealthily. "I couldn't sleep…"

"Me neith—"

He grabs my upper arms and pushes me gently but firmly onto the bed. "...or stop thinkin' about you."

"Are you serious?" I ask. A knee-jerk response. Even though I was just lying in bed obsessing over him, I wasn't prepared to have my wildest dream fulfilled so soon. "Or is this some kind of joke?"

"I don't know." Bucky crawls onto the bed and slides in next to me. "Is it?"

He swoops in and presses his lips against mine—the taste of whiskey and Altoids. So I'm not delusional! The past twenty-four hours have all been a big game of foreplay between us.

It occurs to me that this is the first time in five years I've made out with a man who isn't Ted. I wonder if *he's* been with anyone since our breakup. It's been over a month, so it's not entirely outside the realm of possibility that he's met someone else. And yet I still feel a distant sense of being tethered to him—like what I'm doing right now could somehow qualify as cheating.

No.

I'm not going to ruin this by thinking about my ex-fiancé.

I close my eyes and center myself back in the present moment. The feeling of Bucky's stubble, nose, chin. He's a passionate kisser—urgent, aggressive, ravenous—just like Ted was when we first met. Just like every closeted man I've ever been with. I think it's because they spend so much of their lives with their same-sex desire buried somewhere so deep inside them that when they finally get the nerve to act on it, it's like they're kissing for both the first and last time ever. They have lives and lies to get back to, so they approach the whole thing with a *just-this-once-and-then-it's-out-of-my-system-forever* kind of attitude. The result is a voracious degree of sexual appetite. I think about how, in Ted's case, I was able to translate that appetite into an actual relationship. Perhaps it's not so far-fetched to think I could do the same with Bucky.

"This is crazy," I murmur into the hot space between our mouths. "Are you sure we should be—"

"Nope." He digs his teeth into my neck as his hands roam up and down my body. "Are you?"

"Nope." I squeeze his ass—*his famous, ESPN ass*—and die a little inside. "Not at all."

This exchange of words should be akin to pumping the brakes, but instead it's like flooring the gas.

The kisses become more urgent, the touching more crucial. We're naked under the covers within thirty seconds. I instruct my fingertips to remember what they're feeling right now—every inch of Bucky's skin, body hair, muscles—as future proof that it really happened.

As he goes down on me, he says, "I've wanted to do this forever."

Somehow I intuitively understand that he means *this*—the act of fellatio on another man—and not necessarily *this*—the act of fellatio on me specifically.

"You're so perfect," he whispers as his hands dig into my hips and my lower back.

It's so, so good. Perhaps not technically as good as someone who's done it a million times before—but better. There's an innocent sloppiness to his technique that suggests he's not thinking about it all.

We trade positions, and I nearly pass out from the rush of feeling him in my mouth. His legs spasm as he moans in pleasure. He presses a nearby pillow over his mouth to muffle the sound, which makes me want to make him come even more.

"Go slower," he whispers. "I don't want this to end."

I bring my mouth back up to his in an effort to delay the inevitable, but it's too late. Between him having never been with another man and me having not been with a man who isn't Ted for over five years...neither of us is able to last much longer.

When it's over, I grab an undershirt from off the floor and clean us up.

Bucky just lies there on top of the covers, his biceps and pecs aglow with a thin layer of sweat. He exhales heavily and bites his lip.

I wish I knew what he was feeling right now. Revelation? Regret? Satisfaction? Fear? He opens his mouth to speak, but stops before a word gets out.

I poke his thigh. "You dropped your towel on purpose earlier, didn't you?"

I say it in a lighthearted tone that I hope signals to him that he doesn't have to freak out over what just happened.

"Yeah," he says softly. "I—"

But then he sits up and his demeanor does a complete backflip.

"You can't tell anyone about this," he says in a desperate whisper. "Shit. Damn. Why can't I control myself around you? It's like something inside me is hell-bent on lettin' you in on all my secrets—"

"Don't worry." I stroke the hair on his hard chest. "Your secret's safe with me..."

He tenses up. "I don't have a secret."

"You literally just used that word."

"Well, I didn't mean to. Nothing that happened in here is a big deal. We were just lettin' off a little steam...that's all."

"Yeah, no, totally." I squeeze my eyes shut before they have a chance to fill with tears. I really should have known this was the turn he was about to take. "I get it. You're not gay."

That last sentence hangs in the air for a moment too long, echoing in my head amid the silence between us.

Bucky reaches for my arm. "Maybe I shouldn't have come up here. I don't want you to get the wrong idea…"

"I just told you, it's fine."

He sighs. "I really like you, man. A lot. It's just that my life would damn near be over if anyone thought I was a—"

"Fag? Homo? Got it." I grab my boxer briefs from the foot of the bed. "That label is for guys like me. Guys like you can just 'let off steam' and call it a day."

His face falls. "Come on, now. I didn't mean it like that."

I dig my knuckles into my eyes in an effort to manufacture some stoicism. "It's all good," I lie. "I get what this is. And I promise I won't tell anyone."

Bucky takes a quick breath, like he's going to thank me, but cuts himself off before he can say another word.

25

I awake to the sensation of a vibrating phone under my pillow. Kate's calling, and I'm just groggy enough to forget I'm avoiding her.

"Hiiii," I groan.

"I'm so sorry about yesterday," she says. "I shouldn't have been harassing you."

Her unsolicited apology is so unexpected that I'm positive I've misheard her. "You're... What are you?"

"I said I'm sorry," she repeats through a tiny laugh. "I've been so unfair to you this weekend. I shouldn't have been asking you to spy for me."

I'm so glad I picked up. "I couldn't agree more."

"Honestly?" she continues. "I've just been projecting. You know how before Patrick I was always with cheating jerks? I think this whole bachelor party thing has, like, triggered all the old scars they left on my psyche. Which is so silly! I know Patrick is a good guy. He'd never do that to me."

All my muscles relax into the warm sensation of a resolved conflict. And without any effort on my part! Is there anything better?

"It's all good," I say through a yawn. "And you're right—Patrick would never do anything to hurt you."

"Really it's all Melanie's fault," she adds. "She came over Thursday night and was just telling me all kinds of horror stories of things she'd heard about Wilson's bachelor weekend up in Vermont."

"Patrick didn't go to that one, right? I remember it fell on NFL Draft weekend or something."

"Right," Kate confirms. "Thank *God*. Anyway. So Greeny was dating this girl back then—Steph or whatever—and she and Melanie had gotten close. And Greeny told Steph everything, and then *she* told Melanie everything."

Shit. Who knew Greeny was a gossip who loves drama? I'm glad he's single right now—no girlfriend to report back to.

"There were these illegal strippers there doing all kinds of stuff," Kate continues. "Apparently they had the guys lick whipped cream off their bodies. And then they put on a sex show"—she lowers her voice—"can you believe that?"

"Seriously?" I swallow a held breath. "There's no way that happened."

"According to Melanie, it did." Kate clicks her tongue. "Anyway. So she also mentioned that Bucky was there, and apparently he stayed upstairs the whole time because he didn't wanna risk bad press. So then when I talked to Trista yesterday and she mentioned that you and Bucky were hanging out alone on Thursday night, well—I'm sorry. I jumped to the worst conclusion I could think of. It was stupid of me. I didn't mean to accuse you guys of that."

My chest tightens at how she basically knows everything, and yet has somehow convinced herself that she doesn't. Unless she does and this is all just a loyalty test? If I admit that everything she just described is exactly what happened Thursday night, I pass. If I continue to deny, I fail. Shit. No! This is Kate. She might be a little insecure, but she's not a manipulative mastermind. I can take this conversation at face value.

"That party was like three years ago," I offer. "Why would Melanie just be telling you about it now?"

"She was probably saving it for this weekend," Kate says. "Just to give me something to stress about. Bitch."

"Have I told you lately that your friendship with her is toxic?" I ask. "She's always competing with you and, like, undermining you."

"That's just how she is," Kate says. "I don't take her all that seriously—which is why I believe Patrick when he says none of that stuff has been happening at his party..."

"You talked to him?"

"Yesterday. He assured me that you guys have just been playing poker and cornhole every night. So that made me feel better." She pauses. "You were right the other night. If I'm going to marry him, I really do just have to trust him."

"Exactly." I glance at the mirror and notice a deep red mark in the upper left corner of my chest. Jesus. I don't think I've had a hickey since sophomore year of undergrad. "And I'm sorry I've been short with you the past couple days. It's just been so much work organizing this party. I so wasn't born to be an event planner." I force a chuckle. "You caught me when I was overwhelmed."

"Don't even worry about it," she says. "I shouldn't have been pestering you so much. I trust Patrick! And you."

I release a giant exhale now that we've slipped so easily back into our friendship. "It's all good."

"So what's going on with you?" she asks. "Have you been able to get your mind off of Ted?"

"More than you could ever imagine," I mindlessly reply while pressing my fingers against the hickey Bucky gave me.

"Really?" Kate's voice curls up with intrigue. "Please, do tell."

"Nothing," I protest. "I don't know why I said that."

"Dom."

"Kate."

"What's going on?" she asks.

Shit! I've fully talked myself into a weird trap.

"I'm just groggy," I insist. "Last night was a long night... Your fiancé stole all my money at poker."

But she won't let up. "What are you hiding?"

"I'm not hiding anything," I tell her—which happens to be exactly what someone who's hiding something would say. "I'm..." Stammering, is what I'm doing. "Tired. I just told you I didn't get a lot of sleep."

"I know you, Dom. Something's going on..."

"Nothing's going on."

"Just tell me what it is."

"There's no 'it' to tell you about!"

Kate huffs as the line between us grows quiet. I close my eyes and am instantly bombarded with thoughts of Bucky—a million tiny flashbacks from our encounter last night. His lips, his hands, his—

"Spill," Kate demands. "What did Patrick do?"

"Patrick? He's not the one—" I cut myself off upon realizing that my knee-jerk instinct to clear Patrick's name has thrust me into yet another trap. I just can't win.

"So *someone* did something?"

"No! That's not what I—"

"Oh! Oh my God. Duh." Kate sounds like she just solved the riddle of the sphinx. "Bucky...*you and Bucky!*"

No.

No, no, no, no. This can't be happening. What the hell did I say to make her jump to such an extreme (yet correct) conclusion? Am I really that easy for her to read?

My mind flips through a slideshow of nightmare scenarios. Bucky outed to Trista, to Patrick, to the press. His entire life and reputation in a tailspin. Bucky blaming me, hating me, assuming I told Kate out of spite or resentment or some cliché urge to gossip.

Bucky...in pain.

I launch into a panicked speech of damage control. "You absolutely can't tell anyone, Kate. This is serious. I gave him my word that I wouldn't say anything, and I really meant it." My heart races as the words spill out. "We were drunk. He made it clear last night that it's never going to happen again, and he says he's not even gay, anyway, so it was probably just a—"

"Whoa, whoa, whoa." Kate lowers her voice. "Gay? What are you talking about?"

Oh.

Fuck.

"Nothing." I catch my breath and compose myself. "I think I misunderstood you. What exactly did you mean when you said *me and Bucky?*"

"I was talking about you guys having that conversation the other night," she answers. "I thought you were finally gonna admit that you *did* encourage him to dump Trista." She pauses. "So wait a minute. You and Bucky...hooked up? Oh my God."

I blink hard to stave off tears. It hasn't even been twelve hours since I promised him I wouldn't tell anyone, and I've already managed to commit the ultimate betrayal. I want so badly to just hang up—slide down onto this cold bathroom floor and disappear. But if I don't engage with Kate right now, there's no telling what she'll do next.

"Dom?" she asks. "Are you okay?"

"You have to promise you won't say anything," I repeat. "This cannot get out."

She pauses for a moment, as if weighing her options. Trista is one of her best friends, so I know it's going to be hard to keep such a huge bomb from her. But Kate has to know this is a unique circumstance. She works in media and is marrying a sports attorney; she of all people should understand what's at stake for Bucky.

"His secret is safe with me," Kate says. "Only an extremely shitty person would out someone before they're ready to out themselves..." Her voice trails off. "But babe, how did this even happen? And are you okay? You really don't sound okay. I know you're not the 'secretive one-night stand' type."

Now that she's showing concern for my wellbeing, I'm overcome with the urge to ask her for advice. Last night was quite possibly the most surreal experience of my life—it might feel good to validate the experience by confiding in someone. Especially after the pain I felt when he left in a blaze of regret.

And so I let it all pour out like gasoline—from the unlikely shed-bonding to yesterday's kitchen towel-drop to last night's unreal climax. Kate gasps intermittently, but otherwise she absorbs the revelations silently as I ramble on and on and on. I realize just about halfway through that I sound like a cross between a gushing, infatuated schoolgirl and a bitter, jilted ex-lover. I guess I'm equal parts of both right now—and will probably continue to be until I have a chance to face Bucky in the light of day and figure out where his head is at.

"So I don't know what to do," I finally conclude. "How am I supposed to act around him now?"

"I think you have to act as normal as possible. Something like this...you have to just pretend it never happened." She exhales slowly. "God. I can't believe Bucky is gay. It's so—"

"Please never say that sentence out loud ever again."

"But he is! Poor Trista. How does she not know?"

"Just because he has the capacity to hook up with a man once doesn't necessarily mean he's gay," I explain. Even though, in Bucky's case, I hope it does.

"Well he's definitely not straight," Kate says. "No straight man would just come into your room and make a move like that."

I remind myself that she has no idea Patrick basically did the exact same thing with me back when we were teenagers. Even if it was just experimentation on his part.

But Bucky last night—that was something else entirely. That was a man giving in to a desire he's had his entire life. I could feel it in his touch, in his breath. It was like when I first started sleeping with men in college—losing that lifelong cone collar.

I sigh. "You know what? We shouldn't be talking about this. Please forget we ever had this conversation."

"You're right." She recenters her breath. "But back to Trista for a just a sec—she's heartbroken, you know. She's not mad at *you* anymore, and she's still coming to the bachelorette. But it doesn't change the fact that he dumped her over the phone. That's barely any better than Berger dumping Carrie via Post-it note in season six of *SATC*."

She pronounces it *Sat-C*, as per our custom.

"She should've never been mad at me in the first place," I say. "We barely even talked about her the other night! I still don't understand what that was all about."

"Maybe he was looking to sleep with you this whole time," Kate suggests. "Maybe he wanted to make sure he was single so he wouldn't feel guilty when it finally happened…"

"I don't think so." As much as I'd like for that to be true, I can't discount the look on his face after we finished up last night. It was pure panic—the face of a man who realized he'd just put every-thing he loves at risk in service of a single thoughtless impulse. Not a man who'd just executed some kind of well-thought-out plan. "He's..."

My voice trails off as my mind spirals through a thousand worries.

How am I ever going to face him today? I know my tenden-cies. After I sleep with a guy who I feel even remotely inferior to, it's all I can think about. I obsess. I get weird and needy and insecure, afraid he'll ghost me any second if I say or do the wrong thing. It's a toxic, twisted cycle—and it was one of the primary reasons I stayed unhappily coupled with Ted for so long. At least when you're with someone, you don't have to deal with all the emotional self-worth bullshit that goes along with casual sex. And I'm especially not prepared to start dealing with it now, on this weekend of all weekends. With Bucky of all people.

"Dom?" Kate asks. "Are you still there?"

I struggle to catch a breath. "Yeah."

"Don't worry too much about this," she says, as if she's been reading my mind for the past minute. "Everything is going to be fine."

26

Everything is going to be fine. I repeat it to myself over and over like a mantra as I stick my head under the scalding stream of my morning shower. *Everything...is...fine.*

Normally talking to Kate about the drama of the day makes me feel better—even if just on a surface level—but this time I'm left with nothing but regret. This wasn't just some anonymous Tinder hookup. It was a professional athlete who happens to be her fiancé's best friend and *her* friend's very recent ex.

I should have never picked up the phone. Or at the very least, I should have been way more careful when she grilled me. Even if I didn't intentionally bring up the topic of Bucky's sexuality, I should've found some way to backpedal and convince her that she'd misunderstood what I was saying. And if that didn't work, I should have just shut the call down with as little information as possible. Why did I have to indulge in a whole discussion about what our hookup means for *me*?

I'm sure Ted would have much to say about all this. He always loathed my tendency to lean on Kate or Patrick (depending on the subject) for boozy therapy sessions about the most intimate details of our personal lives.

"Why do you need them to validate your feelings all the time?"

he'd ask. "It's like nothing in your life counts unless one of them tells you it does. Some things can just be private, you know."

I used to think he was just mad that I was telling other people about what an asshole he could be, but now I realize he had a point. Perhaps I do need to learn how to process some things on my own.

I dry off from the shower and squint at my adult acne-prone face in the mirror. I can see the oily beginnings of a breakout forming on my left temple.

As I apply several preventative dabs of Clinique clinical clearing gel, I'm reminded of the last time I ran to Kate for advice when I shouldn't have.

It was a warm afternoon in April, and I was at work, where our CEO had this up-and-coming musical duo from Sony Music perform for us at lunchtime. (One of the perks of working for a streaming startup is that we get treated to intimate showcase performances from recording artists every so often. You know, instead of fair pay.)

It was a husband and wife team, and their chemistry was palpable. The woman—a petite brunette hippie—sat at the piano and gazed lovingly into her lumberjack husband's eyes as she played a whimsical accompaniment and seamlessly blended her soprano with his baritone.

I'll never forget that look she gave him. You could tell she didn't even realize she was giving him a look, it just came so naturally, glowing with admiration. A look that said: *You are perfect just the way you are.* The unconditional love between them was palpable.

And it made me want to scream.

All I could think about was how the only looks Ted ever gave *me* were ones that said: *You are a defective human, and you're lucky I chose you anyway.*

And she was playing that godforsaken piano! The one in the center of our lobby that employees are expressly prohibited from touching. The one that taunts me every day as a constant physical reminder of the creative fulfillment that is sorely lacking from my life. She was living this perfect fantasy of music and love that I could only ever dream of.

The jealousy swirled around in my head all afternoon until it eventually gave way to a mini panic attack. At which point I left work early and headed straight to Kate's office.

"You should have seen them," I moaned from the fluffy chair facing her desk. "They were legitimately in love. And they used the office piano! I didn't even know that thing was in tune, the way no one else is ever allowed to touch it."

"Are you kidding?" she asked. "I wasn't even there, but I can tell you right now it was just performative bullshit. They were on a stage! I doubt they even *like* each other."

"Ted and I haven't had sex in six mon—"

"He loves you, Domenic." She flipped her shiny blonde hair. "He wouldn't be marrying you if he didn't. And it's common to go through dry spells." She paused for a moment. "Granted, six months is a tragedy, and you need to do something about that ASAP. If you had a vag, it'd be drier than the Sahara right now."

"Thanks," I deadpanned. "But how can we make love when all we ever do is fight?"

"It's totally normal to fight with your significant other!" she assured me. "I'd be more concerned if you weren't fighting. You know Patrick and I fight all the time! And we're perfect for each other."

"That's true." I relaxed into the softness of the chair. "No real-life couple is that happy after so many years."

"Nope," she said. "Anyway, I didn't realize you still played the piano? Why don't you ever play for me?"

"I don't still play the piano," I said. "I don't know why I even mentioned that."

"Maybe it's because you…want to pick it up again?"

"Maybe I do," I admitted.

"Then do!" she said. "Tell Ted to buy you one as a wedding present."

Her response was so effective at snapping me out of my funk. I still knew in the pit of my stomach that Ted and I had long-surpassed any normal amount of dysfunction—something was fundamentally off between us—but having a surface-level conversation with Kate was just what I needed to refresh my supply of denial and have faith that we could at least make it to the wedding and figure things out from there.

"Thanks for talking to me about this." My gaze shifted to the menagerie of cheap makeup compacts and mass-produced face lotions lined up on her desk. "Do you have anything for oily skin? I can feel a stress-blemish forming because of this."

"Of course I do, babe." She pulled out a tube of Clinique clinical clearing gel—the same one I'm currently applying to my temple like a neurotic parent slathering their pasty toddler in SPF 90—and passed it to me. "But stop worrying! Everything is going to be fine."

She was wrong back then, and I'm pretty sure she's wrong now.

27

The house is steeped in eerie silence as I creep out of my room and meander toward the lower level. Eventually I find Patrick sitting alone in the kitchen, draped in a seersucker Brooks Brothers robe and reading from the ESPN app on his phone. The emptiness of the space mixed with my volatile emotional hangover prompts me to greet him by asking the one question I know I shouldn't:

"Where's Bucky?"

Patrick looks up. "Good morning to you, too."

"Sorry," I stammer. "Morning."

"Graham took off before any of us woke up," he says.

"He just left?" I ask through an internal flood of disappointment. "He didn't say bye?"

Patrick shrugs. "Must've been in the middle of the night. I got up to take a leak at four, and he was already gone."

My hand trembles as I grab a banana. "Why would he do that?"

"He probably just had to get back to training," Patrick says. "At least he was able to make it out here for a couple days, anyway. More than I expected. And I'm glad you finally got to know him better."

My body temperature increases. "What do you mean by that?"

"Just that you guys spent a lot of time together the past couple days." He says it with caution, like I'm a mysterious package that might explode if opened. "You're acting weird. Are you alright?"

"Yeah. Where are the other guys?"

"They took the pontoon out," he says. "I wasn't feeling it."

I stand up. "Got it. I think I'm gonna go get some sun."

He narrows his eyes at me—a mix of concern and suspicion—but lets it go. "Alright, man. We still have a couple hours before the brewery."

I excuse myself to the back patio while Patrick goes to his room to get ready.

I close my eyes and stick my face up to the sky. For a moment, my thoughts take a back seat to the comforting sensation of heat on my skin.

Eventually I open my eyes back up and survey the picturesque landscape. My gaze shifts down to the lighthouse shed, which then causes my mind to wander back to the topic of Bucky and his secrets. As nervous as I was to face him again today, it's even worse that he disappeared without warning. Now I have to live with this uncertainty of how he feels about last night. No tone of voice to analyze, no body language to dissect.

Was he really that disgusted by what happened between us?

Before I realize what I'm doing, my feet begin marching toward the lighthouse. I pass the beach, the dock, the Adirondack chairs. Mystic Harbor glistens ahead of me, vast and blue, as I arrive at the tiny white wooden door and creep inside.

The teal L.L.Bean sleeping bags are still splayed out on the floor from Thursday night. I crouch down and begin to roll them up. Somehow it feels like I'm mourning yet another breakup right now. Which is a crazy thing to feel! All we shared were a few deep conversations and one night of drunken passion.

But I guess that was it. The vulnerability of it all. The

simultaneous rush and fear of trusting someone. Sure, it's easy to dish to Kate about a hookup or complain about how my fiancé and I aren't having sex—but the stuff I talked about with Bucky felt like the kind of stuff I would normally keep to myself. In a way, it was more intimate than what we did last night.

I push my hurt down as I toss the first sleeping bag back into its spot between the folding chairs and the kayak paddles.

As I reach for the other one, a slew of noises begins to erupt outside on the water. First it's waves, then it's the pontoon's motor. Followed by Wilson's and Greeny's voices as they pull up to the dock. I squeeze the sleeping bag and freeze in place, careful not to make a sound.

"What was her name again?" Greeny asks. There's a highly detectable sense of frat-boy mischief in his tone. "Candy? Mercedes?"

"The brunette was *Kitty*," Wilson answers. "The redhead was *Lexus*."

They both laugh.

"And which was the one you pounded at the end of the night?" Greeny asks. Wait. Pounded? "I was so bombed all I remember is you disappearing into the bedroom with a pair of floating D-cups."

"Listen, asshole," Wilson barks. "We paid for it up front—someone had to make use. It's not my fault Cooper is too whipped to accept a proper send-off."

"You really took one for the team," Greeny cracks. "I'm sure your wife will understand."

Wilson scoffs. "Melanie? Gimme a break. If I waited around for when *she's* in the mood, I'd only get laid twice a year." He emits a sadistic little laugh. "Besides, it's not like you didn't have your chance. Not my fault you had whiskey dick."

"Dude," Greeny says. "I did not. I just used that as an excuse to, you know, not contract hooker-herpes. My buddy from the gym got it last year—it's not fun."

They laugh and then fall into silence for a few moments. Sounds of shuffling and packing echo in the air, followed by wet footsteps along the dock. Their conversation picks up again as they head toward land.

"You're really not worried about Melanie finding out?" Greeny asks Wilson.

"How the hell would she find out?" Wilson asks. "The spy wasn't there."

"Domenic?" Greeny asks as my pulse spikes at the mention of my name. "What makes you think he'd say anything?"

Wilson scoffs. "Dude, he tells Kate everything. And Kate tells Mel everything. And all three of them are gonna be back here in a few weeks for the bachelorette party."

I squeeze the sleeping bag harder—so hard my nails go white. All this time I've been going through hell trying to keep Kate in the dark, only to be presumed guilty anyway. Meanwhile, Wilson conveniently forgets it was Greeny who blabbed about *his* bachelor party three years ago.

"You're not giving Dom enough credit," Greeny counters. *Thank you, Greeny.* "He wouldn't throw Coop under the bus like that. He's basically one of us."

Wilson bursts into cruel laughter. "What have you been smoking? You forget he's gay or something? More power to him—he can bang all the dudes he wants—but get real. He wasn't in OKB. He'll never be one of us."

Greeny sighs. "C'mon, man. It's not 2011 anymore."

"Whatever," Wilson says. "All I know is that Mel can grill him all she wants to at the party next month. As far as he knows, I didn't even get a lap dance."

Their conversation continues, but their voices fade as they get closer and closer to the house. The last thing I hear is an eruption of laughter after one of them seems to slip or trip or hit his foot on something.

My head spins as the shed returns to silence and I assess the damage.

Wilson cheated on his wife—another secret to add to the list. As if I didn't have enough of them already. And of course! *Of course* I'd find out this way—while I'm here of all places. The shed of lies.

But what really stings is the way he talked about me—triggering every insecurity I've had this weekend with six little words:

He'll never be one of us.

I can't help but wonder if Patrick has ever had the same thought.

28

Y ou've been the weirdest combination of quiet and drunk all day," Patrick says to me as we head out to the beach for sunset beers. We've just returned from the brewery, where I got positively hammered on pale ales in an effort to erase my mind. The other guys trail several feet behind us, obnoxious as ever. "Everything okay with you?"

"Yep," I lie. The lighthouse pops out at me from across the beach, which prompts a flash of memory. "You hear back from Buckley yet?"

I probably sound way too invested, but the alcohol in my system has killed my ability to feign indifference. I miss Bucky. Between his absence and the conversation I overheard at the dock this morning, I've felt distinctly alone all day.

Patrick throws an arm around my shoulder to prevent me from tripping over myself and tumbling down the hill. "Bucky, you mean, drunk-ass?"

"Ob-viously," I slur. "I meant him."

"Dude, this is like the tenth time you've asked me." Patrick checks his phone quickly and confirms there's still no answer. "He probably just saw my text and forgot to reply. He does that all the time. He's fine. Why are you so concerned?"

"I miss him," I blurt. Dangerously. "I mean…"

The footsteps behind us accelerate at this exact moment.

"Did I just hear Diva Dom say he misses Graham?" Wilson taunts in his abrasively arrogant drunk-voice. "Aww. Isn't that precious?"

"Fuck you," I blurt. Even more dangerously! But I can't help it. My resentment toward him has been festering for hours.

Wilson releases a smug giggle. "Damn, bro. Defensive much?"

His dismissiveness only pisses me off more.

"Fuck *you*," I repeat—this time drawing out the second word for effect. "What-the-fuck kind of name is Wilson, anyway? What are you, the volleyball from *Cast Away*?"

Greeny stifles a laugh.

"Ooooh," Wilson mocks. "Good one. Never heard it before."

"Dom." Patrick squeezes my shoulder. "You alright? What's going on with you?"

"Nothing's going on with me," I tell him. "*Wilson* is a piece of shit who cheated on his wife the other night…but nothing's going on with *me*."

Wilson runs forward and steps in front of me, puffing his chest out. "What'd you just say?"

"You! Heard! Me! Asshole." I need to calm down. This is turning into a scene from high school, back when I'd start fights I couldn't finish and Patrick would have to swoop in and save the day. But although my mind knows better, my mouth is drunk and incapable of staying shut. "Now get out of my face."

"I'm warning you right now," Wilson barks. "If you say anything to Melanie, I swear to God I'll kick your ass—"

"Guys," Patrick butts in. "Come on. Just chill."

Wilson huffs and then exhales, like he's willing to follow Patrick's orders if I am.

But I'm not. This dark part of me wants to take everything out on Wilson. His cruel betrayal of Melanie. Bucky's wordless rejection of me. My inability to ever measure up to Patrick. My broken engagement. Everything!

"Go ahead," I dare him. And then I grip the base of my beer bottle tightly and thrust my hand forward—splashing him right in the eyes. Who the hell am I? A Real Housewife of New Jersey? "Kick my ass."

Wilson's shiny, dripping face is overtaken by pure animal rage.

"Gladly," he says. "Let's fuckin' go."

He pushes me in the chest so hard that I fall backward. My ass slaps the ground and I almost slide down the hill, but I'm able to grab onto a handful of grass—just enough to steady myself as I dig a foot into the dirt.

"Get up," Wilson continues. His body hovers over mine like a death threat. This guy was probably such a bully in high school; I can't imagine how or why Patrick ever became friends with him in college. "Let's do this."

A shockwave travels up my body as Wilson literally kicks me while I'm down.

"Hey! Hey!" Patrick grabs Wilson from behind and pushes him down to the ground. "That was too far, man. What the hell?"

"So now *you* wanna go, Coop?" Wilson quickly bounces back up and wipes the remaining beer off his face. "Control your friend over there."

"Dude!" Patrick says. "You're the one who kicked him."

"Only after he threw his beer in my face like a little bitch!"

Patrick shakes his head. "Why do you have to be such a dick?"

"Me?" Wilson shoots back. "What about him? It's your bachelor party, and your own best man has been nothing but a wet rag and a spy for your girlfriend."

I jump up to my feet and prepare to defend myself, but Patrick snaps back at Wilson before I can formulate a coherent sentence.

"You know what, man?" Patrick says. "Maybe you should leave."

"I should leave?" Wilson huffs. "That's real nice, *brother.*" He draws the word out like a taunt. "I'll remember that the next time you need—"

"Coop, come on," Greeny interjects. "Wilson's just a little heated. He's been drinking. He shouldn't drive. Let's all just calm down—"

"No! I'm calm," Wilson protests. "I'm not drunk. This party blows anyway." He shoots Patrick a death stare. "You've changed, man. I don't know if it's Kate or"—he gestures at me like I'm not even here—"or what. But you're fuckin' soft, dude. It's embarrassing as hell."

With that, he throws his beer to the ground. It rolls down the hill toward the beach, oozing, leaving a trail of wet foam on the grass. He marches up in the opposite direction and slams the sliding door shut as he enters the house, presumably to pack up and take off.

Nobody stops him.

"You alright, bud?" Patrick asks as we continue walking, his arm around me now.

"I'm fine," I tell him, instantly sobered up by the throbbing pain in my hip. "Sorry I ruined your last day. I shouldn't have thrown that beer in his face. I was just so—"

"Wilson's an asshole," Patrick says. The most accurate statement I've heard all weekend. "He shouldn't have reacted like that."

"Kind of harsh to send him home, though, no?" Greeny asks. "He's our friend." He turns to me and slaps my back. "But that was messed up, the way he attacked you, man. I'm sorry about that. I don't know why he did that."

I acknowledge his statement with a grim nod, and the three of us keep walking in silence until we reach the beach. We settle into the crescent of Adirondack chairs as Greeny hands out fresh beers from the mini cooler he brought along.

"Wilson will be fine," Patrick finally says. "He didn't seem that drunk. And if he is, he knows better than to drive. He'll just stay in his room and sulk for a while."

And so we all shrug and sip and move on—as if that entire altercation never even happened. Which is crazy, because for me, it's easily the most confrontation I've had in my entire adult life. My instinct is to replay, dissect, cry, scream, and analyze the entire episode until I've fully processed and made peace with the fact that there is a person in the world who actively wants to kick my ass right now.

But instead I absorb the nonchalance the guys are exhibiting. They couldn't be more chill, swapping stories and sports stats and stupid jokes. I mostly stay quiet, but I contribute a light laugh every so often to maintain the appearance that I'm at least somewhat present.

Across from us, the sun sets against the sky and water—a fireball descending smoothly through shades of blue—as I continue to breathe, drink, breathe, drink.

It feels like an eternity has passed since I showed up here on Wednesday, plagued with worry that something bad was going to happen this weekend. If only I had known just how many of those bad things were in store—and yet here we are. Patrick was right. Worrying was a waste of time. Those things were going to happen no matter how much I tried to avoid them.

We survived.

And what I take the most comfort in is the fact that, when shit blew up and punches flew, Patrick stood up for me. He hasn't done that since we were kids—and I honestly wasn't sure he'd do it today. But he did. His two worlds clashed—much like when he was faced with the decision of selecting a best man—and this time he chose me.

That has to mean something, right?

july

The Bachelorette Party

n the nineteen days since the bachelor party's abrupt end, my obsession with Bucky Graham has become malignant—such a one-sided, all-consuming fixation that I'm basically Kathy Bates in *Misery* at this point.

Not in the sense that I've considered locking him in a room and slowly torturing him for days on end. (I swear I haven't.) But in the sense that he is a public figure and—given how much contact we've had (absolutely none) since our night together—I might as well just be a delusional stalker-fan at this point. I don't have his number, so I can't text him. I have considered asking Patrick for it on several occasions, but I'm terrified of the ensuing interrogation that would take place. I could try to message him on Facebook or Instagram, but all his social handles feel very professional and are likely monitored by several members of his team. So in the end, it's as if I'm nothing more than a thirsty groupie.

He started playing golf again the week after he missed the Travelers Championship. As far as the general public knows, he tweaked a nerve during a practice round. (His publicist deserves a hell of a raise.) At the 3M Open last week—which he won—an NBC Golf reporter asked him how "recovery" was going.

"Back pain is no joke—put a real hitch in my get-along for a minute there when I had to miss the Travelers," he told the camera in his signature drawl. "I was too weak to whip a gnat. But this win is the confidence boost I needed before headin' into the Open next week."

And then the anchor passed it back to the studio, where all the analysts applauded his ability to rebound so quickly.

"It's because he was never actually injured!" I screamed at my flat screen, alone in my stuffy Financial District apartment with a pint of edible cookie dough and a magnum bottle of Cupcake cabernet. "He was just busy having gay sex"—*wipes cookie dough off upper lip*—"with ME!!!"

Perhaps I've become unhinged.

But have you ever stared at the TV while the last guy who ghosted you is praised for his perfect drives and impeccable putting game? It's a very specific form of torture.

All I could think about when I saw his hand grip a nine iron was how that same hand was gripping *me* mere days ago. I still think about it at least a few times a day. I can't *not* think about it, because if I don't, then it will be like it never happened. And in some way, that would be even worse than the agony I'm putting myself through obsessing over him. It's a vicious cycle.

The only silver lining is that it's been great at forcing closure from my failed engagement. Ted fucking who?

And I know. It's pathetic that I somehow let that one night with Bucky turn into such a big deal. If I were better at casual sex, I'd be able to appropriately compartmentalize it as an isolated hookup with a sexually frustrated "straight" dude. Those hookups happen all the time. It's basically why Craigslist was invented. Some men can screw several anonymous closeted cases per week and move on with their lives. Why do I have to be the kind of man who—instead of accepting casual sex for what it is—involuntarily scribbles hearts on his mental composition book?

Then again, this wasn't just an anonymous hookup. It was a transformative moment of passion with the unlikeliest of partners.

I can't stop fantasizing about telling Patrick the truth, absorbing his reaction like fuel for my gas tank of self-worth. *Turns out the straight frat bro you ditched me for in college is just as gay as I am! How about that?*

And it's not just the sex I keep thinking about. It's all those private moments we shared leading up to the sex—the heart-to-hearts in the lighthouse shed, out on the pontoon—they almost felt like falling in love. That couldn't have all just been in my head.

Which is why Kate is killing me right now, on our drive up to the Mystic house, asking me if it was all just in my head.

"Maybe he was drunk and horny and doesn't even remember it," she says from the passenger seat. "Not that I'm saying you're forgettable, babe. I just feel like I know Bucky pretty well. I can't imagine him being anything but straight. It's like"—she throws her freshly moisturized hands up—"beyond the realm of possibility."

"He flirted with me every time we were alone," I explain to her for the hundredth time. "And *he* came into my room that night. I don't know if he's gay or bi or what, but he knew what he was doing. It wasn't an accident."

"I know, hon." Kate reaches across the console and rubs my knee. "Listen, I need to tell you something. And please don't freak out…"

She exhales and opens the window, ushering in a gust of salty shoreline air. Just knowing that we're about to be back in Mystic makes my stomach twist with memories of last month's party. The twisting is exacerbated by Kate's cryptic tone. She's about to drop some kind of potentially crushing information on me. I can feel it.

"What?" I ask.

"Don't shoot the messenger, okay? I just thought you should hear it from me."

"Fine, fine, yeah. What is it?"

She steadies her voice. "Bucky and Trista are back together."

My hands almost lose control of the steering wheel. Granted, Bucky and Trista's breakup was never made public—I may or may not have checked Trista's Instagram several times over the past three weeks in search of a melodramatic "starting over" post (or Notes app screenshot, as influencers are wont to do)—but they also haven't been photographed together since the breakup, either. I figured they were just timing it strategically—to align with a new campaign Trista had to promote or something.

"That's impossible!" I tell Kate. "Trista hasn't been to any of his tournaments since he started playing again." The hopeless romantic in me loves that part of televised golf—seeing the camera pan to the players' wives and girlfriends. It's especially fun (and/or gut-wrenching) when a player wins a tournament and they show him pull his partner in for an epic embrace, right before victory-marching with her to the clubhouse from the eighteenth hole. "She wasn't even at the 3M last week, and he *won* that!" Did I imagine what it would be like if he were the first openly gay golfer and I was his big gay husband who ran out to celebrate his victory with him? No. Except yes. "He had to walk back to the clubhouse alone."

"She was booked!" Kate says. "She has a career of her own, you know."

"So they haven't even seen each other since the party?"

"No. But they've been talking."

"I see." This makes me feel somewhat better, even though it shouldn't. The fact that Bucky even considered getting back with Trista is clear confirmation of his desire to fully wipe our fling from his mental record. "Well, maybe when they see each other again he'll realize that he's really—"

He's really what? In love with me?

"Oh, babe." Kate's voice deepens as she cuts me off. "Listen, you deserve so much better than him. He's not even remotely available. You deserve a guy who will be proud to claim you—you know what I'm saying?"

"Like Ted did," I mumble.

"Right," she says. "Except someone who's less of a jerk."

Kate is absolutely right, and I appreciate that she wants the best for me. But there's a difference between understanding the concept of self-worth on an intellectual level and actually practicing it. Especially when the alternative to self-worth involves hooking up with the sex-on-a-stick professional athlete you've fantasized about for years.

"And if you ask me," she continues. "Trista deserves better than Bucky, too. With his career the way it is, he's incapable of being in a relationship with *anyone*. Man or woman."

I sigh. "Their relationship is all for show, anyway. He told me as much last month."

Kate's eyes widen. "What? Are you serious?"

Oh. I didn't mean to let that slip.

But I guess I'll have to go with it. "Aren't all celebrity relationships kinda full of shit?"

"Not theirs!" Kate says. "At least Trista doesn't think so. Ugh. I feel so bad about this. Maybe we should just tell her?"

"Tell her what?"

Because surely she can't mean...

"The truth about what happened between you and Bucky that weekend. She *is* my friend. It feels so wrong to be lying to her. I don't wanna have to choose sides, you know? And I hate being responsible for keeping secrets."

"It sucks being thrust into the middle of two of your best friends' relationship drama," I say without thinking. "Doesn't it?"

"Are you trying to say something about me and Patrick?"

"No." Damnit. Why did I have to go there? "That's not—"

"Because if there's something he did at the bachelor party I should know about, then please, by all means—"

"Patrick has assured you several times that you have nothing to worry about!" I nearly miss the exit to Mystic but jerk the car over to the right lane just in time. "Listen, this weekend is going to be fun. It's not about me or Trista or Bucky or whoever else. We're going to be celebrating *you*."

Kate exhales and runs a hand through her straight blonde hair.

We drive the backroads to the Mystic house in silence. I hoped my little speech would cleanse the air between us, but instead it resulted in a million particles of unresolved tension. By the time we pull into the driveway, my thoughts are all dominated by the return of that anxious voice in my head. It's even louder and clearer than it was the day I arrived here for Patrick's bachelor party last month.

Something bad is going to happen this weekend.

30

~

Kate's older sister, Paige, greets us in the foyer, fully decked out in a nautical capri-blouse combo straight from the latest Ann Taylor LOFT summer line.

"Sissy!" She pulls Kate into a hug. This is only my third time ever in Paige's presence—she lives in Arizona with her husband and kids—but she's exactly like I remember her from Kate's surprise thirtieth birthday party last year. A control freak soccer mom who transforms into a party girl once you throw a glass of rosé in her hand.

She releases Kate from her embrace and gives me a quieter, more church-like hug. "Hi, Dom! Thanks so much for keeping our girl entertained while we got the house ready for"—she lights up with a cheesy grin—"Kate's *Last Fling Before the Ring!*"

She points into the living room at a giant banner hung over the stone fireplace with the catchphrase printed on it in that ubiquitous Pinterest craft lettering. You know, the one that's all bouncy and thick and cursive-looking. Bridesmaid font.

Paige squeezes my wrist and squeaks. "Do you love it? I love it."

"Shut up! I'm obsessed." These words actually come out of my mouth. Paige's energy has reminded me of the role I'm expected to play this weekend: sassy gay sidekick. "You're killing it, girl."

"The font is called Shalma," Paige explains. "My girlfriend in Tucson turned me onto it. She has an Etsy shop—I'll give you the link. But first! Let me show you guys around."

Kate rolls her eyes. "Paige, this is *my* fiancé's family beach house. I think I know my way around. Where are the other girls?"

"They're all out on the beach." Paige's bubbly tone deflates just enough to suggest they have a healthy amount of buried sibling animosity between them. "And you've never been here after *I* decorated it for your bachelorette weekend. Now let's go."

Paige proceeds to drag us through the entire house. Each bedroom has been labeled with a name on the door (in that font) and there is an erect-penis-shaped bar of soap suction-cupped to every bathroom sink.

"Give a handy to wash your handies!" Paige sings as we hover in the master bathroom. And then calms herself down. "It's not too much, right?"

"I love me some peen soap," I assure her while leaning forward to give it a sniff. "Is that lavender? Divine."

As it turns out, the bathrooms are just the tip (pun intended) of the iceberg. We encounter several more dicks upon our return to the living room—a bowl of penis-shaped lollipops on the coffee table, a penis pillow tucked neatly onto each of the accent chairs, penis confetti tastefully strewn about the various accent surfaces.

Here's an interesting difference between most straight women and gay men: although both species are romantically attracted to men, their feelings toward the primary male appendage are often in total opposition. For lots of women I know, penises are simultaneously a mystery and a joke—something you might get pleasure out of (*if*—and this is a big *if*—it's properly used), but otherwise they're just these unremarkable nuisances.

For gay men, penises themselves are a huge part of the

package (pun also intended! It's just too easy) when it comes to sexual attraction. It's like when Kitty's...kitty...was in my face and Greeny was like, "Man, this is the best view in the world." That's how I feel about a good penis! Which is why it would never occur to me to completely desexualize them and turn them into disembodied party favors.

"I thought the volume was bordering on crass, but your friend Trista went on a little shopping spree at the sex store," Paige explains with a coy giggle.

An echo of the patio door sliding open reverberates from the kitchen. Melanie saunters into the living room a moment later.

"Girl!" she exclaims as she pulls Kate into a tight hug. "I was wondering when your sexy ass was gonna get here."

Melanie's gaze shifts over to me and instantly freezes over into a look of pure disdain. "Oh." She purses her pink lips. "Domenic. You came."

Yes, that is unvarnished hatred she's serving. Because as it turned out, Wilson *was* drunk and he *did* drive on that last night of the bachelor party—and he swiftly got pulled over and booked for a DUI. The kicker? It was his third DUI within the past ten years. Which means that his license was instantly revoked, and he may even have to serve jail time at some point. (The exact sentence is still TBD.) And so now he and his wife blame *me* for all of it. Not, you know, the fact that the bastard clearly has a pattern.

Normally the knowledge that someone on this earth harbors negative feelings toward me would be enough to trigger a break-down, but it's amazing how one's mind can prioritize levels of anxiety. I've spent the past three weeks so obsessed with the Bucky situation that I've barely taken time to acknowledge that I have a new enemy in Melanie.

But now that she's in front of me, it's all I can think about. There's no worse feeling than being actively disliked.

Don't hate me, I wish I could say. *Hate that piece of shit husband of yours instead. He said mean things about you the entire bachelor weekend, and I defended you! And he cheated on you with a stripper!*

Dump! His! Sorry! Ass!

"Wouldn't have missed it for the world," I say instead. And then I pull Kate close to me, as if to signal that I'm better friends with the bride than she is and so she needs to be nice. "You look great, by the way." I actually mean this. She's gotten an auburn dye job and a fresh keratin treatment since I last saw her; the resulting look is very Emma Stone circa *La La Land.* "I'm loving your new hair."

Melanie fakes a smile. "Thanks. Yours, too."

Meanwhile, I've sported the same basic-ass Supercuts haircut since literally the nineties.

"So..." Paige begins in a clear effort to cleanse the energy of the room.

She's interrupted by Trista, who makes a slow-motion entrance from the kitchen. My heart skips at the sight of her swimsuit model physique. She's wearing a lime-green bikini, draped in some kind of a sheer white sarong.

All I can think about is her body smooshing up together with Bucky's.

The image makes perfect sense, really. Two very fit, very beautiful people—each one the respective quintessence of conventional femininity and masculinity. They're a heterosexual American dream. I'm gay and pining after her boyfriend, and even *I* find something oddly comforting about the image of the two of them posing for a Christmas card together.

Wait. Is Trista looking intently at me right now, as if she can read my thoughts? Oh no. She's looking intently at me right now, as if she can read my thoughts.

"Hey, Dom," she says with an arched (and meticulously waxed but still full and luminous) eyebrow. Why is she greeting *me* first? Does she know something? She knows something. "I've been waiting for you to get here. I have a million questions for you."

My throat dries up like a piece of expired jerky. "Oh. About what?"

She addresses the other girls while pulling me off into the great room. "We'll be right back."

We end up standing below a skylight in the corner, hovering by the shadow of my beloved grand piano.

I swallow a pang of dread. "So...what's up?"

Trista just stares at me, biting her lower lip. I'm terrified of making eye contact with her—lest mine give me away—so I shift my gaze around the room like an SNL caricature of a socially awkward nerd.

"I don't know how to say this," she begins before trailing off. "I..."

She goes quiet again.

The only explanation for any of this strange behavior is that she knows about Bucky and me. Or at least harbors a suspicion.

"Listen," I say through a shaky voice. "I'm not sure what you think you—"

She cuts me off with a hand. "You know a lot about music licensing, right? That's what you do for work?"

I've never been so happy to field a question about my bullshit job. "Yup! I do it every day."

Trista looks just as relieved as I am. "Great. So, like, my friend and I want to start this podcast about professional swimsuit modeling in the age of Instagram. And we're hoping to use '7 Rings' as our theme song. How can we do that—like, legally?"

"You mean the Ariana Grande song?" I ask.

She nods.

"It would cost money," I explain. "And you'd need approval from the publisher. Which, for this song, would actually be more like eight publishers—Ariana's, plus those of all her cowriters, plus it has that *Sound of Music* interpolation, so you'd need to run it by Rodgers and Hammerstein—"

"You know what?" Trista interjects. "Never mind. That sounds like a clusterfuck. We probably won't even do the podcast, anyway."

"Oh." My back stiffens at the realization that this was all just a pretext. "Anything else, then? Or..."

She laughs. "Why are you so nervous?"

"I'm not!" I lie. "Just a little wiped from the drive up."

She pats my chest. "Maybe take a nap before dinner? I know Paige has us on a jam-packed schedule." Her voice softens into a menacing whisper. "Something tells me it's gonna be a *looong* night."

31

plop down on my bed and take a gander at the itinerary.

Paige printed out professionally designed copies for each of us on premium cardstock covered in pink glitter, confirming the fact that her itinerary kicks my itinerary's ass.

Trista wasn't kidding; it's going to be a long night. And I can't even take a nap, because I have less than an hour to get ready for dinner—seared bay scallops with sautéed watercress and roasted cherry tomatoes—which Paige is currently preparing in the kitchen. Then we'll be pregaming at the house until nine o'clock, at which point a limo is scheduled to arrive and take us to Providence, Rhode Island for a night of bar-hopping.

There's a parenthetical instruction next to the dinner menu: *Be sure to wear your shirts tonight. They're in your welcome bags!*

I dig into the L.L.Bean beach tote Paige sent me upstairs with and look for said shirt. It's buried under several room-temp bottles of Evian and a trial size tube of Advil, folded neatly, with a note on top:

A bride is nothing without her tribe! Xoxo. Paige.

P.S. Don't forget to bring your markers to dinner!

There's a package of multi-colored Sharpies attached to the note, which I assume is for some kind of arts-and-crafts drinking project she has in mind. I unfold my shirt—a plain white cotton tee with "Bride Tribe" printed in big magenta letters on the front. The back is an entirely blank canvas, and—damnit. She's gonna make us draw on our shirts.

But this is Kate's weekend, and I'm going to be a good sport.

I repeat this to myself like a mantra as I jump into the shower and try to psych myself up. This is going to be fun! With Paige in charge of the planning, all I have to do is sit back and go with the flow. And not spill anybody's secrets.

Even if Melanie continues being snide to me, I will not tell her that her husband cheated on her last month. Even if Trista grills me about what happened the night before Bucky broke up with her, I will not tell her that he and I hooked up. And even if Kate corners me in a drunken stupor, I will not tell her that Patrick licked whipped cream off a stripper's breasts.

All I have to do is keep my mouth shut.

I dry myself off with one of Mrs. Cooper's terry cloth towels and get dressed. This "Bride Tribe" shirt is a perfect fit, but it still looks absolutely ridiculous on a six-foot-tall Italian-American man with bushy eyebrows and a thick dusting of facial hair. And I'm sure it will look especially so when adorned with various colorful bachelorette-themed doodles. I shiver as I imagine the five of us in our matching tops, trotting along the streets of Providence between gay bars, and—yeah. It is imperative that I get blackout drunk as quickly as possible.

I apologize in advance to my poor liver.

32

How is it possible that I'm already halfway blotto?" I whisper to Kate as we steal a post-dinner moment in her bedroom. This expensive Chardonnay paired nicely with the scallop dish Paige served for dinner, but I've been guzzling it like light beer—despite its considerably higher alcohol content. "Does it sound like I'm complaining? Because I'm not."

"Drink up, bitch." Kate laughs and clinks her glass to mine. "But also pace yourself! We have a full night ahead of us."

"You know who needs to drink up? Fucking Melanie. Like, can't we just bury the hatchet already? Jesus. I didn't even do anything to her and she's been cold-shouldering me all night long."

Kate rolls her eyes. "She just needs a scapegoat for Wilson's heinous behavior. As per usual. God forbid she actually face the fact that her husband is a worthless manbaby."

She fixes her hair in the mirror and readjusts the fit of her white "Bride" shirt (no "Tribe" on hers) and turns to me. "Did Paige tell you exactly what the deal is with these shirts and the markers? What are we supposed to be drawing, exactly? I'm thoroughly confused."

As if summoned, Paige pokes her head in to make an announcement. "Living room in five!"

I turn to Kate. "Guess we're about to find out."

We careen into the living room, where Trista and Melanie are sitting cross-legged on Mrs. Cooper's infamous Restoration Hardware rug—the one I meticulously inspected for whipped cream stains just a few weeks ago. Paige settles into the love seat across from the coffee table, and Kate and I each plop into a chair—the same chairs that Patrick and I sat in while Kitty and Lexus paraded their bodies in our faces. This room is just dripping with illicit flashbacks.

"Okay, so everyone has their markers ready and their bevvies full?" Paige asks.

We all nod.

"I did this at my girlfriend's bachelorette last year and it was *so* fun," she continues. "So basically it's like a game of Never Have I Ever—but with a twist."

"Never have I ever caused someone to get a DUI," Melanie blurts—shooting me her hundredth glare of the evening.

"I'm sorry..." I tell her, finally buzzed enough to snap back. "...that your husband is trash."

Melanie gasps. "Oh my God, Kate! You're gonna let him talk to me like that?"

"Can't we just get along?" I ask before Kate can respond. "I didn't realize he was going to drive, okay? He just disappeared without telling anybody."

"After you splashed beer in his face," Melanie hisses.

I scrunch my eyebrows at her. "Okay! So let's say it *is* all my fault for setting him off. Is it also my fault that he had two priors? Clearly your husband has a problem. In the immortal words of Sinead O'Connor, *fight the real enemy.*"

This elicits a few giggles from around the room. I'm clearly excelling at the sassy gay sidekick act, deploying iconic pop culture references with ease (even in the heat of battle).

Melanie lowers her head in pissed-off resignation. "Whatever. I shouldn't have brought it up."

"Anyway!" Kate chirps. "As the bride, I demand we give this vibe a makeover starting *now*."

She raises her glass and we all cheers her, and somehow it actually works to relieve the tension.

"Now Paige," Kate continues. "How does this stupid game work?"

Paige squints at her sister. "It's not stupid! It's fun!"

"I've played it before," Trista chimes in. "It actually is fun. One person throws out a 'never have I ever'—and if you *have*, then you have to let that person draw a symbol on your shirt to represent what it is you've done. Right?"

Paige lights back up. "Exactly. Thanks, girl."

With that, Kate is converted. "Bride goes first!" she says. "Okay, let's see." She scans the room before landing on Trista and making a sneaky little grin. "Never have I ever done it on an airplane with—"

"You don't need to finish that sentence," Trista interjects while raising her hand. "We get it." She looks around for other raised hands and comes up short. "Seriously? No one else?"

"A fun fact about me is that I literally never leave my seat on airplanes," I explain. "There's too much emotional and physical labor involved."

I will gladly risk a bladder infection before subjecting myself to the whole rigmarole of unbuckling and interrupting my seat partners and—oh, my God—potentially having to *knock* on the *door* to make sure no one's in there.

"You're such a freak," Trista teases. "I love it." She addresses the room. "And we were flying private, thank you."

"Drink, bitch!" Kate says with a maniacal laugh.

She and I are definitely the messiest people in the circle right now, so I appreciate her effort in forcing the rest of the group to catch up.

"Okay, so Kate, since you asked the question, you need to draw on Trista's shirt." Paige relays the instruction like a Sunday school teacher. "Perhaps an airplane?"

Kate pulls out a black marker and creates her masterpiece right below Trista's left shoulder blade. It's ostensibly the airplane Paige suggested, but my vision is kinda blurry so it also looks like a cartoon penis to me. Then again, we're surrounded by cartoon penises—from the confetti to the coasters to the napkins—so they've fully seeped into the front of my consciousness at this point.

"Nice penis, Kate," Melanie cracks.

So it wasn't just me!

"My turn," Trista says. "Never have I ever...had a threesome."

I raise my right index finger and take a guilty chug of wine.

Everyone just stares blankly at me. There's nary a raised hand in sight.

"It was just one time!" I explain. "In college. It was awkward and crowded, and I pulled a muscle in my ass. Overall, would not recommend."

Trista's eyes widen. "Three guys? Or two guys, one girl? Or—oh, my God—*two girls*?"

"Three guys," I answer. "It was a lot. Imagine if all the party favors in here came to life."

Kate laughs. "How did I not know about that? Slutty McSluttington over here."

Trista crawls my way and draws what she assures me is three little stick figure men in a heart on my back. "You other bitches need to start confessing to shit!" she tells the group.

"Now it's your turn," Paige instructs me.

I decide to go with something I know all four of these women have done before, mainly because these shirts will never get filled up if we keep moving at this pace. "Never have I ever used a tampon. Or a bra. Or birth control. Or a Gillette Venus razor—"

Kate punches my arm. "We get it."

"That was a good one!" Paige offers. "Well played, Dom."

I make my way around the circle and draw a tube of lipstick on the back of everyone's shirts in hot pink Sharpie. Melanie goes next and manages to draw a car on everyone's backs. I find it hard to believe that Wilson has never asked *her* for a vehicular blowie, but we have to take her word for it.

We continue to chip away at the white space for the next hour—our shirts now have doodles of everything from an iPhone to a Christmas tree to a human butt and more on them—until Paige gives a twenty-minute warning before the limo arrives.

"One more!" Kate says. "The bride demands it. Paige—you go."

Paige scans the room, rubbing a piece of penis confetti through her fingers. "Never have I ever…hooked up with a guy who was… you know." She lowers her voice to a whisper. "Uncircumcised." She sits up and gasps. "Oh my God, I can't believe I said that!"

I nearly spit out my Vodka Red Bull. (Had to switch from the Chardonnay when I realized we still have an entire night of bar-hopping ahead of us.) Then I raise my hand slowly and take another huge sip.

"You've *never?*" I ask Paige, thinking back to the handful of *Uncut Gems* (sorry! had to) I encountered in my long-ago single days. And also the one I encountered just last month, in this very house. "It's not that uncommon."

"It must be." Paige gestures around at the rest of the group. "You're the only one who drank."

"But Trista!" I blurt without thinking. "What about B—"

I cut myself off upon realizing that I've allowed myself to become entirely too sloppy and reckless.

Kate squeezes my wrist under the coffee table—a threat. I'm sure she is having the same internal meltdown I am right now. Shit! Okay. Think.

"—ündchen," I finish. "Gisele Bündchen! You've done photo shoots together, right? You're friends? I'm sure she saw a few uncut D's before she married Tom Brady." Trista's eyes narrow at me in suspicion as I continue to stammer. "Because she's from Brazil, you know? And circumcision is really only the norm in America..."

"I'm not an idiot," she finally interjects. "You were clearly talking about Bucky." She takes a dramatic breath. "How would you know what my boyfriend's penis looks like?"

This would be a great time for the critical thinking skills of a sober person, but alas there are none of those here.

"I don't," I protest. "I just meant that Bucky's—I mean—"

"You saw it, didn't you?" Melanie asks. "When? Why?"

"No! I didn't say that." But I might as well have. "I just meant that..." A light bulb goes off in my head. "The ESPN Body Issue!" I turn to Trista. "The whole world has seen your boyfriend naked."

"That's a sports magazine, not *Playgirl*," she replies. Okay. That was a very dim light bulb. It definitely just made things worse. "He didn't pose full-frontal. I was at that shoot. He had a pouch covering his junk the entire time."

"Yeah, no, obviously—that was a joke." I force a nervous laugh through my grinding teeth. "Actually? Bucky mentioned he was uncut in casual conversation at the party last month. I didn't *see* it. But now that I think about it, maybe I misheard him."

"This is a very weird conversation!" Paige says before Trista can even react to the absurdity of my defense. "Listen, girls—and Dom—we need to get ourselves together for the limo. I'm bringing a case of water so we can hydrate on the way up to Rhode Island."

Kate exhales. "Paige, you're a genius."

"Yes!" I say. "Hydration is key."

Everyone gets up and shuffles around, but Trista's eyes continue to grill me like a I'm a twelve-ounce sirloin. I make a beeline for the powder room and shut the door. Here's hoping I can pee away the flood of shame that has just spread throughout my entire body.

Okay. So I'm peeing, I'm peeing, I'm peeing, and...

Nope. It's still there.

I finish up and pivot to the sink.

I will act normal and cool for the rest of the night, I instruct my reflection as I wash my hands under the ornate waterfall faucet. *Normal and cool. Cool and normal.*

But this plan is immediately foiled when I shriek upon reentering the hallway. Because Trista is standing right outside the door.

"We need to talk," she says. "Like, now."

33

This one-on-one with Trista is going to be decidedly less chill than our earlier conversation about music rights. I know this because Trista just shoved me back into the bathroom and locked the door behind us.

"I knew it!" she whisper-screams. "I just knew it. This is what I wanted to ask you about earlier, before I chickened out and made up that dumb excuse about the podcast. But I should have asked you directly, because I *knew* it."

"Knew what?" I need to play as dumb as possible. If I can't put this fire out now, then the entire night—Kate's night—will be ruined. "This is all just a weird misunderstanding, I think."

"Don't make me say it out loud." Trista leans against the wall and tugs at her shiny dark-blonde hair in frustration. I avoid eye contact, instead focusing my gaze on the "Bride Tribe" letters printed across her shirt. "You know what I'm talking about."

"I really don't! I barely even know Bucky—the bachelor party was honestly the first time we ever hung out in any meaningful capacity."

"What was so meaningful about it?" she asks.

"That's not what I meant."

"Then what did you mean?"

"The limo is going to be here any minute," I deflect. "We should really go outside."

Trista huffs and crosses her arms. Then her face contorts into something that almost resembles a smile.

And now she's laughing.

"I'm not mad at you," she says. "I don't *blame* you. I'm not stupid. I've had suspicions since well before Patrick's bachelor weekend."

Her assurance puts me a little more at ease. I believe her—she's not stupid. The fact that she shoved me in here to have this conversation privately (rather than performatively, in front of the entire group) already indicates that she's a far more reasonable person than Melanie is, for example. Not that Melanie sets the bar very high, but still. I'll take what I can get at this point.

"Bucky didn't cheat on you," I tell her. "If that's what you're worried about."

"I actually believe that he didn't," she agrees. "He made sure to break up with me over the phone *before* you guys hooked up—like that makes a difference." She rolls her perfectly made-up eyes. "It's just like him, though. God forbid he ever be the bad guy."

"I did not have sexual relations with that man," I tell her—fully assuming a Bill Clinton-y Southern accent, because of course that's where my mind would go right now.

"Was that your best Bucky imitation?" she asks through a small chuckle. "Needs work."

I lower my head. "Sorry. That was uncalled for."

"You don't need to lie." Her voice assumes this matter-of-fact cadence, like she's a cop bargaining with a suspect. "How about this? I'll tell you the full unvarnished truth, you do the same for me in return, and we keep it all between us?"

She extends her arm toward me for a handshake, but I leave her hanging.

"The unvarnished truth about what?" I ask. "This is silly!"

She straightens her posture. "I know something happened at that party. Bucky has been acting weird for weeks. We haven't even seen each other since he got over his 'back injury' and went back on tour. I honestly have no idea why he bothered getting back with me. Or why I agreed."

"That's not..." is all I can say before I run out of words.

I'm normally the perfect audience for this type of grievance. If she were any other female friend or acquaintance, I'd launch right into one of two speeches—either the *I'm sure there's a good explanation* or the *kick that jerk to the curb, girl!*—depending on which one she wanted to hear. But the man in question in this conversation is Bucky, whom I happen to be darkly obsessed with at the moment.

She takes a quick glance at herself in the mirror. "I guess it's just easier for us to stay together. The PR process around making the breakup official would be such a pain."

I nod. As if I can even remotely relate.

"You know what it's like to have sex with him?" she asks.

Let's see. If memory serves, I'd have to say: *passionate, ferocious, thirst-quenching.*

"Of course I don't," I tell her.

"It's like he has a virtual reality headset over his face," she says. "He doesn't see me. His mind is always elsewhere, always trying to get it over with and go back to swinging a golf club."

So he's (probably) just as gay as I am! During the few heterosexual experiences I had back in high school, I did the same exact thing—closed my eyes and kept my mind tuned into whatever gay porn I had most recently devoured online. It's Chapter One in the *How to Have a Beard* textbook.

Except Trista never asked to be Bucky's beard, and I now experience a rush of sympathy for her. She deserves to be with a man who wants her as much as she wants him.

"So then why have you stayed with him so long?" I ask.

She sighs. "I guess I've always just dealt with it because sex isn't that important to me, anyway. And he's always been such a charming southern gentleman. He treats me like a human being. That's hard to find when you've been on the cover of *Sports Illustrated Swimsuit*."

"It must be so hard going through life as the epitome of conventional American beauty," I tease.

"I'm serious!" she insists. "I am constantly pursued by every type of guy imaginable. You should see my DMs—it's exhausting. And it's all bullshit, because none of them know anything about me as a person. They just view me as this object...a prize or something. Bucky's not like that. He's always respected me. And we do have fun together. Even if we're not in *love*."

She shakes her head. "And it's not like I'm so un-self-aware. Bucky and I look amazing together. I was always willing to ignore my doubts if it meant we could have this perfect relationship that enhances both our brands."

"You *were* willing?" I ask. "Does that mean you're not anymore?"

She presses her back against the wall and slides down until she's curled in a ball on the floor. "I don't know. What do you think I should do?"

A part of me wants to engineer this entire conversation toward a breakup, just to see. If the results are anything like the *last* time their relationship was spontaneously terminated, it could potentially work in my favor.

But I can't do that to Trista. Not when I know all too well what it's like to cling to a dysfunctional relationship purely because it looks good on paper. That was literally Ted and me just a few months ago. And as painful as our breakup has been, it'd be thousand times worse if it were incited by a total outsider. Ted and I had the luxury of addressing our problems on our own terms. Bucky and Trista deserve the same.

"The unvarnished truth?" I plop down on the floor next to her. "I think this is a conversation you need to have with your boyfriend."

"You're really not going to tell me what happened that weekend?"

"Even if what you think happened did happen…wouldn't you rather hear it from him?"

She squeezes her eyes shut. "I knew it, I knew it, I knew it."

Trista's fingers claw at the coral bathroom rug beneath our feet. Shit. She definitely thinks I just confessed to sleeping with her boyfriend.

"I'm not saying it did happen," I desperately add. "I'm just saying that it's not my place to comment one way or the other. It's a question you need to ask him yourself."

As I say it, I realize I'm basically encouraging her to call him up and grill him about our night together.

"Actually?" I try to backpedal. "If he had something to tell you, he'd tell you. So maybe don't ask him anything at all." She remains silent, eyes still closed. "Trista? Hello? Please don't get the wrong idea about any of this. I've been drinking… Let's just try to have fun tonight. I promise you have nothing to worry about from me."

She slowly opens her eyes and releases the rug from her grasp.

"Thanks for this," she says. "You've actually helped a lot."

"I have?"

She peels herself off the floor and extends a hand to help me up. "Yes."

I accept. "And...you're not going to mention this conversation to Bucky?"

"No." She fixes her hair in the mirror and adjusts her shirt. The airplane Paige drew on it earlier got smudged already—hopefully from spilled booze and not a stealth tear I didn't see her cry just now. "I know he'll just lie to me anyway."

There's clearly so much left to unpack here, but it's not actually any of my business—and anything I say to help will probably just make it worse. "So we're cool?"

"We're cool," she says through a sad little laugh. "We're also gonna need a hell of a lot more booze for this limo ride."

34

Maybe it's because we're all a little more used to each other's company, but the mood in the limo is the best it's been since this whole thing began. We're laughing, we're drinking, we're dancing in our seats to a throwback playlist of club bops from the early aughts. Even Melanie and I are getting along. It's impossible to remain bitter when "Bootylicious" by Destiny's Child is bumping on the speakers of your private party-mobile to Rhode Island.

"You know what? I love you *guyssss*." Kate says this about halfway through the trip—her tiny arms spilling over the shoulders of Paige and Trista—and I think it might be the happiest I've ever seen her. "I still can't believe you organized such a perfect weekend just for me."

I feel more justified than ever in my decision to mislead her about Patrick. Even though his behavior at the bachelor party was generally tame (compared to Wilson's, at least), there's still no telling how she'd have reacted to hearing about where his mouth had been that weekend. She might've called the wedding off entirely. And then she wouldn't have *this*.

"It's just getting started, bitch!" Trista hoots.

She looks at me and winks. We did a rapid-fire round of shots after our emotional Bucky moment in the powder room. I still have no idea if I made a huge mistake by talking to her—it's entirely possible she'll forget all about her promise not to say anything once the booze wears off and reality sets in—but the ceremony of the shots was enough for us to feel like we'd exorcised Bucky and formed a strange new bond of our own. At least for tonight.

We get to the bar—an uber-gay nightclub called Gotham—in an hour that feels more like fifteen minutes.

The air is thick with sweat particles, dim shards of light reflecting off a disco ball, and the bombastic sound of a nineties Mariah Carey club remix. It's sensory overload, yet somehow I feel like we've managed to catch the attention of literally everyone in this place.

Then I remember we're wearing matching "Bride Tribe" shirts with doodles all over them. Half the patrons here probably want to drop a house on our asses right now.

We line up at the bar for a round of shots, at which point the bartender's jaw basically unhinges and falls to the sticky floor. He's a shirtless, hairless twenty-something who reminds me of myself ten years ago—back when I had a speedy metabolism and the will to manscape.

"Shut up!" he shrieks. "Trista Harlow! Oh, my God. My girlfriends and I are *ob-sessed* with you." Right. I almost forgot we had a semi-famous person with us. "Can I please get a pic for my Insta?"

Trista laughs and hurtles her petite body over the bar to join him for a selfie. Then *she* pours the shots for all of us, which the bartender comps before running off to tell his coworkers about the celebrity sighting.

"That was amazing," Paige marvels. "Does that happen to you a lot?"

Trista flips her hair. "Kate didn't tell you I have fans?"

"I knew you had fans," Melanie snickers. "I just thought they were all sleazy straight men with neck beards."

Trista smiles and throws her a lighthearted middle finger.

"Back to *me*," Kate says. "The bride!"

Right as she says it, the music stops. And then a voice comes on the speakers instructing everyone to "welcome the legendary Miss Anita *Cock*...tail."

The crowd instantly splits in half and shapeshifts into a crescent, forming an audience around a spotlit "stage" surrounded by shiny gold curtains. By no effort of our own, our group ends up front and center in the first row.

"Shit," I whisper to Kate. "Should we bail?"

"Are you kidding?" she asks. "This is totally why we came here! It's a bachelorette rite of passage."

For someone who's a beauty editor at a top media outlet, you'd think her finger would be a little more on the pulse. This drag queen is going to eviscerate us! That's what they *do* to bachelorette parties at gay bars.

Anita Cocktail immediately zeroes in on our group. She's wearing a strappy leopard print dress, platform stripper heels, and a giant bloodred wig. The queen has legs for days, I'll give her that.

"What do we have here?" she coos into her mic. "Looks to me like a fresh gaggle of basic bitches in the wild!" She turns and makes a face to the audience. "Forgive me, I meant to say a '*bride tribe*.'"

"That's right, bitch." Trista matches her attitude perfectly. "This is Kate—"

"It's her *Last Fling Before the Ring*!" Paige says—into the mic—thereby confirming Anita Cocktail's characterization of our group. Should I make a run for it? Maybe I should make a run for it. "Woo!"

"Just precious," Anita says in response. She turns to Melanie. "And what do you have to say for your little crew?"

Melanie glares at her in distrust. Which is essentially the same reaction I'm inclined to have. I normally love a sassy drag queen, but this one seems bloodthirsty.

"Wait a minute," Anita continues. "What's this I see?"

By the time I realize she just singled me out, Kate thrusts me forward and introduces me to the crowd as her "BFF and fiancé's beautiful best man."

Anita Cocktail twirls her synthetic red hair. "Call him whatever you want, but I know a token gay when I see one. Hey! Sweetie!" She snaps her fingers—adorned with fluorescent blue nail polish—right in front of my face. "Blink twice if you're being held against your will."

The audience erupts into laughter at this, so I go along with it and perform two very obnoxious winks. Anything to make Anita go away so we can be audience members and not the main event.

"Message received," Anita says with a wink of her own. "Help is on the way!"

Finally, she moves on to her next victims—an all-over-each-other gay couple who appear to have about a thirty-year age gap between them.

The sight reminds me of the last time I was in a similar situation—five years ago.

Ted and I had been seeing each other for just a few months. He was barely out of the closet at that point, and he had still never been to a gay bar. I assured him it was not our scene, but he wanted to have the experience anyway, so we walked into a random drag show downtown one Friday night after pregaming somewhere else. That night's host was in the middle of her introduction when she spotted us stumbling into the front row. She strutted over and looked us up and down like she was a human TSA body scanner.

"This Patagonia-vest-and-Dockers look you've got happening is *such* a choice," she said to Ted. "You're straight, aren't you?"

"Nope," he replied. "Actually—"

"I turned him," I blurted into the mic, wincing at myself even as I said it. Like I was trying to brag about the impossible.

The drag queen rolled her cartoonishly made-up eyes. "Keep tellin' yourself that, doll face."

I shake the memory out of my blurry mind as Anita Cocktail finishes her audience-banter routine. She launches into a lip sync performance of "Bad Girls" by Donna Summer, at which point I excuse myself to grab a round of hard seltzers for the group.

"Hey!" Melanie sidles up to me at the bar. "Figured you'd need help carrying drinks. Plus I hate that drag queen. I feel like she was being rude to our group for no reason."

I totally understand why bachelorette groups are often derided at gay clubs—they're seen as straight tourists invading spaces specifically designed for queer people—but I also understand the idea that gay bars should be welcoming to *everyone*. Especially groups of women who just want to get wasted without the prospect of being hit on or harassed by straight men. It's a nuanced debate, and one that doesn't need to be had right now. Not while I have this perfect opportunity to bury the hatchet with Melanie by bonding over a common enemy.

"Same! That drag queen was the worst!" I chirp. *Anita, forgive me.* "Listen, I really am sorry about what went down at the bachelor party. Sucks it had to end like that."

"I'm sorry," she says. "I shouldn't have taken it out on you. I of all people know how Mikey can be."

We solidify our truce with a pair of tequila shots and zip through the crowd back to Kate, Paige, and Trista—all three of whom are dancing in place with their arms around each other like a miniature row of drunken cancan girls. We hand out the drinks and realize we're one short, so I head back to the bar to retrieve it.

On the way, my phone vibrates with a series of texts from an unknown number.

> Hi. Sorry to text during the party.
> Coop gave me your number.
> Can you go someplace private and call me?
> It's Bucky.

35

'm pretty sure no one has ever exited a building faster than I just
have. The neon signs of competing bars and nearby convenience
stores bleed into each other as I steady myself on the concrete
sidewalk and hit *Call*.

He picks up on the first ring.

"Hey, bud."

"Hi."

He sounds tired or nervous or both. "I don't mean to make a
big thing out of this—the girls can't hear you right now, can they?"

"They're inside. I'm outside. So why'd you take so long to text
me? It's almost been a month." Shit. This is coming out weirdly
needy and passive-aggressive. I slap myself out of it and conjure
my best bro-voice. "Congrats on your victory at the 3M Open last
week. That was a hell of a tournament. I watched all four rounds."

"Yeah, thanks, man." His words are short and clipped. That
relaxed, casual twang he spoke in during all of our heart-to-heart
conversations last month is nowhere to be found. "Listen, uh,
Trista sent me a text earlier saying that she 'needs to talk.' I hate
to ask, but you didn't tell her anything, did you?"

So this isn't about me. It's about Trista—whose oath of silence
may have been insincere after all.

"What would I have told her?" I ask.

"C'mon," he says. "You know what I'm talkin' about."

"Nope." I need to hear him say it out loud. "Can you elaborate?"

He lowers his voice to a whisper. "About what happened that night. Between us."

Aha! So there's an *us*.

"I didn't tell her anything about that night," I assure him. "But dude, she has a ton of suspicions about you. So maybe you should—"

"What the hell do you mean by that?" he snaps.

"She said you're not exactly the most *present* lover." Maybe I can inspire him to come out to her first. That has to be better for all involved, right? "If you know what I mean."

The line goes silent, except for the *whoosh* of several frustrated breaths on Bucky's end.

This was a stupid idea.

"What the fuck, man?" His voice descends into a pissed-off drawl. "Y'all have just been talkin' about me all night? Is that it?"

"Not all night," I protest. "Literally it was a two-minute conversation."

I take a second to formulate my next line of defense, but then it hits me: Why the hell should I have to defend myself at all? *He* initiated our hookup. *She* cornered me in the powder room. *I* was exceedingly careful not to confirm or deny her suspicions. None of this was my doing. The only mistake I made was during Never Have I Ever when I accidentally blew the whistle on his uncircumcised...whistle.

"I think you need to be talking to Trista about this," I finish. "Not me."

"No shit! You think I wanna be arguin' about this with a—"

"With a what?" I fume as a siren blares in the distance. "A fag you just 'blew off steam' with?"

He ignores my outburst. "She won't pick up her damn phone. Where are y'all at right now, anyway?"

"Some gay club in Providence," I hiss. "You should join."

"I don't have time for this," he says. "It's two a.m. where I am—I should be asleep right now. I need to rest up for the third round of this tournament tomorrow."

"Give me a break." My brain is in full fighting-with-a-boyfriend mode right now. He might as well be Ted. "You don't tee off until two-fifteen."

Shit. That definitely sounded stalkerish.

"How do you know my tee time?" he asks.

"It's…" I stammer. "ESPN was on at the bar, and I happened to see the lineup for tomorrow."

"Really, man?" Rather than flattered by the interest I've clearly taken in him, he sounds absolutely appalled. "You expect me to believe they're playin' golf highlights at a gay club?"

"Whatever," I huff. "Forget I said anything."

He sighs. "Listen, I'm sorry if I gave you the wrong idea. I got nothin' against gay people—but I'm *straight*, alright? I thought you were cool with that. I thought I made it clear." A pause. "Damnit. I knew that night was a mistake."

"You *did* make it clear." I hate myself for being on the verge of tears right now. "And it *was* a mistake."

I hang up before any more damage can be done.

It was delusional to ever expect anything from Bucky. I've hooked up with closeted men who had a hell of a lot less to lose than a bajillion-dollar golf career. They don't just come out of the closet after hooking up with the one magical gay man to convince them it's all worth it. They need to do the work on their own. I of all people should know that.

I storm back into the club and belly up to the bar alone.

My body spasms as an unexpected hand latches itself onto the small of my back. I turn around and see that it belongs to a random man—probably in his forties—with dark facial hair, bushy eyebrows, and a plain black V-neck shirt.

"Sorry," he says. "Didn't mean to startle you."

"You didn't startle me."

He grins. "I have a tab going. Let me buy you a drink?" He extends his hand for a shake. "I'm Mario."

"Domenic." I scan the club for the bachelorette group and see that they've got a little circle going at one corner of the dance floor. The drag show must have ended when I was outside. "Nice to meet you. Thanks for offering to get me a drink, but—"

"My pleasure," he says before I can finish my faux-protest. "It would be an honor to serve a real-life member of the infamous 'Bride Tribe.'"

"Please accept my apologies," I groan. "We were so obnoxious earlier, weren't we?"

He smirks. "Nah. That drag queen was just busting your balls. As drag queens are wont to do."

We clink beers. Everyone else in the bar fades from my awareness as I decide to fully invest myself in this stranger. I'd normally consider him a little too Italian for my liking—I've never been attracted to clones—but he is a living man, and he is giving me attention. And after the interaction I just had with Bucky, those qualities are the only ones I need right now.

"Wanna dance?" I ask.

He smiles, and we make our way to the floor. Our bodies instantly connect, groins grinding against each other to Beyoncé.

The room spins. The disco ball appears to be twenty disco balls. But that's just how disco balls are, right? All reflective and fragmented. I still have my wits about me enough to look at Mario and determine that he is handsome and non-creepy enough to make out with.

My eyes involuntarily close the second our mouths connect. His breath is all tequila and his face is all stubble and his hands are all up in my waistband. Here's a guy who has no reservations about letting an entire nightclub full of sweaty strangers know that he's attracted to me. What's Bucky's problem? This is the 2020s! Surely being an out gay man and a professional golfer aren't mutually exclusive propositions.

I close my eyes tighter and shake him out of my mind as Mario's hands grip my ass harder and harder. I push myself closer into him and bite his lip. His fingers feel dry against my skin—almost like sandpaper—but I embrace it. We grind and kiss and grind and kiss. His hands continue to clandestinely explore the terrain along my boxer briefs. I open my eyes for a moment and remember that we're in the middle of a crowd, but the music is loud, the lighting is dark, and everyone else seems to be in their own world anyway. I squeeze them shut again and surrender to his touch. I'm all his right now.

"Wanna get out of here?" His breath is hot in my left ear. "I'm staying at the Omni around the corner."

"Sure," I say without thinking. Whatever he wants. "Let's do it."

36

It's as if all the liquor I've been drinking tonight catches up to me in a single *whoosh* the instant we step outside. Brain blurry, knees wobbly. One look at the sidewalk triggers a flashback of my phone call with Bucky earlier, adding a sharp sense of dread to the mix.

"You good?" Mario asks, his own shaky arm loose around my neck.

I lean into it anyway. "Sure."

A few sloppy steps later, a voice calls out my name from behind. I nearly lose my balance and collapse as I turn around to see who it is.

Kate runs forward, shooting me a death glare. "What the hell are you doing?"

"Nothing." I flop my hand toward my escort. "Kate Wallace. This is...Luigi."

"Wrong Nintendo brother," he whispers to me through a laugh. "Hi, Kate. I'm Mario."

She is not amused.

Mario seems to register the "Bride" on her shirt. "Congratulations!"

Things rapidly get blurry from here.

Kate is still not amused, that much is clear.

She's...yelling at me?

I watch myself morph into an angry drunk. I thought I had let go of my resentment toward Kate for having expected me to babysit Patrick last month, but no. Now I'm the one who's yelling. Something about how Anita Cocktail was right. I'm tired of being used. Sick of being a token, an accessory, a spy, a secret-keeper, *a fucking side character!* Every frustration I've kept to myself over the past month shoots out of me like a round of bullets.

More yelling on both sides.

Me making a decision I already regret.

And I'm gone.

37

~~

It's morning and I'm naked under hotel sheets. And you know what? With his sleeping face illuminated by the soft glow of morning light, my hookup partner kind of does look like his eponymous video game mascot. This has to be a joke. I fucked Super Mario last night. What is my life? Who am I? What time is it?

The answers to those first two questions are a mystery at this point. But the nightstand alarm clock tells me it's seven in the morning.

I sit up and stretch and—wait. Shit. A pre-blackout image of Paige's fancy printed itinerary comes rushing back to me. The limo was scheduled to leave Providence five hours ago! Everyone must have left without me. And I'm still an hour away from Mystic. Kate must be so worried. Pissed. Both.

"Dude." I poke Mario in the shoulder, which causes him to stir a little. "Wake up."

"Morning, handsome." He rolls over and pulls me into his armpit before he realizes that I'm actively freaking out. "What's wrong?"

"My friends!" I squeal, as if that explains everything. My head is throbbing. "I left them last night. Do you remember if we talked to them? Where's my phone?"

"Oh." Mario sits up against the headboard, his dark chest hair glistening in the rays of sunshine pouring through the open hotel curtains. "Yeah, you were being pretty brutal to them before we took off. You don't remember?"

"No! What did I say?"

He furrows his brow. "You went off on the bride. Told her you were sick of being 'the Stanford to her Carrie' and that it was time for you to be your own Carrie." He laughs quietly. "I've only ever seen a few episodes of *Sex and the City*, but even I picked up on the reference."

"I said that? Out loud?"

"You really don't remember?" he asks. "Jeez. You really *were* wasted. I knew I was doing the right thing by resisting your relentless sexual advances last night…" He winks. "As tempting as they were."

Oh. So I *didn't* fuck Super Mario last night. I just ripped my clothes off and tried—and failed—to seduce him. Even better.

"How am I going to get home?" I wonder aloud. "Shit!"

Mario rubs my knee. "We talked about that last night, too. I can give you a ride down to Mystic. I'm headed to New Jersey today, anyway. Connecticut is on the way."

So that handles the problem of how to get back to the house, at least. If I'm even still welcome there. It would be nice to check my phone for reassurance that I haven't been entirely friend-divorced over this, but of course it died sometime overnight. And naturally Mario's charger is incompatible.

"Thank you so much." I spot my white "Bride Tribe" T-shirt on the floor across the room. The ink from the various colored Sharpies looks smudgy and bloodstain-like in the light of day—a rainbow crime scene. "Can we leave immediately?"

We dress quickly, he packs his bag, and within fifteen minutes we're zooming down I-95 in his weathered Ford pickup truck. Despite having only known him for a few extremely drunken hours, I feel comfortable in his passenger seat. It's like riding with an old friend or cousin or something. He's the first guy I've ever hooked up with who would fit right in with my family. He's got that works-with-his-hands, Italian-on-both-sides vibe. Unlike the uber-preppy Ted, who my father never had any idea what to do with.

"So what do you do for work?" I ask.

"Ah, this conversation…" he says. "Again."

"Oh. I'm sorry. I should've warned you that my conversation skills while blackout drunk are unparalleled."

"It's fine," Mario says. "I'm a lobsterman up in Maine. I'm headed down to Jersey to visit a relative. I thought I'd make a pit stop in Gay Providence on the way." He cracks a small smile. "Glad I did."

"You don't have to do that," I say via reflex.

"Do what?"

"Pretend you like me just because I passed out naked in your hotel room," I murmur. Where the hell is my self-esteem? Oh, right. In the hands of Bucky Graham. "So you're a fisherman! What does that entail? I must confess my only point of reference is *I Know What You Did Last Summer* starring Ryan Phillippe and the iconic Jennifer Love Hewitt."

"The correct term is lobsterman. And you said that exact sentence last night." Mario flicks his blinker and passes an SUV on the left. "Remember? And then I told you I'm more of a Sarah Michelle Gellar fan myself."

I take a swig of water and beg the Advil in my system to start doing its job.

As I gaze out at the smear of green highway signs, a memory surfaces of our transition from club to hotel. We did have an entire conversation about our professional lives. I told him all about how I hate my job and only pursued law to keep up with my straight best friend. He told me how he had no choice but to pursue lobstering because it's what his father and grandfather before him had always done.

For a moment I wonder what my life would have looked like if I'd done the same thing as Mario—eschewed college altogether to follow in my dad's blue-collar footsteps. I'd probably feel even more unfulfilled than I do now, sure, but also? I wouldn't be caught in a web of WASP drama all summer. I'd probably have a diverse group of friends from an eclectic mix of backgrounds—people I could *relate to* rather than try to *keep up with*.

And now I remember pieces of the fight with Kate. I can see her face outside the bar as I ran away from her. She didn't even look angry—just broken.

"What else did I say to my friend last night?" I ask Mario. "Was I horrible? Something tells me I was horrible."

He exhales. "You definitely exploded a bit, like you had a lot bottled up against her."

"Which is so crazy," I say. "Because I really love her! It's not like I resent her or anything."

"Really?" he asks. "Because after it all went down, you were telling me how you feel like she and her husband-to-be are self-absorbed, entitled rich kids who wouldn't know struggle if it bit them in the ass. And that they expect you to drop everything and be this perfect 'best-man-slash-relationship-counselor' for their 'perfect straight wedding,' yet they barely seem to care that *your* wedding was ripped away from you not even two months ago. I'm just paraphrasing here." He pauses. "Sorry about your ex-fiancé, by the way. That sounds like a tough break. Who is he? I promise I won't tell anyone."

"Why would you care who my ex-fiancé is?" I ask.

"I'm bit of a golf nut," he says. "And you said he was a closeted pro golfer."

So I was describing Ted as Bucky? What a fun, fucked-up twist from Drunk Me! And also a ridiculously dangerous one. Judging from Bucky's tone yesterday, there is no doubt that he will destroy me if I start spreading rumors about him.

"Please tell me you're kidding," I say. "And remind me never to drink again."

Mario ignores my plea. "You said that in addition to his secret gay engagement, he also has a secret doping habit. So judging by players who have noticeably beefed up in recent years...if I had to guess..."

Please don't say Bucky Graham.

"Bucky Graham?" he asks. "That dude was *ripped* in his ESPN Body Issue shoot."

Yes, I'm well aware.

"My ex was not a pro golfer." I wince in my seat and force out a laugh. "This is embarrassing, but I lied. I have no idea why— probably because I thought it would sound cool or something. But my actual fiancé was just an anonymous asshole named Ted who works in finance."

"Ted," Mario says flatly. "Like the stuffed bear in those Mark Wahlberg movies?"

"As opposed to your name," I tease. "Which carries absolutely zero cartoonish connotations."

Mario releases a deep, kind laugh. "Touché. Well, I'm sorry it didn't work out. But at least you ended things before it was too late."

"Yeah?"

He taps the steering wheel. "Take it from someone whose divorce was just finalized a few weeks ago. I was married to my wife fourteen years, had three kids, the whole thing—before I finally decided I couldn't pretend anymore." He shoots me a quick, reassuring look. "So if you ask me, you're still ahead of the curve."

"You don't look a day over forty," I tell him.

"Thanks?" he says. "I'm forty-four."

"You were exactly my age, then. When you jumped into your hetero-sham marriage." I pause. "No offense."

He chuckles. "None taken. It was a sham. I was way too consumed with what other people thought of me back then. But you know what? I wasn't entirely unhappy at first. My wife and I looked great on paper, and that was actually enough to keep me satisfied for way longer than you'd think. Does that sound weird?"

"Nope." That's exactly how I feel about my entire relationship with Ted. And my legal career, for that matter. Things that have only ever made me happy in that they checked all the boxes. "Not weird at all."

"Society's approval is a hell of a drug." He flicks his blinker and pulls off at the Mystic exit. "Even if it only exists as a concept inside your own head."

38

'm greeted at the front door by a positively enraged Melanie.

"It's called a 'Tribe' for a reason!" she whisper-screams. Apparently the other girls are all still asleep. "You abandoned Kate on her night." She lowers and tightens her voice. "All for a piece of ass."

"I'm seriously so sorry," I plead from the front stoop. I consider clarifying for her that I did not *actually* get a piece of ass last night, but then realize it's entirely beside the point. "Can I please come in?"

"Honestly, Dom. I don't know." She crosses her arms. "I think it might be better if you go home and let us finish the weekend as just us girls."

Of course the only awake bridesmaid would have to be the one with a preexisting grudge against me. I thought we'd made something of a truce last night, but it clearly wasn't all that strong.

"Come on. Please? I know Kate wouldn't want me to leave."

"You do, do you?"

"Yes." I step forward. "And by the way, you are the ones who *let* me run off with some rando when I was drunk off my ass. I could've gotten murdered." I pause. "And/or chlamydia."

"Kate tried so hard to stop you! But you lashed out at her."

"Listen, I really want to try to make it right. Can you at least let me come in and charge my phone and shower? If Kate wakes up and says she wants me gone, then I'll leave."

Melanie purses her lips and stares at me in pity for a few moments before finally relaxing her shoulders and letting me in.

"Thank you." I rocket up the stairs toward my room. "I really am sorry."

I close the door and jump into the en suite bathroom for one of those scalding post-drunken-hookup showers that you hope have the power to cleanse you not only of dirt but also shame, embarrassment, and general unworthiness.

But no such luck. I'm still a hot mess after I wash up. Just a clean hot mess.

I throw on a beachy button-down and linen shorts before plunking down on the bed for a catch-up session with my phone. There's an endless backlog of missed texts and calls—from Kate, Ted, Bucky, Patrick, an unknown number, and—okay—breathe. Let's just start from the beginning.

At midnight, Kate sent a picture of Mario and me on the dance floor. His hand is fully down my pants and I'm slobbering all over his face, oblivious to the fact that Kate was even watching—let alone documenting. Her accompanying message is simply: Slut.

And that's all I got from her all night. Which is a bit surprising. If our fight was really as bad as Mario and Melanie made it out to be, wouldn't she have yelled at me via text after it was done? Then again, if it wasn't so bad, wouldn't she have checked in on me at some point?

Twenty minutes after Kate sent the picture of Mario and me, I forwarded the picture directly to Ted. I didn't include any text, probably because I figured the picture would speak for itself. *Look what you gave up! I'm so over you! Another man finds me attractive! Ha!*

But in reality, the actual subtext of the picture was more like: *I have unresolved feelings around our breakup, so here's a pathetic photo of me contracting mouth herpes from a stranger.*

I know this because Ted replied almost instantly with: If you have unresolved feelings around our breakup, please contact me like an adult instead of sending me a pathetic photo of you contracting mouth herpes from a stranger.

Next up is Bucky, whom I also sent the make out shot to.

Lose this number, he replied.

Next I have a string of unread texts from Patrick—all of which are basically variations on What did you say to Kate? and Call me now!

Ignore. At least until I can make up with Kate.

And the unknown number is Mario. He texted me his name last night at around one, and just ten minutes ago he checked in to say that it was great meeting me.

I set the phone down and rack my brain for ideas on what to do next. Thinking about the level of damage control required of me right now makes my entire body go numb. Where did all my anger even come from last night?

That phone call with Bucky was rough, yes. And sure, I clearly haven't had enough time to process all my emotions surrounding my breakup with Ted. But Kate and I have been in a good place since the bachelor party. Why did I have to take it all out on *her* of all people?

"Dom." Speaking of the bride, she is now calling for me from outside the bedroom door. Her voice is stiff with purpose. "Are you in there? We need to talk."

39

The sand is a mushy blend of hot and damp beneath our toes. Kate's blonde bedhead floats messily in the salty breeze as we stroll along the water. I breathe it all in for a few moments before launching into my apology.

"I had no idea what I was saying," I explain. "Bucky and I got into a fight on the phone, and then I just lost it. I was so wasted and—"

Kate cuts me off with a hand. "Why would you have called him in the first place? It was my party. You should have stayed with the group. But of course that would have been too...what was it? *Token gay best friend* of you."

"I seriously do not remember saying that."

"Well, you did. And a whole bunch of other stuff about how Patrick and I are horrible friends who don't care about you as a person."

She scoffs before continuing. "I'm sorry if you feel like we didn't make a big enough deal about your breakup with Ted—or if you're jealous that our relationship is stronger than yours was—or whatever—but what were we supposed to do? Cancel our own wedding in solidarity with you?"

I'm determined to make this a conciliatory moment, so I can't say what I'm really thinking, which is that *at least Ted and I knew how to communicate without the assistance of an unwitting third party in the middle.*

"You're right," I say instead. "It wasn't fair to unload all of that onto you. And it's not really how I feel."

"It obviously is!" she says. "Why can't you just admit that you're pissed at me?"

"Because I'm not!" I insist.

Kate ignores this statement entirely. "It really hurts that you'd accuse us of not caring about you as a person. Have you really forgotten about all the times we've been there for you over the years? I mean, third year of law school alone—you stayed in our guest room basically every night because you were so convinced you'd have a heart attack in your sleep."

"I was dealing with chronic palpitations! Those can be a sign of—"

I cut myself off and redirect. This is so not the time to be defensive.

Especially because Kate just made a valid point. She and Patrick *have* always been accommodating to my various neuroses. Or at least they were—until I started dating Ted and my neuroses became his problem.

"That's fair." I decide to throw her a kernel of truth. "I guess I was still upset about how you put me in the middle of everything at the bachelor party. Expecting me to spy for you, threatening to call off the wedding if I let Patrick do anything bad—as if I were responsible for his behavior."

I stop myself there, remembering that Kate still doesn't know the full truth about what he did that weekend.

"I thought we'd already squashed that," she says.

I shrug. "Looks like I still wasn't over it."

She tilts her head, like she just remembered something. "You know what's so interesting? Patrick and I have actually had debates over which one of us is friends with the real you."

My ears heat up. "The real me?"

"When it's just you and him, you're all beer and football. When it's you and me, you're all rosé and *SATC*." She pauses. "Of course he swears he knows you better than anyone in the world, but I've always thought my version of you was the realer one." Another pause. "*That's* why I asked you to watch the bachelor party for me—not because I view you as a 'token.'"

"I know you don't." Her explanation makes a certain kind of sense, and now I feel bad for thinking the worst of her. "I'm sorry for accusing you of that last night. I really am."

"Maybe you're just too much of a people-pleaser," she continues. "It's like you'll do whatever it takes to make the people around you comfortable." She releases a deep sigh. "And maybe I have taken advantage of that over the years…but it's only because I've always assumed you *like* playing the role of the gay best friend."

She's has a point. I've never complained about the dynamic between her and Patrick and me before. Because, for the most part, I actually do like it. There's something special about being able to float between their two worlds so seamlessly—indulging both the hypermasculine and ultrafeminine sides of myself. It wasn't until this summer—when they each expected my allegiance to fall expressly on one side—that I started to resent it so much.

"I should have told you when it started to become a problem," I admit. "Sooner. And more calmly. Instead of keeping it bottled up until it exploded on a sidewalk in Rhode Island."

She allows a small chuckle. "I'm sorry for not recognizing it on my own. I guess anyone would hate being in the position you were in last month."

"Don't apologize," I say. "I'm the one who messed up in this situation."

She hits my arm. "You really—*really*—did. Ugh. I could have killed you out there last night! And you know, maybe I have been treating you like Stanford Blatch this weekend—"

"You totally haven't—"

"But this is my bachelorette party! If ever there's a time I get to be the Carrie, it's now."

"I know. That is absolutely correct."

I rub her back for a moment. She doesn't swat my hand away, which I figure bodes well for the objective of this talk. We walk silently for a few moments until we reach the dividing line of the neighbor's beach, at which point we turn around. The act of reversing direction serves as an effective final step in smoothing over the friction between us.

Kate squeezes my wrist. "I was so worried about you when you walked off. Thank God that man ended up being normal."

I lighten my voice into dishy gossip mode. "He's a lobster fisherman."

"Shut up!" she says. "That's the hottest thing I've ever heard."

"I know, right? Too bad he lives in Maine."

She laughs. "Of course he does."

And just like that, for the moment at least, we're back on solid ground.

40

The five of us pile into Paige's rented soccer-mom minivan for the drive to lunch. It's a stark contrast to last night's party limo, but much preferred on my part. Less risk of getting obliterated and lashing out at the bride with buried resentments.

Our destination is Mystic Pizza, a cheesy little restaurant in the center of town that served as the basis for the famous eighties movie of the same name. I was obsessed with *Mystic Pizza* as a child—wearing out my VHS copy whenever I was home alone, marveling at the fact that my best friend's family had a house there, drowning in anticipation of my next summer stay with them.

In retrospect, it's sad how I idealized Mystic via that movie. It's a story about haves and have-nots; Julia Roberts's character Daisy comes from a working-class Portuguese family and struggles with feeling inferior to Mystic's wealthy seasonal residents (including the charming law student with whom she eventually falls in love). Given that I always stayed in Mystic with a family of wealthy seasonal residents myself, it's remarkable how I never acknowledged that I had far more in common with Daisy than I did with my hosts.

We get to the restaurant and file into an oversized booth below a giant wall of Hollywood memorabilia. A kitschy shrine to the restaurant's fifteen minutes of fame.

"I love this place," Paige says, gesturing at a signed headshot of Queen Julia. "So fun!"

"The pizza's actually good, too," Kate adds. "A little greasy, but totes worth it."

Before I can chime in with my enthusiastic agreement, our waitress swoops in from stage left.

She's wearing a tight tank top and short shorts. Her face is obscured by a wavy blanket of thick brown hair as she leans over the table to distribute menus and silverware, but there's something familiar about her aura and the way she arches her back—inherently sensual, like a Victoria's Secret mannequin or something.

She stands upright.

Time freezes as our eyes meet.

I almost choke on the sip of water I just took.

Because it's Kitty.

"I remember *you*," she says—specifically to me—curling her dark pink lips into an amused smirk. So much for going unrecognized. "What are you doing here?"

"Oh, just here for the nostalgia." I hope my tone makes it clear to everyone at the table that *I have definitely never licked this woman's whipped cream-covered breasts.* I laugh nervously and point up at the TV that plays *Mystic Pizza* on a loop in the corner of the dining room. "Julia Roberts at her finest."

Melanie and Trista eye me suspiciously from across the table.

Paige buries her face in a menu.

Kate pokes my arm. "Are you gonna introduce us to your friend?" She playfully rolls her eyes and addresses the waitress. "I'm Kate."

"Oh, right." I can feel a bead of sweat forming between my eyebrows. "This is…" It occurs to me that I only know her by her stripper name. And of course her hair is covering all but the first letter of her name tag. "J—"

"Jill," Kitty finishes for me. She must have taken pity after noticing that I'm perspiring from every pore in my body. "Nice to meet you. Are you all ready to order or do you need more time?"

Melanie throws an eager hand up. "Just a few minutes, please." She proceeds to grill me once Jill's out of earshot. "How do you know that girl?"

"Family, uh, friend," I stammer. "My...cousin...Vinny. He used to date her. Way back in the day. I'm surprised she remembers me, to be honest."

Paige perks up. "Isn't that a movie?"

"*Mystic Pizza*?" I ask. "Yes—it's literally playing on every screen in here."

"*My Cousin Vinny*," Paige clarifies. "How funny that you actually have a cousin Vinny!"

"Oh, yeah." I force a chuckle. "People always say that."

"She seems nice," Trista offers. The first words she's said to me all day. "Why didn't it work out with her and Vinny?"

"The usual," I improvise. "They grew apart."

Kate nods. "Interesting."

"Speaking of breakups," Melanie jumps in. "What's going on with you and Bucky?"

I thoughtlessly open my mouth to answer, but thankfully Kate pokes my thigh hard enough to make me realize that the question isn't directed at me.

"Who knows," Trista answers. "I'm so embarrassed. He must think I was such a mess, FaceTiming him from the limo at two in the morning and yelling at him. In the middle of a tournament weekend! He's never going to forgive me."

"Please," Kate says. "You weren't that bad. Maybe a little

combative…but he deserved it for phone-dumping you last month!"

So there was a limo FaceTime altercation last night, and Kate didn't tell me on our walk earlier. She's hiding something.

Paige taps the table. "You *were* being kind of mean to him."

"Yeah," Melanie agrees. "Especially when you called him—"

"We don't need to rehash," Trista snaps. "I don't want to obsess about it."

"Why did you call him *gay*, though?" Melanie asks. "He's not…"

"I was drunk!" Trista looks at me with apologetic eyes, and in this moment I realize that I may have ruined Bucky's life. Even though I didn't explicitly tell Trista his secret, our conversation last night still led her to draw a firm conclusion about his behavior in Mystic. Of course she was gonna bring it up during their next argument! She's only human. "It was stupid."

"Wait a minute." Melanie looks at Trista—then at me—and gasps. "The uncircumcised penis from yesterday. Oh, my God." She slaps my wrist from across the table. "You hooked up with Bucky! That's how you knew."

I can tell she's been waiting for a chance to bring this up. Probably since the moment I made that slip last night.

I could kill her. "Me and Bucky? Do you have any idea how ridiculous that sounds? Come on."

"I'm just putting two and two together."

"Well how about you take your two and two and shove it up your ass?" I snap. "Jesus. I know you hate me, but please— for Kate's sake—can you try to veil your contempt for, like, two seconds?"

Melanie clutches her necklace.

"Kids!" Paige launches into mom mode. "This is Kate's

weekend. And we are going to have a *nice* lunch. This will not be a repeat of last night—got it?"

"I apologize." I throw my napkin on the table. "Excuse me for a moment."

I slide out of the booth and march to the men's room, which I decide will be a metaphorical car wash of sorts. I'll enter with frustration and bitterness but will emerge cleansed of it. I owe as much to Kate. I even splash my face with water to literalize the intention.

It almost works.

But then I run into Jill, a.k.a. Kitty, on my way back to the table.

She pulls me into the waitstaff drinks station and speaks in a low whisper. "I'm sorry. I should've told you I work here so you'd know not to come for lunch with the fucking *bride*."

I match her whisper. "How'd you know she's the bride?"

"Please," she says. "Your table just screams Basic Bitches on a Bachelorette."

"What are *you* doing here?" I ask. "I thought you were... committed to the work you do in your other field?"

"You think I get jobs like that every night? I'd never be able to walk straight. Especially with the way your *friend* jackhammers. God bless his wife." She lowers her voice. "Oh, my God. Which one is she, exactly?"

I almost consider describing Melanie to her, but I need this conversation to end as soon as possible.

"That's so not important," I say. "Can you do me a favor? Can you make a random reference to my cousin Vinny at some point while waiting on us?"

Her eyes light up. "I love that movie!"

"Not the fucking movie," I whisper-scream. "I gave them a fake backstory for how we know each other, and I'd love if you could casually corroborate it. You used to date my cousin—who happens to be named Vinny."

"Really?" she asks through an amused grin. "All the names you could've chosen for a made-up cousin, and you went with Vinny?"

I roll my eyes. "I didn't exactly have time to think about it."

"You're so adorable." Jill/Kitty grabs the soda gun and pours two Cokes. "Yeah, whatever you want. That Vinny was a real jerk to me when we were goin' out." She pauses. "How was that?"

"Perfect," I confirm.

She laughs. "Oh. Did you guys find the present we left you, by the way?"

I immediately know what she's talking about. "No! And we looked everywhere for it. Where did you plant it? You have to tell me. That house belongs to the groom's rich family. They'll freak if—"

"Simmer down. It's in the umbrella holder right by the front door."

"No, it's not." As if I wouldn't have thought to look in the one receptacle designed specifically for long, tubular things. "I remember checking there."

"Well, check again. It's definitely in there."

"How are you so sure?" I ask. "It's been weeks."

"That night was memorable," she says. "Mostly because of you! Lexus and I still talk about how funny you were when you and the groom licked that whipped cream off our tits. It was one for the books."

I can't help but smile at the thought that I left an impression.

"That it was," I reply. "Thanks for the intel on the double-sided dildo. That could have gotten ugly if the bride had found it."

She laughs. "You got it, babe."

I exhale and creep around the side of the beverage station toward the dining room. But guess who's standing right there, as I turn the corner.

Of course.

Melanie.

The first words out of her mouth: "I heard everything."

41

Melanie is calm and collected—pleasant, even—for the rest of lunch. She dabs the grease off her pizza, sips her seltzer, laughs at her friends' jokes as if everything is peachy keen.

If she were anyone else, I might take comfort in this. But this is Melanie. She is merely filing the information away for later, plotting its detonation for a time that will have maximum impact. The only question is *when*.

I grow especially paranoid about the answer to this as we pile into Paige's soccer-mobile for the second stop of the day—a nearby vineyard for a wine and rosé slushie tasting. Once she has alcohol in her system, there's no telling when she'll release the kraken.

As Paige pulls up to the lush green oasis that is Stonington Vineyards, I remember that I've been here before.

With Ted, four summers ago. He loved the setting so much that our single tasting turned into five straight hours of day-drinking, and we had to book an impromptu hotel room for the night. I had suggested that we give the Coopers a call—they'd surely have been happy to let us crash at the Mystic house—but even back then Ted wasn't a fan of my idolization of them. I thought it was cute that he felt threatened by Patrick, but over time he revealed that what bothered him most was the imbalance of it all. By the frequency of how often I asked myself—when either of us were ever presented with a decision to make—*what would Patrick do?*

"You gotta cut that out," he'd demand. "Do you think Patrick has ever lost a second of sleep asking himself, *What would Dom do?*"

Maybe he had a point.

But then again. If I had asked myself "what would Patrick do?" more often over the past twenty-four hours, I'd be in a hell of a lot less shit. I never would have blurted about Bucky's uncut penis, I never would've let Trista corner me in the powder room, I never would've deserted the party to go hook up with a random lobsterman at the Omni hotel, and I never would've engaged with Kitty when she tried to pull me aside into the beverage station. I'd have avoided drama naturally, because I wouldn't be such a magnet for it.

"This place is beautiful," Kate observes as we head through the parking area toward the tasting room and lounge. There are rows and rows of grapes on the horizon, backdropped by lush green hills. "I love it already."

A pigtailed hostess guides us to a rustic wooden bar tended by a tall, dark, handsome man in a tight little shirt.

"Does *he* come with the tasting?" Trista mutters under her breath as we settle onto our stools. I can't tell if this means she's over Bucky already or just trying to take her mind off of him by flirting with a stranger. "Break me off a piece of that."

The bartender stands up a little straighter and shoots our group a smile from halfway down the bar. Then he struts over to us and gasps upon getting a closer look at Trista.

"Holy shit," he exclaims. "Trista Harlow? I must be dreaming."

She flips her hair back, relaxes her shoulders, and giggles. This must be the exact reaction she was going for. "Big *Sports Illustrated* fan?"

He laughs. "Actually, I'm a golf fan. Shouldn't you be at the tournament right now? "Your man is heading into the sixteenth hole..." He twists his neck around to look up at a TV that's mounted in the corner.

"Look!" Paige chimes in, pointing up at the screen. "There he is."

I squint to get a better look. It's a picture-perfect day on the links at Royal St. George's Golf Club in England. A pair of white golf pants (my favorite on him) hugs Bucky's ass perfectly as he sets up at the tee. On top he's wearing a light blue Nike golf shirt, and his tight crew cut is covered with a white Callaway cap.

He executes a flawless, super-charged drive—exerting so much force that his clubhead almost seems ready to break loose from the shaft upon impact. It's a Par 4, but he hits the ball so far that it nearly lands on the green. This Incredible Hulk–esque display doesn't go unnoticed by our bartender.

"Your man really beefed up this year," he says with a heavy dose of insinuation. "Dude's jacked."

"He's not on PEDs, okay?" Trista doesn't miss a beat. "He just works out a lot and drinks a ton of protein. Ever heard of it?"

I wonder if she knows the truth about Bucky's doping history and is just covering for him, or if she's truly ignorant to it. Either way, it's clear she's not ready to stop publicly pretending they're a couple.

The bartender puts his hands up. "I didn't say nothing. He sure did recover from that back injury quickly, though."

Trista gives him a middle finger. "Shouldn't you be serving us a sampling of every wine you have?"

He smiles. "Touché."

We taste three whites, a rosé, and two reds. I try to keep a close ear on Melanie—waiting for her to cause a scene—but the more wine I drink, the more shamelessly my attention wanders up to the TV screen. Bucky's the current leader, so the broadcast is showing a lot of him. I'm hypnotized by the way his arm muscles glide and churn every time he takes a swing, like moving parts of a perfect machine. He's in the zone. You'd never guess he felt "isolated" out on tour, as he confessed to me last month, or that he recently had a brush with the (PGA) law. The vulnerable and anxious Bucky I got a glimpse of during our private moments in Mystic is nowhere to be seen. He's back to normal. Back to cocky. Back on top.

My heart sinks as I realize something.

Bucky only latched on to me that weekend because he thought his career (and life) was over. He was fresh off a failed drug test, still waiting on the details of his suspension. His world was actively falling apart, so of course he avoided his best friends and phone-dumped his girlfriend and indulged in a gay hookup fantasy.

He never had any feelings for me. I was merely a distraction from rock-bottom.

"Dom?" Kate asks. "Hello?"

I snap myself back into the moment. "Sorry. Hypnotized by the golf."

She side-eyes me. "Right. Listen, we're ordering full bottles. Which wine was your fave?"

"I'm not gonna—" I start to explain why I don't want to get drunk today, but her eyes are giving me a very strong nonverbal message: *You need to guzzle some wine and start being fun ASAP.* "You know what? The Dry Riesling would be divine."

We get a couple bottles in ice buckets and migrate outside. All the better to stop me from obsessing over the TV screen.

"I came here with Ted once," I tell Kate as we settle into a circle of stone seats around a dormant firepit. Trista and Melanie sit across from us. Paige meanders out into the grass for a quick FaceTime with her husband and kids.

Kate squeezes my arm. "Oh, babe. If I'd known that, I would've told Paige to pick someplace else—"

"Don't be silly!" I really wasn't looking for sympathy. "I'm not sure why I even brought it up. Just thinking out loud."

"Why did Ted leave you, anyway?" Melanie asks me.

"He didn't leave me," I lie. "It was a mutual split."

"Dom finally realized he can do better," Kate chimes in, graciously corroborating my story. "Which he *really* can."

Melanie purses her lips. "Ted always seemed like a nice guy to me."

I bite my tongue and sip my wine.

"Anyway!" Trista chirps. "Kate, how are *you* feeling? Less than a month to the wedding. You must be so excited."

Kate flashes a grateful smile. "Girl, I'm on such a *cloud*. And did I tell you we're doing the Maldives for our honeymoon right after? A wedding gift from Patrick's parents." A pause. "Well, one of our wedding gifts."

"They really spoil that boy," Melanie says. "Don't they?"

"They have to," Kate replies. "They're loaded, and he's their only child."

"Well," Trista says. "I for one appreciate their generosity. Without it we wouldn't have such a swaggy beach house to stay in all weekend!"

Kate sighs. "Ugh, you guys. I just love the Mystic house so much."

Melanie raises an eyebrow. "It sure has been getting quite a bit of use this summer. Hasn't it, Dom?"

She's clearly fishing, but I refuse to take the bait. "I wouldn't know. This is only my second weekend up here."

"Right. The first one being Patrick's bachelor party…" Melanie narrows her eyes at me and swoops in for the kill that I know she's been waiting for since lunch. "…where you licked whipped cream off of our waitress's boobs."

Kate spits out her wine.

Trista's jaw drops. "Our waitress?"

My body temperature skyrockets. "No—"

"I knew you were acting weird around her!" Trista continues. "That whole 'my cousin Vinny' thing sounded so made up."

"This is ridiculous," I fume. "Melanie, can you please give it a rest?"

Kate turns to me. "Oh my God. There *was* a palpable weirdness between the two of you. Every time she came to the table you tensed up and, like, shivered."

"Because she was a stripper!" Melanie says. "Worse." She shoots a look at me. "Dom, just tell her what happened. Don't make me be the one to say it out loud. Kate deserves to know the truth about Patrick."

"Why are you doing this?" I ask Melanie. "We're supposed to be celebrating Kate, and you're over here trying to tear her down."

Kate slams her wine glass on the ground and sits up in her seat. "What is the 'truth' about Patrick?"

"He slept with her," Melanie says. "Patrick slept with that waitress. I heard it from her own mouth when she was talking to Domenic at the restaurant."

Now I slam *my* wine glass down and sit up in my chair. "That's a blatant lie! You have no idea what you're talking abou—"

"Guys," Trista interjects with a hushed tone. "People are looking at us. Can you not do this here? If someone recognizes me, this fight will get recorded and end up on social media."

"You're right." Kate's eyes start to water, but she holds it together. "We need to go back to the house."

I gesture at the bottles of wine between us as a last-ditch effort to delay the blowout, but Kate reads my mind and cuts me off before I can even say anything.

"*Now.*"

42

The minivan is a hotbox of tension.

"What the heck did I miss?" Paige asks from the driver's seat, clearly unprepared for this level of dysfunction. "I check in on my family for five minutes and a total war breaks out?"

"You didn't miss anything," Kate says flatly. "I'm not talking about it. No one speak until we get home." She swings her pretty blonde head around and looks at me. "Especially you."

I wish I could follow her command, but I can't let Melanie's character assassination on Patrick continue to linger unchallenged. "But—"

"I'm serious." Kate's voice and eyes are daggers.

Melanie rubs her shoulder from the backseat. "I'm so sorry, babe."

Kate throws Melanie's hand back at her.

I stare out the window and rack my brain for reasons as to why Melanie would tell such an extreme lie, and then I realize the obvious. She thinks it's the truth. She misinterpreted the conversation by the beverage station.

For a moment I consider piping up and setting the record straight—telling the entire car that it was Wilson who hooked up with the stripper—but if I do that, then I'm admitting there was a stripper in the first place. And ideally I'd like to get out of this whole thing without confessing to anything whatsoever. That way—even if Kate does turn it into a whole thing—I can at least still tell Patrick I did nothing but deny, deny, deny.

So I bite my tongue for the rest of the excruciating ride back to the Mystic house.

When we finally arrive, Paige and Trista disappear into their rooms (per Kate's orders) and the three of us settle into the living room for what I assume is going to be a very uncomfortable episode of *Oprah*. (Or—who am I kidding? *Maury*.)

Melanie and I each take a seat in one of Mrs. Cooper's accent chairs.

"Can someone please tell me what the hell that was all about?" Kate asks. She's perched on the love seat, glaring at us like we're in time out. "Which one of you is lying? And why?"

"Dom is covering for Patrick," Melanie says. "Isn't it obvious?"

"Melanie is just trying to cut you down like she always does," I retort. I wish I could come up with a better motive for Melanie creating such an elaborate lie, but this will have to suffice for now. "She's jealous of you marrying Patrick because *her* husband is a piece of shit."

"Fuck you," Melanie barks.

"So it was all just made up?" Kate asks. "Our waitress isn't a stripper? The bachelor party last month was totally innocent?"

I swallow my guilt and search for a way to answer this that's technically true. "For the millionth time, Patrick did not cheat on you."

Melanie rolls her eyes and flips her hair. "If I'm lying, you won't mind if I get up right now and dig through the umbrella holder. Will you?"

Shit! How could I have forgotten?

Kate sits up. "What's in the umbrella holder?"

My throat tightens. "I don't—"

"Your fiancé's whore left her dildo in there as a parting gift," Melanie interjects.

Kate's face falls. I think she's been wanting to believe me this whole time—despite knowing on some level that I'm not being entirely truthful—but it's clear that Melanie just made a power play. She has proof—and it's lurking just a few feet away from us.

Melanie shoots out of her chair and runs over to the front door. She returns seconds later with the sex toy dangling from her fingers like it's roadkill she peeled off the highway by its tail.

"So gross," she hisses. And then throws it at me. I can tell she's loving this. "How could you have let that happen?"

The first defense that comes to mind is that it's just another one of Paige's many penis party favors. But what's the point? This thing has a realistic dick vein running through it. It's clearly not decorative.

I take a deep breath and dig for the nerve to tell the truth. Maybe I'll lose Patrick over it, but if I keep lying then I'll lose Kate. And really, losing one of them will be losing both of them anyway; they're a package deal. I was never *not* going to lose them in this scenario.

"Fine." I straighten my posture and breathe calmly, already feeling a strange sense of relief at getting the truth out in the open. "I'll tell you everything."

"So you *have* been lying to me?" Kate asks.

I flash her a genuinely apologetic face. "I wanted to be honest with you from the beginning. It's just that I was sworn to secrecy at the bachelor party, and I couldn't betray Patrick's trust. But at this point it looks like doing so is the only way to exonerate him from Melanie's accusations, so here we go." I start from the beginning. "They were only here for a few hours one night. Two strippers. They gave us lap dances—"

"Before or after you and Patrick licked whipped cream off their tits?" Melanie asks.

"Patrick *also* licked our waitress's boobs?" Kate asks. "And I just sat there and ordered my pizza from her like an idiot? Oh, my God."

"He did more than that," Melanie says. She pauses for effect and rubs Kate's back under her hair. "That pig. I could kill him for what he did to you."

"That's not true!" I say. "It was only me who licked our waitress's boobs. And her name is Jill. But she's known professionally as Kitty." You know what? These details aren't necessary. "Patrick licked the *other* stripper's boobs. And it was only for a split second, and only because they forced him to do it as some kind of bachelor party ritual. He did not enjoy it at all."

Melanie rolls her eyes. Kate pulls her hair back and silently rocks back and forth.

"Anyway," I continue. "Kitty did have sex with someone that night—but it wasn't Patrick." I sit up and direct my attention at Melanie. This is my moment. "It was Wilson. And it was Wilson who hired the strippers in the first place."

"He's lying." Melanie slaps my arm. "You're lying."

"Come on, girl." I glare right back at her. "We all know Patrick would never do that to Kate. He's a good guy. I wouldn't be friends with him if he wasn't. And I seriously wouldn't have kept it from you, Kate, if he did cheat on you. I promise! I only kept the strippers from you because, as someone who was there, I knew it would sound worse than it actually was."

"He licked a tit!" Kate snaps. The absurdity of that sentence coming out of her mouth almost makes me laugh. "And how do you explain *this*?" She gazes down at the sex toy resting on the floor—looking like a discarded hydroponic cucumber—and studies it for a moment. Her eyes widen, I presume because she is realizing that it is double-sided and is putting two and two together. "Oh my God, did they—"

"Yes." I shrug. "I wasn't there for it, but I was told there was a lesbionic recital of sorts."

Melanie shoots up and grabs her purse. "You know what? I'm not doing this."

She pulls her phone out and heads for the back patio door. Her voice echoes through the air as she greets Wilson with, "Babe? Tell me you didn't screw the entertainment at Patrick's party last month."

And then she slams the door shut.

Alrighty then. So Wilson is surely going to want to kick my ass now more than ever. But I can't think about that right now. Not when Kate's right in front of me, silent and stoic, her mind sorting through a million possible actions and outcomes, I'm sure.

After what feels like hours, she lifts her head from her hands and speaks. "I can't marry Patrick."

Her voice has a quality of inevitability to it. As if she had been prepared for this possibility all along. And a part of me wants to just let it happen—stand by and watch as she burns her relationship to the ground. Maybe it's time she and Patrick finally face consequences for their toxic communication patterns and trust issues. But if I don't get Kate to change her mind right now, then Patrick will consider his cancelled wedding to be my fault. And I refuse to be the big gay scapegoat in all this.

"He didn't even do anything!" I plead. "The whipped cream? Please. That was nothing."

"He lied to me!" Kate counters. "That means it's something. What if Ted had licked another guy's dick at *his* bachelor party? You would've forgiven him just like that?"

"That's not fair," I say. "You and I both know that boob-to-dick is not an apples-to-apples comparison."

"You know what I mean," Kate mumbles through a tear. "It's not even the stripper. It's that he's been lying to me every day for the past month." Her wet eyes cross the line from sadness to anger as she turns to me. "And *you*. You've been lying to me!"

"I didn't want to! But I had no choice. You admitted yourself this morning that you guys put me in an impossible position."

"You don't get to be the victim right now," Kate declares. "And you did have a choice."

"It was a bachelor party! Everybody lies about those! It's the reason why that Las Vegas tourism slogan even exists. *What happens in—*"

"You're right," she says, stopping me dead.

"Then why are you so upset right now?"

"Because you knew I was having second thoughts about marrying Patrick! You are the only person I told that to. And you still decided to lie to me about this."

"The stuff that went down at the bachelor party doesn't tell you anything you haven't always known about him, Kate. You always knew he had douchey friends. He was a frat boy! That is part of why you fell in love with him in the first place."

"Exactly!" she says. "But I've changed. And I thought he'd changed with me." She pauses. "I thought I was clear with you about how *that* was why I needed you to be honest with me about what went down that weekend."

I can't help rolling my eyes. "Did you really think I'd feed you information that could potentially ruin the life of the oldest and best friend I've ever had? I mean, come on."

"That's bullshit," Kate says. "I'm a better friend to you than Patrick ever was. And you know it. If it weren't for me, he would've chosen Bucky as his Big Gay Best Man."

The way *Big Gay Best Man* rolls right off her tongue terrifies me. She's clearly not burying Bucky's secret anywhere all that deep.

"I love you," I tell her. "But it's just different with us. Patrick has always had my back."

"Give me a break," she huffs. "You and Patrick haven't been true best friends in years! I'm the one who brings you guys together at this point. I'm the one who *gets* you."

"You get me?" I scoff. "My wedding was *cancelled*, and you barely even acknowledged it! I could have used a shoulder to cry on, but instead you found a way to manipulate me and make it all about you."

Kate scoffs right back. "As if you'd ever cry real tears in front of me—or anyone! I tried to be there for you when Ted left, but you wouldn't let me. You always shut down, Dom. You don't *do* feelings. I was just following your lead."

"Cute attempt at psychoanalysis," I say. "But you should stick to the mascara reviews."

"I don't know why I even invited you here." Kate stands up. "You've contributed absolutely nothing to my bachelorette party other than bullshit and drama."

"I'm sorry I didn't play my role to your liking," I hiss. "Perhaps next time you can equip me with the *Vogue* article on how to be a better Gay Accessory."

"If you really think that's how I look at you, then why did you come? Why are you even friends with me?"

I stand up. "That's a great fucking question."

We look at each other from opposite sides of the room as it falls into silence. Echoes of the words we just hurled at each other reverberate in my mind, and it becomes clear that I've fought myself into a corner. There's no coming back from the grenades I've just launched.

The only thing I can do is leave.

43

~

It takes me several seconds to figure out where I am when I open my eyes. At first I expect to be in the Mystic house—listening for the sounds of a summer breeze, water crashing against rocks in the distance. But no. A car alarm drones outside my window, reminding me that I'm alone in my New York apartment.

And it all comes rushing back. I massacred my two very best friendships.

After the fight with Kate, my phone blew up with pleas from Patrick to call him. I couldn't answer while I was driving—through tears—and by the time I got home all I wanted to do was pop an Ambien and pass out.

His texts had made it clear that all he wanted to do was chew me out for telling Kate about what happened at his bachelor party. As if I hadn't twisted myself into a million knots trying to avoid doing exactly that. He probably thinks I just gleefully spilled the beans during some kind of bachelorette party gossip sesh.

And the thing is? I don't feel like bothering to defend myself. To do so would inevitably lead to groveling for his forgiveness, which would only reinforce the notion that Patrick is inherently superior to me. And I'm getting so sick of subscribing to that belief. I've held onto it for my entire life, and look at where it's gotten me.

So Patrick can hate me. He can revoke my title of best man and uninvite me to the wedding. I can't apologize to someone who put me in this position in the first place. Kate has made it abundantly clear he'll be happy to replace me, anyway.

My thoughts are interrupted by the vibration of my phone from the nightstand.

Seeing "Front Desk" on my screen is a cruel reminder that I cannot afford the luxury apartment I'm currently sulking in. Paying rent without Ted's help over the past three months has already knocked a giant chunk out of my savings. By the time this lease is up, I'll have none left. I've known this for a while, but I've been plugging my ears to it like a child—*la, la, la*—while distracting myself with the parties all summer.

"Good morning, Mr. Marino," the doorman says when I answer his call. "Just letting you know Patrick Cooper is here. I sent him right up."

"Great," I chirp out of habit—despite the fact that this is a disaster. Another thing to do now that I'm *alone*-alone: update the pre-approved visitor list at the front desk. "Thanks."

I throw on a pair of sweatpants and wait by the door for Patrick to start knocking. I might as well get this over with. As much as I dread the conflict, there is cold comfort in the thought of the closure that will follow it.

The ding from the elevator goes off down the hall, followed by Patrick's footsteps (more like stomps), followed by Patrick's knocking (more like pounding).

"Open up, dude." *Pound.* "I know you're home." *Pound.* "I saw your car on the street."

I crack the door, and he whooshes in like a storm, looking like a personal trainer in his workout clothes. Clearly he hasn't been that distressed if he stopped by the gym before showing up here unannounced.

"Look, man," I begin. I can hear my voice automatically descending an octave, and it pisses me off that—even at a time like this—my instinct is to match Patrick's tone. I clear my throat and attempt to speak more naturally. "I tried really hard not to say anything, okay? It was just that Kate—"

"She's calling off the wedding." He slams his fist against my kitchen counter and catches his breath. "What the hell happened at that party? What did you say?"

"It was *Melanie*."

"Oh, Melanie?" He strokes his chin. "You mean Wilson's wife? The one who told him she wanted a divorce last night?"

"Holy shit."

"Yeah." He scoffs. "You somehow managed to break up Bucky and Trista, too." He gives me a slow clap. "Nice job destroying pretty much every relationship in my wedding party. What a great best man you are."

My reflex is to de-escalate. "I didn't do anything on purpose, okay? The stripper from your party was our waitress at lunch the other day. Melanie overheard me talking to her, and then" —I throw my hands up—"everything just snowballed from there."

"Snowballed?" he sneers. "More like you just couldn't keep your mouth shut. You never could. Ever since we were kids and I had to fight all your battles for you."

"So you think I actively decided to destroy everyone's relationships?" To hell with de-escalation. "Who would do that?"

"I don't know, man. Maybe someone whose fiancé just left him? Someone who's trying to make everyone else miserable now that he's alone and doesn't have a punching bag to take all his shit out on anymore?"

"Fuck you," I shout. "Maybe I did use Ted. And maybe he left me—but you know what neither of us ever did? Lie. Which is all you and Wilson and Bucky have been doing all summer! It's not my fault you all got caught." I pause for effect. "It shouldn't have been my job to cover for *any* of you assholes."

Patrick digs his knuckles into his eyes and collapses into a kitchen chair. "I trusted you, man. You think it was easy to have my bachelor party knowing that there'd be someone from the other side there? I thought you understood how important it was for me to—"

"The other side?" I ask. "The other side! Right. It's not like we're lifelong friends or anything."

"You know what I mean."

"I know exactly what you mean." Now I'm the one who's about to punch the counter. "I wasn't supposed to be there, because that was only for your real friends. And I stopped being one of those a long time ago. Ever since you dropped me in college—"

"*I* dropped *you* in college? What kind of revisionist history bullshit is that?"

"It's the truth. I came out of the closet, and you couldn't deal with having a gay friend—so you went and did the straightest thing possible and joined a fraternity."

Patrick scoffs. "You're the one who distanced yourself from me. I was just following your lead. You wanted to reinvent yourself, so I let you." He sounds totally serious right now, like he actually believes this. "You were never in our dorm room. I spent so many nights alone that first month of school while you were sleeping at your boyfriend's house. I *had* to rush Omega Kappa Beta. How else was I supposed to have a life?"

Damn. I haven't thought about that boyfriend in years—which is wild, considering how fully my world revolved around him for the nine vivid months in which he allowed me to believe our relationship was monogamous.

But I was eighteen! Of course I fully threw myself into my first boyfriend. It doesn't change the fact that something fundamental had changed between Patrick and me the second I told him I was gay. I know I didn't imagine that.

"If you really felt like I was ditching you, you could have said something to me." I cross my arms. "You loved that I was gone all the time."

Patrick opens his mouth to speak, then stops short. His face is unreadable—a blank canvas onto which all I can do is project years of his smug superiority and my pent-up resentment.

I stand up. "Do you have any idea how much I have killed myself trying to keep up with you in life? Everything that has come easy to you has been so hard for me. I hid my sexuality for all of high school because I needed to have the perfect girlfriend, just like you. I ran countless miles on track—in much shittier shoes than you!—trying to catch up with your impeccable race times. I'm crippled with law school debt because it just *had* to be NYU—"

"This is all my fault? I didn't tell you to do those things—"

"You didn't fucking *have* to!" I scream—and suddenly it becomes clear to me that I'm acting unhinged—two expletives away from throwing a dish against the wall.

I collapse onto a kitchen chair and heave a sigh.

"Dude," Patrick says from across the table. "Calm down."

"You only maintain your friendship with me out of pity, don't you?" I say it quietly this time. "I know your first choice of best man was Bucky."

His face falls, and he slumps down into his chair, defeated. He doesn't actually address the statement I've just made. A part of me was hoping Kate had made that up, but his muted reaction makes it clear that she didn't.

Several seconds of silence pass.

"Did you even hear me earlier?" he finally asks. "Kate wants to call off the wedding."

He rubs his eyes. "I don't know what to do, man. I can't lose her. Not over some random stripper."

As much as I want to stay mad, I can't help but feel bad for him. I know how gutting it is to confront the possibility that the wedding you've been planning for months—the life you've been looking forward to for years—might be ripped out from under you.

"It wouldn't be over the stripper," I tell him. "If she breaks up with you, it would be because you don't see her for who she really is. She's not the 'cool girl' she was eight years ago. She needs more from you now—more affection and better communication. You have a little bit of a bro thing where you never talk about your feelings." I pause. "Making this all about Kitty would be like me saying Ted dumped me because of that spider—when, really, the spider just happened to coincide with his revelation that our problems as a couple had grown so much as to become insurmountable." I'm not sure if I'm comforting Patrick or myself at this moment, but I keep going. "There were years of unhappiness and incompatibility that led to that one stupid little moment."

Patrick buries his face in his hands. The tears are imminent— he's gonna break down, right here on the IKEA kitchen table that Ted and I bought when we moved in together all those years ago.

This is first time I've ever seen Patrick come face-to-face with the possibility of failure—of loss—and it's painful to watch. It doesn't matter that he brought it on himself by lying to his fiancée all summer, or that his life has been impossibly charmed up until now. He's human. And he's suffering. I know exactly what he's feeling, and I wouldn't wish it on my worst enemy. Let alone my best friend.

After a minute of this face-buried silence, Patrick lifts his head. But he's not crying.

His face has assumed an expression of pure rage.

"Fuck that," he says. "Kate and I are nothing like you and Ted. We've always been happy together. We're *meant* for each other." He jumps to his feet, slams his chair into the table, and bolts toward the front door. "And this is all your fault."

44

His breakup is my fault.

"Right. I wield that much power. It couldn't possibly be that your fiancée doesn't trust you. It couldn't possibly be that you're not as perfect and untouchable as you think you are. Go to hell, Patrick!!! I'm glad Kate called off the wedding. How does it feel to face an obstacle for once in your shitty-ass charmed existence?"

Whew—that felt good. If only I had said it to him when he was actually here.

I fall onto the couch and angrily scroll through my phone. The first thing I see is a tweet reminding me that today is the final round of the British Open.

Bucky is sitting pretty at the top of the leaderboard, and he tees off in an hour. Which means I have exactly that much time to find something to do with my day. Otherwise there's a strong chance I'll wind up spending the bulk of it curled up on the couch in a cocoon of self-loathing, watching the man I'll never have swing his way toward yet another Sunday victory.

I send a text to Mario—the lobsterman whose number I still haven't deleted—but it goes ignored. He either decided I'm too much effort or he's already returned home to Maine.

Probably both.

This is the part of being single I wasn't prepared for. Before Ted, I had so many friends and acquaintances who I could have easily called up on a Sunday afternoon and initiated several hours of day-drinking with. But of course I had to be that guy who revolved my entire life around my boyfriend—totally unwilling to consider that he might one day no longer be mine—so those people have long since transitioned from real-life friends to social media thumbnails. Most of them have moved to the suburbs and started families at this point. A cruel reminder that my failed relationship with Ted took place during five of the most crucial years in life-building. The entire second half of my twenties.

So...cocoon of self-loathing it is! Good thing I stocked up on chips and cookie dough last week.

The hours pass in a blur.

Bucky kicks off the round with a double bogey, which immediately knocks him down several spots on the leaderboard.

And it just gets worse from there. His second drive goes into a pond, and every shot after that somehow lands directly in a bunker. He starts to turn it around at the third hole with a birdie, followed by a few pars in a row. But then he starts bogeying again. Meanwhile, all the other golfers are playing at the top of their game.

By the tenth hole, Bucky is no longer even in the top twenty.

"This is just a brutal collapse," the announcer says as Bucky picks up his ball and walks toward the eleventh hole with his loyal caddy, a balding elk of a man whom I've never heard speak but somehow seems British. "For the tournament favorite to unravel in this way—it's a difficult thing to watch."

Bucky's eyebrows form a seemingly permanent acute angle, and his bottom lip is bloodred from being bitten and chewed on for the past couple hours. Gone is the simple smile and Southern charm. He's in pain.

"You hate to see it," the co-announcer replies. "Bucky Graham just cannot get out of his own way on this Sunday at Royal St. George's—and nobody knows why."

But I do. He's in his head, worrying about the potential loss of the life he's worked so hard to build, now that Trista knows his secret.

The last seven holes go by in slow-motion, with Bucky getting less and less screen time as he fades from contention and the announcers shift their focus to the leaders. When all is said and done, Bucky places somewhere in the thirties—a tragic downfall, especially for such a major event.

"You were the clear leader going into this," the announcer says to him in his post-round interview outside the clubhouse. "Tell us. What happened to you out there?"

"I just had a rough go of it today," Bucky says through a clenched jaw. His eyes are two black holes of grief, but somehow he manages to fake a good-natured smile. "But it's like my granny used to say: 'the sun don't shine on the same dog all the time.'" He wipes a bead of sweat off his forehead. "Reckon I was due for a blunder one of these days."

I turn the TV off and close my eyes. I'm not sure if it's mental exhaustion or looming depression or secondhand embarrassment for Bucky or what, but my brain shuts off and I drift into a heavy sleep. It's as if I never woke up in the first place—Patrick never came over, Bucky never blew his shot at the Open.

Several hours pass before I'm shaken awake—just after midnight—to a text message alert. Three little words.

Hey, you up?

Bucky.

45

have no idea why Bucky would send me a booty call after the way we left things in Providence, but it's impossible to interpret the phrase "hey, you up?" as anything *but* a booty call, so I reply to it with an embarrassingly eager yes.

He calls me immediately.

"Mornin'," he says.

"Morning?" I rub my eyes, still unsure if this is reality or just a very lifelike dream. "It's the middle of the night."

"I'm over in England," he explains. Right. So this isn't a booty call situation at all—we're an ocean apart. "It's 6:00 a.m. out here. I played the Open yesterday…"

"I watched it all," I confess. "I'm really sorry."

The line goes quiet for a moment. "Thanks, man."

I want to fully lean into my excitement about his resurfacing, but it's tainted by my confusion. The last I heard from this man, he told me to lose his number.

"So what's going on?" I ask. "Is everything okay? Is this about Patrick?"

"I'm fine." He sounds about as convincing as I would saying that sentence right now, which is to say not convincing at all. "And nah, not about Coop."

"Oh. Okay."

He takes a deep breath. "I reckon I just thought we could talk."

"About...?"

Silence.

Eventually he says, "This probably seems real desperate, huh? I'm sorry." His voice carries the same lilt of disappointment it did when he told me about his suspension that day on the boat. "I've just been thinkin' about you. I ain't hardly slept all night. I don't know what's goin' on with me. My play yesterday was so—"

He cuts himself off, muffling a quiet sob.

My heart hurts for him. "It wasn't that bad. Everyone has an off day sometimes."

"C'mon now." He sniffles. "You know that was a hell of a lot worse than any ol' off day." He catches his breath and steadies his voice. "But thanks for sayin' that. I guess this is why I called. Somehow I knew you wouldn't judge me for cryin' over it."

I understand what he's saying. Crying about a loss to anyone else in his life would be a display of weakness, and people love Bucky specifically because of his strength—not only can he dominate a golf course, but he knows how to keep it together when the golf course dominates him. Instead of breaking down in tears, he'll get a chip on his shoulder that motivates him to push harder next time. Anger is fine, but sadness would ruin the image.

While I love that he feels like he can take his armor off with me, I do have to wonder why he's only ever drawn to me when everything else in his life has gone to shit. If he had performed well on the course yesterday, would I even be talking to him right now? If only I had the nerve to ask.

I opt to comfort him instead. "Listen, there's always gonna be another tournament. Remember when you missed that big putt at the 3M Open a few weeks ago? And the reporter was trying to get you to comment on it, and you were just like, 'my mind's already onto the next round.' And then that whole *Ted Lasso* reference you made about how 'to play well, you gotta have the memory of a goldfish,' because they forget everything after three seconds?"

This actually seems to stop the tears. I can almost hear him smile. "Dang. You remembered that goldfish thing? So you really have been followin' my game these past few weeks, huh?"

"I've tuned into a few rounds," I stammer. "It's not like I've been stalking—"

"I'm just playin' with ya, bud." He laughs. "Goddamn. It feels good to hear your voice again after all this time."

I can't deny the feeling is mutual. Even though we're on opposite sides of the world, even though there's a mountain of unresolved tension between us, his voice is a like warm blanket to me right now. It validates every extreme emotion I've felt toward him over the past month. I wasn't delusional in my obsession—I was suffering from withdrawal.

So I permit myself to smile. "It's good to hear your voice, too."

"And I want you to know I'm real sorry for everything," he says. "I know I treated you two times worse than dirt...especially after that night at Coop's party. It was just that I spent my entire life running away from that feeling. You know what I mean, man? So when I gave into it with you, it scared the livin' crap out of me." He sighs. "And then once they dropped my suspension and I got back out on tour again, I had no choice but to slip back into my old habits. Throw myself into the game."

"So that's why you got back with Trista?" I ask.

"It is," he admits. "But I'm sure you heard by now that it's over. I can't even be all that mad 'bout it. Our split was a long time coming."

I have to ask: "Are you worried she'll tell people about... you know?"

He sighs. "Tryin' not to be. She's a good person. I think I can trust her."

A pang of guilt hits me in the stomach. "I could have been a lot more careful at the bachelorette party, but I want you to know I didn't tell her. She figured it out on her own."

"She told me how it all went down," he says. "I can't blame you. I'm surprised she didn't figure it out sooner."

It feels so good to hear him say this—a two-ton weight off my chest.

"So what's the official story?" I ask.

"We *grew apart*," he says. "And that's all there was to it."

A small part of me wants to push for more details—especially about whether or not he's made any progress in coming to terms with his sexuality—but a bigger part of me knows that if there were anything to tell, he'd tell me on his own.

"Fair enough," I say instead. "So what else is going on with you?"

He doesn't answer right away.

When he finally does, he laughs softly in a way that still sounds laced with tears. "I'm a mess, is what's goin' on with me. That whole 'slippin' back into my old habits'? Throwing myself into the game? It ain't workin' like it used to. Somethin' changed after that weekend with you in Mystic..." He takes a deep breath before letting more words pour out. "I keep thinkin' about what you said that night in the lighthouse. How you used to feel like you had one of those big cones on your head."

"Right. I've since recalled that the proper term is Elizabethan collar." I cringe at the reminder that I explained my coming out experience to him by comparing myself to a post-surgical dog. "I know that was a very weird metaphor..."

He chuckles. "My granny had this ol' basset hound when I was growin' up—Smokey. I remember when he had to wear the cone. Made him crazier than a cross-eyed cowboy, he wanted to scratch himself so bad. We called it the 'Cone of Shame'..."

I don't know exactly where he's going with this, but I'm pretty sure Smokey isn't the end game, so I wait for him to keep talking.

"I guess I'm sayin' I also felt like that. I had gotten so used to my cone, I barely realized I was wearin' it. But then I took it off with you—and man, it felt so good to finally scratch that itch. Now I get what all the fuss is about." His voice is just north of a whisper; I almost can't hear him. "And it wasn't just that. It was every time we talked. I felt like I could be myself around you—not the rich golf star with a perfect life and girlfriend, but the ol' Southern boy who grew up in a three-room shack with his granny, scared to death of bein' called a—"

He cuts himself off. "Man, I'm sorry. I don't even know what I'm over here blabberin' about anymore. I just miss talkin' to you. I miss...you."

I take a moment to process what he's saying. It's not a confession of love or anything, but it's definitely something real.

"I miss you, too."

He clears his throat and returns to a normal speaking volume. "Anyhow. I'm flyin' back to the States in a couple hours..."

"Oh." It occurs to me that I don't know the location of his next tour stop. "Where to?"

He takes a careful breath, like the answer to my question is flammable. "New York."

My pulse quickens. "New York?"

"New York."

"City?" I ask. "New York City?"

"That's the one."

"Oh."

"I got a tournament across the river in New Jersey this week," he continues. "Liberty National Golf Club…"

If he doesn't tell me he wants to see me while he's in town, I will literally track him down and light his Nike golf pants on fire for leading me on like this.

"I'd like to see you while I'm in town," he says, saving me the trouble. "If you're available."

"I'm available," I blurt. "I mean, I think I can find time to hang out."

He smiles through the phone. "Great. I'm actually gonna be stickin' around in the city for an extra six days after the Cup. What with Coop's wedding in two weeks and all."

So Patrick hasn't filled him in yet. Probably because he has absolutely no idea how to tell people he's failed at something in life. (If we were on good terms right now, I'd offer to coach him.)

It's not my place to tell Bucky myself, so instead I focus on the opportunity that his extended stay could present for us. "What do you plan on doing with that full week of free time?"

"That there is a great question." His voice descends into a sneaky drawl. "I reckon I thought we could hang together for a bit. Maybe pick up where we left off in Mystic."

46

Bucky is renting a luxury penthouse in the heart of Tribeca—the kind of place I've previously only ever seen in movies, *Architectural Digest*, and that one Kardashian spin-off show where Kourtney and Kim "took" New York.

The lobby is a maze of marble, stone, and glass. The stoic doormen exude Secret Service–levels of importance in their designer suits.

As I ride the elevator to the top floor—which I've been advised opens directly to the home's foyer—the reality of Bucky's multimillionaire lifestyle hits me in a way I hadn't yet experienced. Even the Coopers' wealth seems modest by comparison. They stay at the Plaza when they're in the city, sure, but they at least have to navigate a hallway to get to their room.

The elevator doors whoosh open.

"Howdy." Bucky stands before me in a white tank and gym shorts. His genuine smile stirs a high in me that immediately drowns out any second guesses I might've had on the way over here. His biceps don't hurt, either. "Sure is good to see ya."

I melt into his hug. "Thanks for the invite."

He pats my back. "Absolutely. Thanks for comin' over at this hour."

"It's seven o'clock," I tease. "This is a totally normal time to meet someone."

He laughs nervously. "Oh. Right. Guess I'm still messed up from the time-switch. You eat yet? I'm not all that hungry, had a burger after training at the course earlier... I can order you somethin—"

"I'm good. Not hungry either."

"Alright, then." His enthusiasm deflates slightly as he readies for his next statement. "So, listen. I don't wanna sound insensitive or anything, but I promised myself I'd give you a list of ground rules when you got here. Just to make sure we're on the same page and all. I hope that's cool?"

I was prepared for this. "Sure, of course."

He takes a step back. "First off, this has to be kept a secret. No one can ever know about us."

Well, then. Perhaps I wasn't prepared for him to be quite so direct about it.

I respond by telling him that I have far too much self-respect to regress into a clandestine affair with someone so devoted to their internal gay shame that they refuse to even entertain the idea of living openly.

Ha! Just kidding. I might be able to grasp the concept of self-respect on an intellectual level, but let's be real. I'm not turning down Bucky Graham.

"That's totally fine," I say instead, lying through the echo of heartbreak in the back of my head. "I understand you're in a tough situation with your career and all."

His shoulders relax. "Exactly. I got too much riding on my image, too many folks lookin' up to me. If I came out of the closet, it would be a whole media circus. I can't have that kind of distraction from my game. 'Specially after this past weekend."

My ears perk up at his choice of phrasing just now.

"So you admit it?" I ask, channeling my inner Regina George. "You're *in the closet.* You're…gay."

He tenses back up. "Looks like it."

It's not ideal that he's so disgusted by who he is (and who *I* am) that he gets so uneasy when I refer to him as "gay" out loud, but I get it. It's gonna take time to undo all the internalized homophobia that's surely been drilled into him all his life. And honestly? Even his tepid "looks like it" strikes me as a big step forward. He's no longer denying the truth of his sexuality—not to himself, at least.

Or to me. Being trusted with such an intimate revelation pretty much guarantees that the existing feelings I have for him will only intensify from here.

"So what are the other rules?" I ask.

"Actually, there's just one." He grabs my hand and pulls me forward. "Follow me."

He drags me through the seemingly endless hallway of this luxury oasis until we come upon a large open space with floor-to-ceiling windows and a brilliant, modern chandelier hanging from above. The floors glisten in the sunlight; the walls display a mix of simple yet elegant artwork and jagged shadows of nearby skyscrapers.

In the center of the room is a black Steinway & Sons baby grand piano.

"You gotta play a little somethin' for me," he says. "Deal?"

I can't find words to respond with, so I pull him into a zealous kiss. Normally the thought of someone asking me to play for them would induce severe nausea, but nothing about this situation is normal. Nothing about Bucky is normal.

"I reckon that's a yes?" he jokes.

"It's a yes," I confirm.

His eyes light up. "Good. I was so worried you'd feel weird about all this, but I had to give it a shot." He gives my arm a playful punch. "Plus it's only fair. I mean, you've been watchin' me do my thing on TV every weekend this past month. But I haven't been able to see you do *your* thing since that day I snuck up on you playin' Chopin at the Mystic house."

Again, all I can do is kiss him.

This time he digs his fingers into my lower back as he reciprocates, which makes me want him so bad.

"Let's save the recital for later," I suggest. "There's something else we haven't been able to do since that day at the Mystic house…"

"I'm right there with ya," he murmurs. "Can't believe I lasted this long since you got here, to be honest."

He leads me on another journey through this sky-high palace until we wind up in the master bedroom. There's a glass-covered fireplace in the center of the room, making this space warmer than any other in the penthouse. All the more reason for us to shed our clothes.

I collapse onto the bed.

Bucky climbs on top of me.

He talks to me urgently through his kisses.

"I want you here"—*breath*—"every night." *Kiss.* "But."

Oh no.

Kiss. "You gotta know I'm gonna be training all day, every day this week." *Breath.* "And then the tournament." *Kiss.* "I gotta warn you." *Breath.* "I'll be on another planet 'til that's over." *Kiss.* "But I still want you here anyway." *Kiss.* "So we can at least do this"—*breath*—"every damn night."

A tiny voice inside of me wonders why he's bringing this all up now—conveniently tempering my expectations of his time while we're deep in the throes of passion. Setting the stage for a relationship built on shame, secrecy, and late-night hookups.

But these worries are erased by the weight of his body on top of me.

Every worry I've ever had in life is erased by the weight of his body on top of me.

"That's fine," I promise. "I'll be here."

He presses into me harder. "Good."

I don't care how small and stolen our moments together need to be. We are going to spend the next seven nights falling deeply, wildly, irreversibly in love. I'm sure of it.

august

The Wedding?

47

~

Mornin'," he says to me from across the California king bed. The sheets are vivid white, a zillion-thread count, and the comforter is the goosiest down I've ever had the pleasure of wrapping myself up in. I've come to realize that beds like this are why rich people always have that glow to them. They sleep better than the rest of us. "I just ordered a big ol' Southern breakfast. My post-tournament tradition. I'm talkin' ham, eggs, sausage, biscuits, gravy...grits. Hope you're ready to get greasy 'round the mouth."

I lean in and kiss him. "Always."

True to his warning, I've barely seen any of Bucky this past week. He was gone for basically fourteen hours a day during the tournament—between practice rounds, warm-ups, press events, and the actual golfing (he gave a solid comeback performance)—but we have woken up in this bed together more often than not. For a few blissful moments as the sun rises each morning, I've been pretending we're a legitimate couple.

And now that the tournament is finally over, I'm hoping to extend the magic several more hours into the day.

"So then what do you wanna do?" I ask my future husband. "After breakfast. I don't know if I told you, but I took the day off."

His face scrunches up in worry.

"You didn't mention that." He gets up and throws on a pair of boxer briefs. I will never tire of the view of naked Bucky Graham. It's so much better in real life than it is in the pages of *ESPN Magazine*. "I'm kinda booked."

Good thing I didn't actually take the day off. This was just a test to see if he'd actually be willing to do something in public with me, in which case I was fully prepared to call out. (I'm fucking insane, I know.)

Judging from how guilty he acts every time he comes and goes from the penthouse—he only relaxes after locking the door and having a whiskey—my guess is that he's still afraid to be seen with an unidentified and possibly-gay male friend. It's not like he's so famous that doing things in public is a huge issue, but he does get recognized by enough sports fans to raise a few eyebrows.

"I'm sorry," he offers in response to my silence. "It's just—"

"No worries," I lie. Damn. Even though I saw this answer coming, it hurts more than I thought it would. There's a chance I've been building up too many expectations for how Bucky would act once the tournament ended. "We can just connect later. Or whenever."

"Listen, man. I knew this would be weird." He squeezes my shoulder. "It's Cooper. He wanted to talk about wedding stuff. Since I'm...you know."

Oh. That's the other thing.

While I've been shacked up in this tower playing house with Bucky, the gap between my two best friends and me has grown exponentially. Somehow they were able to reconcile with each other, but neither of them have felt compelled to apologize to me. Deep down, I always knew they would never follow through with something so messy and humiliating as a last-minute wedding cancellation. They'd sooner get married and follow it up with a quiet divorce a few months after the fact.

They probably used me as the thing to bring them back together—a common enemy. The last I heard from either of them was a text from Kate last week that said: If you don't want to come to the wedding, we understand.

To which I responded: Okay, thanks.

I know. It's silly. If they could forgive each other, surely they could forgive me. Nothing that went down between us was monumental enough to warrant this level of animosity. But I suppose it was just the tip of a larger iceberg of resentment on all sides.

"That's fine." I fake a yawn to assure him I'm totally unbothered by the mention of Patrick's name. "It was nice of you take on the role in my place."

"Not like there's anything to it at this point," he says. "Hard part's over thanks to that rager you threw for us up in Mystic."

I force a chuckle. "Has he mentioned me at all?"

Bucky shrugs. "A couple times, over the phone. He made it sound like the issue was between you and Kate more than anything. I know he wishes y'all would patch it up."

Of course he'd frame it that way now that his life has been put back together. Patrick has always had a gift for moving on as if whatever minor problem he's experienced has simply never existed. If we ever had a fight as kids, all we had to do was not talk for a couple days, and then we'd hang out again as if everything was back to normal. He's not like me—desperate for resolution about every little thing.

"You wanna know what I think?" Bucky asks. "This fight makes about as much sense as a trapdoor in a canoe."

"Can you repeat that in Yankee, please?"

"I'm saying it makes no sense. It's immature!"

"It is," I agree. "But what can I do? Neither of them has apologized."

He opens his mouth—like he's about to suggest I swallow my pride and apologize to them first—but cuts himself off.

"I'm gonna talk to Coop today," he says instead. "It's not right that you miss this wedding over somethin' so dumb. You two got somethin' special. Somethin' he and I don't even have."

"Yeah?" I crack. "What's that?"

"History. Y'all been running together since you were knee-high. I don't know about up here, but where I come from, that means something."

I sigh. "If you try to defend me, he's just gonna think I put you up to it."

"Why would he think that? As far as Coop is concerned, you and I barely even know each other." He pauses. "Right?"

Now might be a good time to admit to him that Kate knows about what we did in Mystic, but I can't. He's still uncomfortable with the fact that Trista knows—if he knew Kate knew, he might fully unravel.

"Right?" Bucky asks again. "Dom'nic?"

"Right! Of course." My stomach sinks as I imagine Kate going scorched earth in the aftermath of our broken friendship. At this point, the only thing that would have stopped her from telling Patrick everything about that night is her loyalty to Bucky. Which I can't say I have the most faith in. But I swallow my fear and hope for the best. "He'd never guess in a million years."

48

~

Bucky's right about one thing. Patrick and I do have history. Ever since we stopped speaking, memories of our shared childhood have been resurfacing in the gaps of my mind, haunting me as I try to focus or sleep or do anything requiring a modicum of mental discipline.

There's one moment in particular I keep thinking about, from back in high school.

(No, not *that* moment.)

Patrick had just gotten this expensive new pair of Nike running cleats for track.

Naturally, I seethed with jealousy. If anyone needed a new pair of track sneakers, it was me. I'd used the same beat up Reeboks for two seasons in a row at that point. The laces were frayed, and the soles resembled a worn-out eraser. The situation got so bad at one point that our track coach noticed and bought me a pair of replacement insoles out of pity.

Meanwhile, Patrick's mom bought him new sneakers every couple months, having heard from her trainer that their performance declines sharply after a hundred miles. (A statistic which I'm now inclined to think is a total crock of shit, but that's neither here nor there.)

I tried to make the case for a new pair to my dad, but he was having none of it. "Are there holes in your shoes?" he asked while inspecting them with tired eyes.

"Not technically," I said. "But—"

"Then there ya go." He scoffed. "Just because your friend's snob parents buy him new sneakers every other week doesn't mean you need them, too."

"Thanks for nothing," I huffed. "As per usual."

My fortune changed one day when Patrick and I came back to his house after practice. There was a box of brand-new Nikes placed neatly on his bed.

"You know what?" Patrick said. "I just broke in the ones I have. They've got a lot of miles left." He picked up the orange shoebox and handed it to me. "We're still foot twins, right?"

I glanced down at our two pairs of feet and released a pathetic chuckle. "Yeah."

"Then take these. I don't want them."

"But—"

"Or I can throw them out." He gestured toward the trash bin in the corner of his boxy teen boy bedroom. "Your call."

"Fine, fine. Don't throw them out." I accepted the box with a strange combination of shame for needing his help and gratitude for having received it. "Thanks a lot, man."

It's a random memory to harp on, but it keeps coming back to me every time I try to convince myself he's a bad guy. He's not. I've just been so fixated on the problems between us this summer that I lost sight of his innate kindness. The man has a big heart.

And so does his future wife.

I'll never forget early on in our friendship, right after Kate and Patrick first made their relationship official. I was cramming for the bar exam—didn't sleep, eat, or bathe for days. My entire life rode on that test. I had the good fortune of being hired at my job prior to taking it, but my company had made it clear that failure was not an option if I wanted to remain employed. And my student loan and credit card debts were so enormous at that point that even just two weeks without a paycheck would have debilitated me.

But my obsession with test prep eventually became counterproductive. I couldn't see that by not practicing basic self-care, I was jeopardizing my chances at success in an entirely different way.

Until Kate stepped in one night. She showed up at my apartment with Chinese takeout, a magnum of wine, and several *Sex and the City* DVDs. It was the pinnacle of Fashion Week—a sacred season in her world—and I had to do a double take to make sure it was really her at my front door in a headband and sweatpants.

"Shouldn't you be at a show tonight?" I asked. "Or a mixer?"

"Both," she confirmed. "But I had to bail, because this is an emergency."

My heart skipped a beat. As if I weren't already on edge enough. "What is it? Is Patrick okay?"

"He's fine." She threw the takeout on my kitchen counter. "But you're not. I'm mandating that you take tonight off from cramming."

"Oh." I exhaled. "That's not happening."

"I'm doing this because you're my new best friend and I love you," she said. "You're on the road to burnout, Dom. I don't know shit about the bar exam, but I know beauty—which mirrors every other aspect of life—and if you don't give yourself some rest, you will fully self-sabotage."

"I have to pass this test—"

"I understand." She put her hand on my arm and shot me a look of concern. "I do. Your job means a lot to you."

"Because—"

"You can't afford to lose it, I know." She popped the cork from the wine and poured us a glass each. "That's why I'm doing this! You will lose it if you don't learn to take care of yourself. So tonight you are going to unwind, okay? No law stuff! No studying, no Adderall, no staying up until five in the morning on an empty stomach. Tonight is all about eating, drinking, living vicariously through four iconic single women in early-aughts New York City, and *sleeping* until noon tomorrow. Got it?"

She clinked her glass with mine. "You'll thank me when you start your week in a perfect state of rejuvenation on Monday."

I found out from Patrick later that the show she missed was her favorite designer's.

In retrospect, the most remarkable thing about the gesture wasn't just that she came over with some takeout and entertainment. It was that she knew exactly what I needed and gave it to me without my having to ask. It was that she spent an entire night with me and didn't once make it all about her. At some point during this summer's ups and downs, I had forgotten about her capacity for selflessness.

At the end of the day, she's a good friend.

And so is he.

And so am I.

And yet here we all are, throwing it away.

49

I shouldn't have come to the office today.

I always have trouble focusing on my work, but today the struggle is above and beyond. I had been doing such a good job of not thinking about Patrick and Kate over the past week—living out this fantasy with Bucky has been the best distraction—but our conversation this morning and all those trips down memory lane brought all the wedding drama back to the front of my mind.

If Patrick isn't harboring a grudge against me, then why is he letting Bucky take over as best man? Why didn't he protest when I told Kate I wasn't coming to the wedding? Why is he so willing to throw away twenty-plus years of friendship over a handful of misunderstandings? And why do I need Bucky to be the one to convince Patrick to talk to me again? Why is—

I can't be thinking about all this right now. I'm on the verge of drowning in all the shit I've been putting off at work. If the stack of contracts on my desk were an architectural structure, it'd be the goddamn Freedom Tower.

The Freedom Tower—Kate's office building. I wonder what she's doing at *her* desk right now. Probably comparing shades of lipstick on her arm, her mind in pre-wedding overdrive, not thinking about me at all. Probably—

Stop! I guzzle the remains of my venti red eye and force myself to focus on my inbox.

Somehow I manage a full hour of uninterrupted work—essentially a day's worth for me—but then I make the mistake of checking my personal email.

There's a note from Illuminated Weddings—the pyrotechnics company that Ted and I hired to execute several lavish fireworks displays at our wedding.

Dear Mr. Marino,

Congratulations on being just six weeks away from your big day! This is a friendly reminder that your second installment of $3,000 is due within fourteen calendar days. Please note that we do not accept cancellations and/or issue refunds less than two months ahead of the wedding date.

What the hell? Ted was supposed to handle this months ago—it was squarely in his column of our wedding cancellation spreadsheet.

I remember because these fireworks were a whole point of contention in the first place. I initially dismissed them as an unnecessary extravagance, but Ted convinced me they were worth splurging on after we watched a video on the Illuminated Weddings website.

I had never seen fireworks like that before. Tasteful, elegant bursts of silver and gold—like a million diamond rings exploding into the sky. And so I agreed to the deluxe package, complete with giant sparklers lining the entrance to the venue and a grand finale show at the end of the night, which our sales rep promised would look even more spectacular when launched over the reflective stream of the Connecticut River. Ted covered the deposit three months ago, so I agreed to pay for the second installment. Which is apparently due in two weeks.

I forward the payment reminder to Ted's email address in a furious huff.

His response comes in right away: Oh. Fuck.

Followed by a phone call.

"Sorry," he says in place of a standard greeting. "That's my bad."

"No shit," I hiss. "I don't have three grand to spend on fireworks we're never going to use. I'm paying rent alone now—remember? I have zero expendable dollars."

"Calm down," he says. "We'll figure it out."

"*We'll* figure it out?"

"I will." He pauses. "Listen, I've been meaning to reach out to you—"

"Then why haven't you?" I ask without thinking. Something about the tone of his voice just now has auto-launched me right back into the hideous tendency I've always had to nag and shame him for every little forgotten detail or flubbed errand. "Not that I care."

I need to dial it back. I'm sounding way too much like the bitchy boyfriend that I used to be and not enough like the indifferent ex I now am. I've barely even given two thoughts to Ted over the past few weeks.

"What did you want to talk about, then?" I ask after he responds to my attitude with the silent treatment. This call is like a Greatest Hits of all our old toxic relationship dynamics. "If not the fireworks?"

"I talked to Kate," he says. "So I just wanted to make sure you were doing okay. I know she and Patrick are basically your only friends—"

"I have other friends," I lie. "My entire world didn't just revolve around you and yours for the past five years." Another lie. "And I'm doing great." And another! "I'm actually in a new relationship."

At least that last one wasn't a total fabrication. Ted doesn't have to know that the relationship I'm referring to is a late-night affair shrouded in secrecy and shame that I constantly have to remind myself isn't just a fever dream.

Anyway, it's better than whatever I had with Ted at the end.

At least Bucky and I have that early sexual chemistry. And we're nice to each other. And I never feel compelled to nag *him*. Granted, that could be because it's all so new and surreal and he wields too much power in the dynamic; it's an honor for me just to blow him. But still. I know I'm not imagining that there's a deeper connection at play beneath it all. The sparks between Bucky and I burn brighter than the ones between Ted and I ever did—even during the honeymoon-iest days of our early courtship.

"A relationship?" Ted asks. "With who?"

"Does it matter?" I answer.

The line falls into silence for a few moments.

"I gotta go," he finally says. "But I wanna talk to you more about this Kate/Patrick thing. Are you free for a drink after work?"

50

For some reason, I say yes. But on the condition that we meet at Rafters, a bro-y sports bar directly across the street from the luxury high rise Bucky's been staying in. He and I don't have explicit plans tonight, but I'm assuming he'll text me at some point with an invitation to sleep over once again. Might as well be nearby when he does.

So here I am in this wood-paneled arena that feels more like a frat house than a bar. The walls are accented with framed football jerseys and hockey sticks. They have several beers on tap but only two wine options—red or white. There's something so comfortable about the unfussiness of places like this.

Right as I begin to text Ted for his ETA, he startles me by plunking down in the stool beside mine.

It's like seeing a ghost. His sweepy light hair is freshly cut, and he's wearing his go-to work ensemble: grey Patagonia vest, blue button-down, khakis. I used to love this look on him so much. Even though it's the standard uniform of every finance douche on Wall Street, the fact that I had attained one such finance douche for *myself* always felt like an achievement.

"Dom." Ted grabs my shoulder. "Did you hear me? I said hello." He scans my outfit as I turn to greet him. "Nice shirt."

I glance down at my torso and realize he's saying this because the shirt is his. He moved out in the middle of a laundry cycle, so I inherited a number of his beloved Bonobos button-downs.

"You want it back?" I begin to unbutton it. I'd rather strip to my undershirt right here and now than allow him to think I'm attached to the hand-me-downs he never bothered to ask for after he left. "Here."

"Please." He smiles. "It's yours now." He flags the bartender and orders a pair of IPAs. "So how was work?" he asks. As if we're just two friends meeting for happy hour and he didn't dump me three months prior to our wedding.

"A soul-sucking slice of pure hell," I lament. "Thanks for asking."

"Right. So the usual." He taps his fingers against the bar as we await our beers. "I was hoping you might have quit by now."

"What's that supposed to mean?" And there it is. Nag-and-bitch mode, activated once again. This man has such a talent for bringing out the worst in me.

"Nothing at all. I'm just saying. I thought being single for the summer might have forced you to confront some of the *other* things in your life you'd been—"

"Is this why you wanted to meet?" I ask. "To judge my life decisions?"

He laughs nervously. "Sorry. No. I wanted to talk about Kate and Patrick." He accepts two frosty pints from the bartender and bequeaths one to me. "I think you're making a big mistake."

"That is literally a judgment of a life decision." I take a swig of beer and it goes down smooth—hoppy but grapefruity. "Trust me, whatever Kate told you is only a tiny slice of the story. This summer has been all kinds of messed up."

Ted wipes his mouth after a heavy sip. My chest twitches as I think about how familiar and close and *mine* that mouth was for so long. I can't help but wonder where it's been over the past few months.

"I'm sure it has been," he says. "But I'm telling you right now, not as your ex, but as someone who still cares about you: you're going to regret it if you don't go to this wedding. These are your best friends. You can't let a misunderstanding undermine so many years of friendship. It's silly."

My voice drops into an enraged whisper. "You're telling me this because you care about me? That's a joke, right? You literally ruined my life, Ted." I gesture at the space between us. "You ruined *our* life—the one we built together! You destroyed it. Everything we knew for the past five-plus years—"

"I *saved* both of our lives." He leans in. "If we had gone through with the wedding, it would have only ended in divorce later on. I mean, come on, you know how unhappy we made each other."

"I was happy enough," I lie.

He stares blankly at me. "You were miserable. You were just willing to suffer through it. The same way you do with your job and your—"

"Why would I be *willing* to suffer through misery?"

He blinks. "Let's see. To keep up appearances. To keep up with Patrick. To maintain some kind of illusion of—"

"You've made your point."

And unfortunately, it's a good one.

Maybe he didn't save our lives—that's a bit dramatic—but I can be open to the possibility that he did us both a favor in the long run. If we couldn't work through our incompatibility during the nearly six years in which we were together, what made me think we'd have been able to do so within the restraints of marriage? Being in his presence right now—after having spent so many feverish nights with Bucky—only reinforces the fact that we never had the life-altering chemistry I've always dreamed of. Ted was merely a safe choice.

"I didn't come here to fight." He puts a hand up. "Like I said, I still care about you as a person. And believe it or not, I was worried about how you'd been doing on your own all summer. But I figured you'd be fine as long as you had Patrick and Kate. Which is why I'm so surprised you're fighting with them. I mean, I know you haven't always had the healthiest dynamic—but it's nothing worth ending things over."

"It's complicated." I have to admit that Ted's sudden concern for my wellbeing does seem genuine, and it would be nice to talk to someone about all this.

So I launch into a play-by-play of how it all went down. From Kate's threats ahead of the bachelor party to Patrick's behavior at said party to the moment it all exploded at the bachelorette. "I basically revolved my entire summer around them and their wedding and their secrets," I finish. "And somehow they decided it was my fault that they almost broke up at the end of it all."

Ted strokes his chin for a moment before coming back with his analysis. "So basically you tried to play both sides—like you always do with them—and it bit you in the ass."

"I had to play both sides," I say. "I didn't have a choice in the matter."

"But you did have a choice. You could have told Kate from the beginning that you refused to be her mole. And you could have told Patrick that you refused to keep secrets from Kate."

"I tried! With both of them!" I tell him. "It didn't work."

"Did you stick to your guns, though? Or did you give in to their demands after they pressed you on it?"

I wince, thinking about how I ultimately did assure both of them I was on their respective teams just to keep the peace. "I shouldn't have had to stick to my guns. They should have known not to put me in that position in the first place."

"I agree," he says. "But in the end, it sounds like you led them to think you were cool with it, so they figured you were cool with it." He pauses. "You know this is all because you're so afraid of even the tiniest bit of conflict."

"That's not true," I counter. "Look at you and me. Our entire relationship was nothing but conflict."

"Right." He laughs. "Myself being the only exception."

"That's because couples are supposed to fight! Friends aren't. Friends fighting is just so...gauche." Pause. "And immature."

"Ah, yes. But chronic avoidance—now that's mature."

"Fuck you."

"And by the way," he adds. "There's a difference between good fighting and bad fighting. All couples have the occasional conflict—but did you really think our level of *constant* conflict was healthy? It wasn't."

I know he's right, but I don't feel like giving him the satisfaction of admitting it out loud. I don't feel like having this conversation at all. "Are you done yet?" I ask.

Ted wipes some IPA off his lip. "I'm just saying I think you should bite the bullet and apologize. I'll admit it was shitty that they put you in that position, but from Kate's version of events it sounded like you're not exactly the most innocent victim in all this."

"Me? I didn't do anything."

"She said you were M.I.A. during a full day of Patrick's party and that you literally skipped a night of her party to hook up with some random lobster guy in a hotel."

I get a weird sort of pleasure in hearing Ted acknowledge that I've hooked up with someone else since we've broken up. I'm sure he thought I'd wallow in carbs and celibacy for at least half a year.

But the pleasure is quickly dwarfed by my realization that Kate might be slightly entitled to her grievance. I think about how Paige was this perfect maid of honor, handling the decorations and schedule and personally catering to the bride's every need throughout the duration of the bachelorette party. My approach as best man was nothing like that. I basically just emailed some bullet points that I called an "itinerary" and then let the chips fall where they may—all while sneaking around with Bucky behind everyone's backs. And then the whole bachelorette debacle. I really should've been more focused on the guests of honor at both parties.

"I'll admit that I messed up," I say. "But only because they messed up first."

"So there you go," he says. "You're all even. If you just reach out to either one of them, this whole thing can be squashed in five minutes."

His logic almost resonates. But something feels wrong about me being the one to reach out. They messed up first, so they should apologize first. And also: Ted has the smuggest know-it-all look on his face right now. The one he gets when he feels like he just solved a problem that only he could solve.

It enrages me.

"Why do you even care?" I ask him. "You left me. I'm not your problem anymore. What difference does it make to you if I go to their wedding or not?"

"It doesn't," he says. "I just want you to be happy, Dom. That's why I left you in the first place. So you could find actual happiness. But clearly you haven't been able to do that." He narrows his eyes at me. "Do you even like this new mystery man you've been seeing?"

So now Ted is accusing me of being miserable without him—but also miserable when I was *with* him. He's basically saying I'm altogether incapable of happiness.

And the worst part is that last question. If I answer truthfully—"the 'mystery man' I've been seeing wouldn't even allow himself to be seen in this bar with me"—I'll just prove him right and confirm that my life is entirely out of control.

"Of course I like him," I say. "What kind of question is that? I'm not a dumbass. I don't need you telling me what it takes to be happy. Especially when you're the one who left me in the first place."

"You didn't even like me," Ted snaps. "You just liked being engaged. You liked the *idea* of having a husband. It didn't matter how much I ever did for you. It wasn't appreciated." He pauses. "And honestly? You say that Patrick and Kate were using you, but I think it's the other way around. You've always used them—fetishized them—to enhance your own self-image. You've never stopped to consider that they are human. After all the shit they've done for you over the years, what have you ever done for them—really?"

"They are literally blessed with perfect lives!" I snap back. "They've never *had* any problems. I'm the one who's gay and broke and alone."

"Clearly they have problems—they nearly called off their wedding." Ted shakes his head. "And what did you do?"

"That's cute," I say. "Because the situation is so cut and dry—"

"I gotta go," Ted interrupts. "I'm sorry this turned into a fight. I'm not sure why I expected anything else." He takes out his wallet and throws cash on the bar for the drinks. "I hope you can work it out with them, though." He pauses before walking away. "And I hope you can learn to love yourself."

"Fuck you!" I yell at him. "You're not my therapist. Or my boyfriend." Ted's already halfway out the door. I might as well be howling at the moon at this point, but something in me needs to say this one last thing—if only to hear what it sounds like out loud. "And I do love myself."

51

Hours pass as I stay planted at the bar, drinking my feelings, scrolling through my phone, stewing over the fight with Ted. This was hardly the first time he's hurled unsolicited psychoanalysis at me, but it is the first time I've allowed myself to acknowledge the truth. That he's right. The problem in our relationship wasn't just him. It was also me. And my problem with Patrick and Kate isn't just them. It's also me.

And Patrick's right, too—he never asked me to try and keep up with him all these years. I took it upon myself, because my self-esteem has always hinged so delicately on some imaginary audience's comparison of the two of us.

The irony is that, all this time I've been pissed at Patrick and Kate for tokenizing me as the gay best friend, I've been doing exactly that to them. By holding Patrick up as this paragon of male perfection, I was just reducing him to a stereotype. And I spent so much time envying the fact that Kate was able to nab the perfect husband and perfect relationship—when she told me she was having second thoughts, I was only concerned about how their hypothetical breakup would affect me.

It's almost enough to make me want to apologize to both of them right now and see if we might be able to patch things up.

I consider sending Patrick a text, but decide to wait until I hear from Bucky about how their conversation went earlier today. But of course for that to happen, Bucky would have to respond to the texts I've been sending him all night. Which he is not.

Are my eyes glued out the window at the entrance to his building across the street? No.

Except yes.

I order another drink and debate the pros and cons of sending another text. How many before I start to seem unhinged? Maybe he wasn't planning on inviting me over tonight after all. But I've spent nearly every night the past week up there. What could've changed?

The bartender slides a fresh beer in front of me, and then the face I've been scanning for all night suddenly appears. Much closer than expected.

Bucky enters the bar.

My eyes light up for a moment at the idea that he saw me sitting here and decided to come join, letting go of all his hang-ups about being seen in public together. He'll explain that his phone died and he's so glad he ran into me.

But my spark of hope is quickly extinguished when I notice that his arm is wrapped around a woman—a gorgeous blonde with long straight hair and a perfect ass. She's smiling up at him as if they're on some kind of date...which is, I realize with a sinking in my stomach, exactly what's happening here.

I slouch in my stool and try to will myself into invisibility. Which would be a lot easier if they weren't headed straight to the bar right now.

Bucky's face turns white as our eyes meet. He almost looks like he might approach my side of the bar—maybe try to play it off to his date as though he's just run into a random friend—but then a stranger approaches him from behind. He flashes the guy a smile and thanks him for what I assume is sycophantic golf-praise. He gives the same smile to a number of other people at the bar, whom I now realize are all staring at him. I should've known he'd be a celebrity in this place. There's literally a mural of Augusta National Golf Course painted above the urinals.

Bucky throws me an apologetic look. *See? People recognize me here. I'm sorry.*

Or maybe it's more like, *Can you please get the hell out?*

Normally I'd oblige, but that's what someone who's afraid of conflict would do. And right now, I'm not that person. I'm actually *craving* conflict.

So I stare at them for a few minutes. Bucky tries to sip his beer naturally, smile at his date. But his eyes keep wandering over to mine between sentences. Finally she excuses herself to the bathroom, at which point I leap out of my chair and race over to his side of the bar.

His posture stiffens. "I can explain."

"Please don't." I'm colder than the frozen margarita that his date left half-full on the bar next to me. "So I take it I'm not staying over tonight?"

He shrugs in regret as I study his face. Deep brown eyes, chiseled jaw, heavy cheeks. Those lips I've been kissing every night for the past week. It all fills me with a primitive sense of jealousy. Wasn't he just mine?

I step forward.

"Dom," he whispers. "Don't do somethin' stupid. Please let me explain later."

I could do what I've been doing all week: acquiesce to his demands, smother my better judgment, settle for whatever scraps of attention he's willing to give me up in the penthouse, late at night, when the rest of the world is asleep.

Or I could believe that I deserve more than that. I could force myself to accept that no matter how deep our connection is—no matter how much chemistry we have behind closed doors—Bucky simply isn't capable of giving me the kind of relationship I'd need to be truly happy. He has too much work to do on himself.

I take a step back. "You don't have to explain anything."

"Can we..." He motions toward a narrow hallway in the back of the establishment. "Let's talk there."

I follow his lead until we're tucked into a corner between two stacks of discarded mahogany bar stools. It feels remarkably private despite the bustling crowd just ten feet away.

"I'm sorry," Bucky begins. "Alright? She's just—"

"It's fine." I straighten my posture in determination. "You've been clear from the beginning about what this is between us. And we both know it's gonna die at the end of this trip anyway, right? So let's just kill it now."

He grabs my waist. "Please don't say that. I need you."

My gaze wanders out to the main bar area, where anyone compelled to squint in our direction could easily catch a glimpse of us. "Careful. God forbid someone see the great Bucky Graham engaged in a moment of public homosexuality."

He immediately lets go.

"I need you," he repeats. "I want you—"

"Clearly you don't! What you want is to keep your image intact as some kind of quintessential—straight—golf god."

"Why can't I have both, huh?" he asks. "As long as *you* know the image is all an act. Why can't we keep this thing between us going, just the way it is now?"

"Because," I begin—and then choose not to continue. He should know why I don't want to settle for such a second-rate arrangement. The fact that he doesn't, that he's willing to put us both through this, is all the proof I need that we're not in the same place in our lives. Maybe we never will be. "We just can't."

Bucky sighs, clearly drained. And honestly? Same. I'm exhausted. Not even with him at this point, but with myself. I should've known better than to latch onto such an unavailable man in the first place. As if the gaping divide between our two sets of life circumstances would just magically close itself if I pretended it didn't exist.

But it does exist. And I'm tired of pretending I'm someone I'm not.

"It's fine," I assure him. "I promise I won't tell anyone about you—your secret is safe with me—but I'm done. I can't go back in the closet for you. Or anyone."

"Don't do this," he pleads. "Dom."

We stare at each other with desperate faces. I swear I can feel his tears being swallowed, the same way I'm swallowing mine. This is how it ends for us. In the darkest corner of a church of masculinity, surrounded by wood paneling and sports memorabilia. The sexual and romantic force between us raging and invisible.

And impossible.

Heart heavy, I step forward to initiate my exit.

But something in him snaps.

"Goddamnit," Bucky whispers. "I fuckin' love you."

He pulls me into a ravenous kiss.

We close our eyes and savor each other's taste, letting the heat between us take over the way it always does.

He tightens his grip on my waist and kisses me harder.

I relax into his strength.

Until he stops.

I blink. "What?"

He pushes me away so hard that my back slams into one of

the spare bar stools behind us. It makes a loud thud as it crashes against the wall.

"Fuck." Bucky's eyes are two rabbit holes of pure terror—fixated on the wide-open space beyond our private nook. The bar full of drunken sports fans being drunken sports fans. "Someone might've seen us just now."

"I doubt that—"

"No," he interrupts, firmly stomping on the flare of hope his kiss had kindled in my chest. "You were right. I'm sorry. We can't do this anymore."

And then he turns and walks away.

wake up in my own bed, which is the worst blow of all. No more mornings with Bucky in his penthouse. Mornings where I could pretend he was mine. Mornings where I could sit down at the piano and pretend *it* was mine. Mornings in which reality didn't exist.

I check my phone, a regressive part of me hoping he might've reached out overnight to initiate a reconciliation.

Nothing.

But there is evidence of a different kind of reconciliation. One between Patrick and I.

Breakfast tomorrow? he asked just past midnight.

Drunk Me must have predicted this massive hangover, because I responded with: How about lunch instead?

Patrick: We're leaving for Mystic at noon.

And then me: Breakfast works.

Patrick: Let's do the diner by your place at 9. You, me, Kate.

Me: I'm really sorry about everything.

Patrick: We'll talk tomorrow. See you in the morning, bud.

I reread it several times until a blurry memory of the conversation surfaces. The way I meticulously labored over every word of my texts back to Patrick, it's amazing they're as concise and unremarkable as they are. But they got the job done. And I stand by my decision to apologize. Something about losing Bucky last night really put the situation with Patrick and Kate into perspective—it was ridiculous of us to ice each other out as long as we did.

An hour later I find Patrick and Kate ensconced in the peach vinyl of a corner booth, an aerial portrait of Central Park quaintly hanging above their heads. He's wearing a Lacoste polo and a Rolex that I haven't seen on his wrist in years. Her hair is pulled back into a low ponytail. She barely has any makeup on, but still looks as fresh and dewy as always. They've already ordered me an iced coffee, which I guzzle immediately.

"I'm so glad I caught you guys before you left," I say. "Thank you so much for this."

The fact that they're squeezing me in at the start of their wedding week—when they surely have a million other things to do—isn't lost on me. It's a repentant gesture in and of itself.

Patrick grabs my shoulder. "Me too, man."

The air goes silent. The three of us exchange expectant glances, no one knowing quite what to say or where to begin. We're like that meme of the three Spider-Mans pointing at each other.

Kate eventually perks up and launches into problem-solving mode. "So. I'll go first." She turns toward me and puts her hand over mine. "Dom, you were right. I put you in an impossible position when I asked you to report back to me about the bachelor party. I should've gone directly to Patrick with my trust issues instead of putting you in the middle. You've been dealing with so much this year, breaking up with Ted and everything, and instead of being supportive I just made it worse. I'm sorry, babe. I really am."

Her apology is very much appreciated, but I can't pretend I'm innocent in all of this. "I'm sorry, too. The way I ditched you at your bachelorette was totally uncalled for. I still can't believe I did that to you on your big weekend. And yeah, it sucked being asked to report back to you on the bachelor party, but I get why you assumed you could count on me for that. And I shouldn't have been so willing to lie to you..."

Patrick clears his throat. "That's my cue. I think we can all agree that I'm the guiltiest party at the table." He addresses me. "I'm sorry, bro. It wasn't cool that I asked you to lie to Kate. And that fight we had at your apartment last week... I'm sorry about that, too."

"It's all good," I assure him.

He leans in. "I know you feel like I've always put you in a different category from my frat brothers—"

I put a hand up. "There's no need—"

"And I have," Patrick admits. Ouch. "But it isn't because I think they're better than you. It's because I think you're better than them. You're the realest friend I've ever had." He takes a moment to formulate his next sentence. I know this can't be easy for him—he's not the heart-to-heart type—so I appreciate that he's trying. "I just want you to know that, regardless of our differences, I've always viewed you as my equal. And not just because our hands and feet are freakishly identical." He laughs. "If anything, *I've* always been kinda jealous of *you*."

"Well, alright." I make a face. "Let's not get carried away."

"I'm serious," he insists. "Like, yeah, everything I've ever wanted has always come easy to me. I won't deny I'm a lucky son of a bitch. But I don't have what you have."

I squint in confusion. "Which is..."

"Drive! You're an entirely self-made man. The only other person I know who can say that is Graham."

The mention of Bucky's name sends a jolt to my chest. I take a sip of water to drown it out. "We're not exactly in the same boat. He's a multimillionaire sports star."

"And you're Senior Counsel at the fastest-growing music app in the world!" Patrick says. "I know you hate your job, but still. That's impressive."

Maybe Patrick's right. Instead of being insecure about my humble origins, I should be proud of them. Instead of being ashamed of my past, I should be grateful for it. Instead of resenting my father for always being so tired and angry during my childhood, I should sing his praises for working his ass off to keep us sheltered and fed.

Patrick taps the table. "So we're good?"

"We're good." I look at him and then at Kate. "I'm sorry again for the way I handled things."

Kate shrugs. "All three of us handled things spectacularly poorly. It's amazing, really. Somehow we managed to concoct a whole seven-layer dip of toxic communication patterns and unnecessary drama out of a single bachelor party."

"A big part of the problem was Wilson," Patrick chimes in. Ah. Perhaps *he* was the common enemy that brought them back together. "Instead of telling you how to act, I should've been telling him. If he hadn't gone and hired those strippers..."

Kate nods. "He's the worst. I'm so glad Melanie is divorcing his sorry ass." She looks at Patrick and then back at me. "We've already told him he needs to be on his best behavior at the wedding. If he tries to start any shit with you, his ass is getting escorted out."

My shoulders relax at the assurance that I'm safe from another Wilson attack.

And then I realize what Kate just said.

"So this means I'm officially re-invited?" I ask.

She smiles. "Technically you uninvited yourself. But yes."

"You guys!" I shriek. I can't help it. "I'm so excited. And seriously, thank you so much for coming here today. I'm sure I would've tried to make up with you via text at some point before Friday…but this is so much better. It will make the actual wedding much less awkward."

Kate laughs. "Can you imagine if you'd actually missed it?"

"I'd have never forgiven myself." I glance at Kate's nails, which happen to be painted a pale pink that reminds me of the sex toy that nearly destroyed their marriage. I suddenly feel compelled to do a wellness check on their relationship—see if they've truly made miraculous strides in building trust over the past few weeks or if they've just decided to temporarily ignore their issues to get through the wedding. "You two are good now? You've worked through all your problems? No more secrets?"

Okay—that came out judgier than I'd intended it to. I release an awkward chuckle to diffuse the tension. "Just want to make sure I'm not in danger of nearly destroying the wedding again."

They throw me a few awkward chuckles of their own.

"We're a work in progress," Kate explains. "We've started going to couples counseling." She squeezes Patrick's hand under the table. "I'm being much more honest with Patrick about my feelings these days. No more 'cool girl'…just the messy, ugly truth."

"Don't let the makeup fool you," Patrick says through a smirk. "It is *not* pretty under there."

Kate slaps his arm playfully. "Clearly we still have some work to do."

"The most important thing is that we love each other." Patrick sits up a little straighter. "I'm the luckiest bastard in the world to get to be marrying this one! I almost messed it up once. I'm not gonna do it again."

Kate makes a gushing face at me and then turns toward him. "Babe! Ugh. I love you so much."

Okay, well, damn. Ted and I tried couples counseling a few times, but it sure as hell didn't produce results like this. If anything, it somehow made us dislike each other even more than we already did.

"By the way, Dom." Patrick taps the table. "I talked to Bucky about it, and he's fine with surrendering the title of best man. So if you're still willing..."

Not too long ago, I would've interpreted this offer as a dig—further proof of me being second fiddle—but now I just see it for what it is. My best friend making amends. "I am."

He flashes a smile. "Great. It was important to me—and him—that you reclaim the title."

"How's he doing?" I ask as casually as possible. "You know, after breaking up with Trista and all."

Patrick shrugs. "Good. He had a first date with some new swimsuit model last night. You guys know how he is. I can't keep up."

"He's not bringing her to the wedding, is he?" I blurt.

Patrick laughs. "It was a first date."

"He's not," Kate affirms. "He was still with Trista when we did invitations and seating. No plus-one."

Patrick looks at me. "Why do you care—"

"So!" Kate chirps. "I'll text you with all the updated details, but basically the plan is the same. Rehearsal dinner Friday...but of course you're welcome to come up and stay at the Mystic house earlier."

I want to lean into my excitement about returning to Mystic, but I can't stop thinking about how hard it's going to be to feign normalcy around Bucky. As if he's just some friend-of-a-friend I haven't seen in two months. As if he didn't impulsively admit that he "fuckin' loves" me last night. I suspect it will feel distinctly like going back into the closet—even though I broke things off with him explicitly because I refuse to do just that.

"When is Bucky coming up?" I ask.

"Friday," Patrick answers. "Why?"

"No reason." Okay. So at least I can steal a few days of beachside peace before having to figure out how to act. "How about I come up tomorrow?"

"Yes!" Kate squeezes Patrick's arm. "You guys. I'm so glad everything's back to normal. This is going to be the best wedding week ever."

53

~

My first day back at the Mystic house is a dreamy montage of summertime bliss—all lawn games, Coors Light, and sunshine. Patrick and I take the boat out and reminisce on high school bullshit. Kate and I stay up late drinking white wine and talking about Drew Barrymore's personal journey. It's as if we never had a falling out at all, as if there is no wedding to worry about—just a lazy summer to relish.

But now it's Thursday, and there's definitely a wedding to prepare for.

Especially where Kate is concerned. She decided to do a (totally unnecessary) twenty-four-hour juice fast ahead of the rehearsal dinner tomorrow. A mild bridezilla energy seems to be intensifying with each shot of wheatgrass, but luckily Paige arrived this morning to start fulfilling her MOH duties—so I've accepted that I'm probably not going to have any meaningful time with Kate until the day of the actual wedding.

Which leaves Patrick, who suggested that he and I play a round of golf today. I scoffed at first, reminding him of the last time we went out on the course together. I lost no less than eleven balls to water, woods, and course-adjacent rich peoples' outdoor entertaining spaces.

But he insisted.

So here we are at the tenth tee.

And in a pleasant plot twist, I've been playing better than I ever have. I even got a birdie on the last hole, which I can only assume is the result of some kind of mysterious osmosis that took place between Bucky and me every time we made love over the past few weeks.

"You're on fire," Patrick says on our cart ride to the fairway. "What's gotten into you?"

"I've been watching a lot of golf on TV lately," I say—which isn't a lie. I just omit the part about only doing it because I've been romantically involved with his other best friend. "I'm just imitating the pros."

"Next time we'll have to play a round with Graham and see how you really stack up." He laughs. "Just kidding. He'd murder us both."

At the end of the round, we stop by the clubhouse for a few beers.

"To love and marriage," I say as we clink bottles.

"To your epic round," Patrick says. "You shot a hundred and ten. Definitely the best round you've ever played." He smirks. "Even if you still finished twenty shots behind me."

"Story of my life," I mumble.

Shit. I hope that came out jokey and good-natured. I'm supposed to be letting go of my latent resentment toward him—and I can certainly feel it receding after what he said at the diner yesterday—but I imagine it will take some time to dissipate completely.

Patrick frowns. "I was just kidding, bud."

"No, I know." I take a swig of beer. "So was I."

We fall into an easy silence for a few moments. He checks his phone, takes a swig, sets his eyes on the expansive green outside the giant clubhouse windows.

"Should we sleep in the lighthouse tonight?" he randomly asks, breaking the silence and causing me to choke on my pale ale. He laughs. "I'm kidding again."

"Good times." I force a chuckle. "Did you ever wonder why we chose to sleep out there? On basically a slab of wood? There was such a nice house—with amazing beds—right up the hill!"

"We thought it was cool," he says. "It *is* pretty cool out there. I don't remember why we ever stopped…" His voice trails off. He leans in and flashes an apologetic half-smile. "Well, that's a lie. Obviously I remember."

He can't be doing this right now—he can't be bringing up that night. It's impossible. It's one of those things you literally never talk—or even think—about. I mean, I've thought about it a lot, but that's because I'm me. But Patrick is supposed to have forgotten about it entirely. I've long since accepted that as far as he's concerned, it never happened at all.

"Do you remember that night?" he asks. His voice is so low, it's almost a whisper.

"Which night?" If he's not going to feign ignorance, I sure as hell am.

He crinkles his eyebrows underneath his white Titleist golf hat. "Dude, come on. You know what I'm talking about."

So he's doing this. He's really doing this.

"Yeah," I finally admit. "I guess I do."

"I'm sorry," he offers. "All the time we spent not talking last week, for some reason I kept going back to that night in my head. Thinking about how I should have apologized to you back then, but never did. I'm sorry, man."

"You didn't do anything wrong," I say cautiously. "It was just—"

"I acted like it never happened. That wasn't cool of me. I mean, sure, I didn't know you were gay yet...but still. I could tell it meant more to you than it did to me."

"What are you talking about? It didn't mean anything to me," I joke.

He puts a hand on his chest. "Ouch, man."

"Maybe it did mean something to me," I admit. "It's not like I was in love with you or anything, but I definitely knew I was gay by then. And for the briefest moment that night, I thought maybe I wasn't alone in that." I take a swig of beer. "But then it became extremely clear that I was alone in it. Which obviously isn't your fault. I mean, you couldn't help that you were straight."

Patrick laughs for a second before veering back into sincerity. "I'm sorry you didn't feel like you could tell me. I know I was the one who set the tone with our friendship." He pauses. "I think I just assumed that you were ultimately on the same page as me. That you just wanted to forget it ever happened, so our friendship wouldn't have to change."

He has a point. I did everything I could back then to make Patrick believe I was on the same page as him about pretty much everything, always. I can't be mad at him for taking me at face value.

"Well," I remind him. "Our friendship did change a little. We never slept out there again after that."

"Right," Patrick says quietly. "That was the one thing."

There's an unspoken understanding that this was our way of sweeping it under the rug. If we never returned to the scene of the crime, we'd never have to acknowledge there was a crime to begin with. "Well, like I said. The house is a hell of a lot more comfortable anyway."

Patrick smiles. We fall into a comfortable silence for a moment, both staring out the window at the golf course, where two teenage boys prepare to tee off at the first hole. They look like best friends—like us fifteen years ago—and I can't help but wonder what their story is.

"So you really didn't have a hunch that I was gay in high school?" I ask him. "Then how did you know I was gonna be so open to doing...that?"

He shrugs. "I guess I figured that if I was a little curious, there was a good chance you'd also be. I think a hell of a lot more straight guys out there have experimented than would ever admit it. How else do they know for sure they're straight?" He grins. "I know that's how *I* knew."

Now it's my turn to feign offense. "Ouch, man."

He smiles. "I'm glad we finally got this out there. Are we good?"

"We're good." I had no idea how much I've always needed this moment to happen. Somewhere deep in my chest, I feel a sharp kernel of shame actively dissolving. "Thanks for saying all this. Your apology actually means a lot to me."

Now that I have it, I'm ready to put the topic to bed forever. Especially because the thought of a past version of myself whose feelings toward Patrick were anything but nonsexual makes me want to vomit directly into my golf bag. "Now let's never speak of that night again."

Patrick smirks. "So it's not going in your best man speech?"

My cheeks heat up—both at the thought of me referencing that moment in a public setting and also at the reminder that I still have to come up with a best man speech, which I've yet to do.

"Definitely not," I say. "But I will be making a reference to the whipped cream tits from your bachelor party." Now Patrick's face is the one turning red. "Kidding!"

Patrick exhales. "Let's never speak of *that* again, either."

I laugh. "What happens in Mystic, right?"

54

With the rehearsal dinner starting in six hours (and the wedding in twenty-four), the Mystic house bustles with activity from caterers and construction crews and party organizers.

Patrick and Kate are out to lunch with their respective pairs of parents—this is only the third time they've ever met, given that Kate's family is from the West Coast—and Paige is busy entertaining her husband and two sons, who showed up this morning.

Which means I'm just sitting around alone, scrolling through my phone and freaking out over the imminence of Bucky's arrival.

The sleeping arrangements this weekend are essentially family only—Mr. and Mrs. Cooper downstairs in the primary master, Patrick and Kate in the upstairs master, Paige and her husband splitting one spare bedroom, and myself in the other spare. Which: thank God. If I had to stay at the nearby Hilton with the rest of the guests, there's a chance I'd end up desperately banging on Bucky's door at the end of the night—drunkenly sprawled out on the hotel carpet like a rabid raccoon coming down from a trash binge.

At this point I just want to clear the air and move on. If we're going to survive being in a wedding party together all weekend, we're going to have to find a way to establish a new—platonic—dynamic.

I also want to thank him, because regardless of the secrecy and shame of our arrangement, he did do one very amazing thing for me last week. He brought me back to my first love: the piano.

And I'm going to keep playing. Even if I have to dig my old Casio out from my dad's attic, it will be better than nothing. I'm also going to find a new apartment. One I can afford on my own. And I'm going to stop doing so many things I don't want to do. Even if I have to keep my legal career going to make ends meet, I can at least seek fulfillment in my free time.

And I'll be a better friend.

Which reminds me: I still need to draft my speech.

I pull up my phone and swipe into the Notes app, but my progress is quickly interrupted by the ring of the doorbell.

Bucky?

I creep out into the hallway and listen for voices at the front door. The wedding planner's tinny voice says *hi, hi, come in*.

Melanie.

"Hey girl," I say once I get to the bottom of the stairs. Hopefully she'll follow my lead and just be fake. I can only imagine how much she blames me for her divorce. "How have you been?"

She narrows her sleepy eyes at me. Her hair's in a messy bun, and a limp garment bag hangs from her forearm. "Where's Kate?"

I motion at the window. "Out, but they should be back in a couple hours. You're early."

"Yeah, well. I needed to get out of that hotel room. They didn't have any vacancies left, so I'm stuck sharing with my soon-to-be-ex-husband."

I tug at my shirt. "Right. Listen, about that. I'm sorry for—"

"Please." She puts a hand up. "I know it's not your fault. He is who he is. It's my fault for thinking he'd eventually grow out of his frat boy bullshit." She sighs. "I'm sorry I took it out on you before. I was such a bitch at the bachelorette."

"Not even," I gush—high on having just resolved a long-standing conflict with such minimal effort on my part. "You're totally forgiven." I recognize something of myself in her eyes—the pain of a shattered marriage. "I have an idea. Let's bury the hatchet—or, rather, *drown* the hatchet—by day-drinking until everyone else gets here."

She lights up. "Hell. Yes."

We convince the catering staff to fix us a tray of piña coladas—complete with dark rum floaters on top—and take them down to the beach. The pure bliss of Mystic Harbor shimmers before us, all gentle waves and perfect sky. Up the hill behind us is the chaos of transforming the backyard into a top-tier wedding venue, all canopies and chairs and pieces of a dance floor that are yet to be assembled.

For a moment I remember the first time I sat in this Adirondack chair earlier this summer—back in June, on that first night of the bachelor party—and almost choke on a chunk of pineapple. A lifetime has elapsed since.

"I haven't been single in years," Melanie groans once we're a few drinks deep. "How am I gonna do it? How did you do it after Ted left?"

"Honestly? I have no clue. And it's been four months. But somehow I've been surviving." I gulp down a particularly rummy sip of colada. "And, somehow, you will, too."

She absorbs this for a moment.

"I don't blame you for leaving us that night in Providence," she says. "If a hot Maine lobsterman were to come onto me right now…" She giggles. "I'd totally miss the rehearsal dinner. Or—hell—the entire wedding." She hiccups. "Ugh. Mike is the worst! I wasted so much time on his stupid ass."

"The worst," I agree. "God, what a prick."

We cheers, and the man-bashing continues for a while until the entire tray of drinks is gone and we're both bloated and sick from all the sugar.

We embark on a sloppy walk of shame up to the house. Our plan is to detox via several gallons of water (both in and on us) before getting ready to consume more alcohol at the rehearsal dinner.

Melanie's in the shower when I happen to peak out the window and see an army of humans arrive in the wraparound driveway. The happy couple and their parents, plus basically the entire wedding party.

Trista, Paige, Wilson, Greeny, and...him.

He's laughing at a joke Patrick just told. His outfit is a crisp salty pink dress shirt and clean light khakis with brown Gucci loafers.

"Dom?" Kate yells up the stairs once everyone whooshes inside.

I silence the drunken butterflies that the sight of Bucky has just induced. "Yeah?"

"Hey!" she says once I make it out to the hallway. Her skin has a sun-kissed glow; they must've opted for outdoor dining. "Can you entertain everyone for cocktail hour while Patrick and I get ready for the rehearsal? Lunch ran a little late."

I nod and run back into my room, where I guzzle a bottle of Evian and reapply my deodorant. It's actually brilliant that I got day-drunk with Melanie on the beach. I don't know how I was ever planning to face Bucky sober.

55

~

The sprawling land behind the Mystic house is already looking less like a beachy backyard and more like a professional outdoor wedding venue.

The wedding theme is "He's Her Lobster"—a nod to the episode of *Friends* where Phoebe uses a lobsters-mating-for-life analogy to prove that Ross and Rachel belong together—so the existing New England vibes of the house have deeply intensified. The dining and dancing tents are draped with ivory and navy curtains that look like they could sail a boat. Strings of nautical lights hover above high-top cocktail tables, which each have these lobster-shaped candles in the center that are far more elegant than any themed candle has a right to be.

Speaking of cocktail tables, I need another drink. My buzz is fading, and it's becoming difficult not to fixate on Bucky's looming presence. So far I've shot him several low-key glances, none of which have been returned.

We're back to being strangers.

"You want another champagne?" I ask Trista, whom I've been small-talking with for the past half hour. It only occurs to me now that perhaps this is why he's been avoiding me all night.

"Is the sky blue?" she asks. "Does a bear shit in the woods? Is my professional golfer ex-boyfriend uncircumcised?"

I choke on my last sip of bubbly. "Uh—"

"Your face!" She laughs. "I'm sorry, that joke was in poor taste. I just knew you were the only person here who could appreciate it."

I laugh because I'm loving Trista tonight—she *is* pretty funny—but her vivid reminder of the famous penis I'll never see again is a bit of a buzzkill.

"Just so we're clear," she adds. "Yes. I'll take another glass."

"You got it. Be right back."

I shake Bucky out of my mind as I make my way to the nearest bar tent.

"Two champagnes," I ask. "Please."

Three separate bars have been set up out here, each one designed to look like the outside of a Maine lighthouse. Meanwhile, the actual lighthouse at the end of the beach has a hundred white chairs neatly arranged in a colosseum-like semicircle in front of it. So that's fun! The infamous Shed of Secrets will be the site of the ceremony.

The bartender passes me a pair of effervescent champagne flutes.

As I turn around to deliver them back to Trista, I crash right into Bucky. A splash from each flute wets his shirt and drips off my wrists.

"I'm so, so, so sorry," I say immediately—as if I'm apologizing not just for the spill but for literally everything. Which I suppose I am.

His eyes meet mine and I swear they're happy to see me. "Don't sweat it. Barely hit me."

"No, I mean..." I lower my voice. "I'm sorry about how we left things the other night. I didn't mean to make you feel—"

"Dom." He places a hand on my shoulder, igniting actual sparks. "It's fine. You're not the one who..." He trails off.

I narrow my eyes to a squint. "Why have you been ignoring me?"

"Because—"

He cuts himself off and looks away.

"What?"

He lowers his voice. "I can't do this."

My throat tightens. "You can't accept my apology?"

"No, it's—your apology is accepted. I just mean I can't be talkin' to you."

"Why not? I'm trying to start over as friends. If we're gonna be in this wedding together—"

"Friends?" he whispers. "You and I both know that's impossible."

And I realize he's correct. The tension between us is still too strong. It's hijacking my nervous system right now, as we speak.

"I need to focus on gettin' my game back," he continues. "Which takes willpower. It takes—" He cuts himself off again and points behind me. "Can we just drop this? I think they're startin' the rehearsal."

"Fine." I hand him the champagne flute that was meant for Trista. "Here. Take this."

He reluctantly accepts it and we head to the beach, where we're immediately swept away into a whirlwind of staging and instruction.

The planners go through the usual rehearsal motions— ensuring everyone knows what they have to do and when. My role as best man doesn't require much. Just stand behind Patrick, hand over the rings when I'm asked to, escort maid of honor Paige back up the aisle once it's all over. The real challenge will be tomorrow at the reception. I still haven't made any progress on my speech.

One good thing about all the rehearsal action is that it helps me to stop thinking about Bucky for a while. Seeing the glow in Kate's face as she practice-walks down the aisle with her dad is the perfect reminder that this weekend is not about me.

But this sense of perspective doesn't last long.

I slip back into the bad place by the time we're seated for dinner. Bucky's stationed directly to my left and Wilson is to my right, which means I'm literally sandwiched between the two people here who want nothing to do with me.

I focus my attention on Paige, who's directly across from me.

"We still need to decide on our entrance shtick for tomorrow!" she proclaims. "You know, for when they introduce the MOH and best man at the reception."

I take a giant swig of the Sancerre that the waiters have been distributing like water. "How about we do an S&M thing? You can whip me."

Paige almost spits out her drink. "Domenic!"

Bucky tries—and fails—to hold in a laugh to my left.

"Just kidding," I say. "I don't know where we'd find a good whip at this stage in the game."

"How about we keep it simple?" she suggests. "Like, the fishing pole. That's a classic."

A harrowing image of Paige casting an imaginary line and reeling me in flashes across my mind, but it's interrupted by the sight of Mrs. Cooper approaching. She's been making the rounds all dinner, thanking each guest individually in lieu of making a toast. She's the quintessence of a WASP-mom—cream-colored silk blouse, diamond earrings, the works.

"Domenic!" she exclaims when she gets to me. "I hate how little I've seen of you this week. I have been positively beleaguered with preparation." She lowers herself to a squat beside my chair and rubs my arm. "How are you, my sweet boy?"

Her maternal energy helps soothe my Bucky-angst. She always talks to me like I'm still the helpless stray I was twenty years ago during sleepover weekends. And I always eat it up.

"Chugging along," I tell her.

"Patrick told me all about that Ted." She says his name like it's a curse word. "I could kill that man for what he did to you."

I shrug. "It was for the best."

"Are you seeing anyone new yet?" she asks.

"Nope." I catch a glimpse of Bucky from the corner of my eye. "Taking a break from men."

"As long as you don't take a break from *women*. You owe me several dances tomorrow!" She chuckles and then launches into a familiar request. "And I don't suppose you'd be willing to treat me to a few songs on the piano at some point this weekend? I haven't heard the thing played in years, darling. It's tragic."

I've been dodging her requests to hear me play for nearly a decade at this point, but now I'm willing to oblige. The thought even makes me smile. "Absolutely."

"I knew there was still hope for you!" She winks at me. "That's why I've never stopped asking you to play for me."

She squeezes my shoulder and then turns toward Bucky. "And what about you, my dear? How are you holding up since the breakup with Trista?"

He swallows the drink in his mouth. "I'm doin' just fine. No hard feelings. Hell, I've barely had time to think about it. I still got two tour stops comin' up after this weekend."

"I'm glad you have the right attitude," she says. "Such a handsome star like yourself will have no problem finding the right woman when you're ready for her."

"Yes ma'am," Bucky replies with a fake smile.

His deliberate performance of heterosexuality makes my stomach turn. I guzzle the remainder of my wine and excuse myself for a refill.

Halfway to the bar, I hear Bucky's voice. "Wait up!"

I turn around to see him running after me.

"Are you talking to me?" I ask. "Is this…allowed?"

"I'm makin' an exception." He struggles to maintain balance once he catches up to me. I'm clearly not the only one who's been drinking my feelings tonight. "This dinner has been killin' me. Sittin' next to you, hearin' your voice. Fuck willpower." He lowers his voice. "How about you come back to the hotel with me tonight?"

I'm almost drunk and horny enough to ignore my better judgment and accept his invitation with no questions asked. But then I remember the revelation I had at the bar the other night. This was exactly why I chose to break things off with him. Because I don't want to settle for someone who needs to get drunk and murmur "fuck willpower" to himself before he can entertain the idea of sleeping with me.

Plus his suggestion is logistically impossible anyway.

"We can't," I tell him. "What would I tell Patrick? I'm just giving up my room at the house to share a bed with you at the hotel?"

His face falls. "You're right. That was dumb. See? This is why I can't be around you. You make me stupid."

"And! Also! Besides. It's just a bad overall idea." Look at me! I'm being strong. "From now on, I need to only be with men who are available. Which you are extremely not."

The air between us goes quiet for a few moments of unbearable sexual tension. I know what I just said was true, but I also know that on some level I am hoping for him to counter it with the suggestion that maybe he could try to be available. Even just the promise of the possibility that he might one day decide to come out may be enough to—

"Yo!" Patrick sneaks up out of nowhere and puts an arm

around each of us. "Look at my two best men, getting along so
well. Who'd have ever guessed?"

Bucky blinks himself into bro-mode. "Hey Coop."

Patrick slaps my back. "Dom, mind if I steal Graham for a
sec? I need him to settle a golf debate between Uncle Moe and my
dad. Shit's getting heated down in the cigar pit."

"By all means." I exhale and let the moment go. "I gotta take
a leak anyway."

The rest of the night is a moonlit blur. I float back and forth
between groups—twenty minutes with Kate and her bridesmaids
here, ten minutes with Patrick's cousins there—but all I can think
about is Bucky's suggestion that I go back to the hotel with him.
Maybe I should've just said yes and worried about the repercus-
sions later. One last hurrah before we end it all for good.

Before I know it, one of the wedding organizers makes an
announcement for all hotel guests. The shuttle's leaving in five.

I scan the crowd for Bucky's head amid the mass exodus, but
can't find him.

Which crushes me. And forces me to admit that I was indeed
hoping we'd reconnect at some point in the evening and make a
reckless decision. Or at least share a stolen kiss or a tight embrace
or something. But perhaps this is for the best. As good as it
would've felt to backslide into another drunken hookup with him,
in the end I know it would be a mistake. To borrow an idea from
Bucky: I need to have some willpower.

Just as I begin my solitary march toward the house—where I
can already see Mr. and Mrs. Cooper preparing a nightcap at the
kitchen island—my phone buzzes with a text.

Meet me in the lighthouse.

56

To borrow another idea from Bucky: fuck willpower.

I barrel down the hill toward the beach like I'm about to reunite with my military husband who just returned from a lengthy deployment. My hand tears the door open like the knob's on fire. Bucky's laying down on a sleeping bag on the floor, his face aglow in blue iPhone light. Without a word, I throw myself on top of him. He tosses his phone to the side and bites my lip. His hands grip my flesh with so much strength it's like he'll fall a hundred feet if he lets go.

Our mouths wrestle for a few more moments before wandering elsewhere.

The soundtrack is nothing but ferocious breathing and water crashing against the dock. The view is nothing but bare skin and a single ray of moonlight sneaking through the ceiling window. The feeling is nothing but toe-curling pleasure.

But what really makes it so good is the fact that up until a few hours ago, I genuinely believed I had touched Bucky Graham for the last time. Now that he's mine again, I savor every inch of him.

There's no telling how much time goes by. We're on another planet entirely. And we stay there, giving each other every last piece of ourselves, until there's nothing left.

57

~

I awake to the sound of a seagull squawking. My ear's pressed
against Bucky's armpit, and for a moment I think we're back at
that Tribeca penthouse he was renting. Then I feel the polyester
of the sleeping bag under my skin. Followed by a throbbing pain
in my lower back as the result of sleeping on little more than a
wooden plank.

Reality comes rushing back to me.

"Dude!" I squeeze his arm and scan the floor for my phone
and pants. "We fell asleep. Get up."

I squeeze him again and again until he's jolted into
consciousness.

He groans. "What were we thinking?"

"We weren't." I find my phone, but it's out of juice. "What
time is it? My phone's dead."

"Mine, too." He sits up and grabs his watch from a pile of
clothes in the corner. "It's nine."

A sigh of relief. "Okay. Three hours until we need to be
dressed and ready."

"Shit, man." Bucky doesn't seem quite as chill. "My tux is at
the hotel. How am I gonna get it and come back without anyone
noticing?"

His fear is not unwarranted. Surely the entire house is up and running by now. The staff is probably already outside completing the setup that they started yesterday. In fact, I think I can hear them bustling just up the hill.

"Uber and a prayer?" I suggest.

"Both our phones went and died! Wait. Do y'hear that? Someone is—"

He's cut off by the sound of footsteps rapidly tumbling down toward the shed. They are unmistakably headed toward our little love shack.

Did I mention we're still fully-ass naked?

Bucky's terrified eyes meet mine as we scramble to get our underwear on. But it's too late. The door swings open without so much as a knock.

58

"Holy sh—" Patrick shrieks as he averts his eyes. He's wearing his old NYU Law tank top and mesh gym shorts. Strange to think this look will be replaced with a wedding tux in just a few hours. "Jesus. Guys. I'm sorry. I should have knocked."

"Coop," Bucky pleads as he pulls his boxer briefs up around his waist. "This ain't what it looks like."

This reaction stings. Given the zeal he showed for me last night, I was hopeful he'd made at least a little bit of progress toward self-acceptance. Not even for my sake, but for his.

"Listen guys," Patrick begins. His voice is laced with concern, but he doesn't seem nearly as fazed by this as he should be. "I already knew about your thing. I don't care."

Bucky shoots several bullets at me with his eyes.

"I didn't tell him!"

"Kate did," Patrick says.

Bucky hits my arm. "You told Kate?"

"Not on purpose!" I say. "She just kind of—"

"Yo!" Patrick says. "We have a much bigger problem right now." He pulls out his phone and shoves it in our faces. "This."

His screen displays a headline from *TMZ*:

Double Bogey! PGA Powerhouse Bucky Graham Exposed for Gay Smooch AND Doping Suspension.

Right underneath it is a grainy cell phone pic of our kiss from the other night. We ended up in the background of a random bar patron's Instagram post, and then some asshole internet sleuth spotted Bucky and me in the background and zoomed all the way in. The camera caught us at that exact second when we closed our eyes and gave in to the kiss out of mindless habit. It's not the most high-def image, but there's no question that it's Bucky. His distinctive side profile gives it away.

"No." Bucky grabs the phone from Patrick's hand and glues his eyes to the article. There's a stack of unused Adirondack chairs in the corner of the shed. He backs up into it and collapses into the top one. "No, no, no, no, no—"

"Doping?" I ask him. "I thought you stopped doing that back in June."

Patrick looks at me. Now *there's* the look of shock I expected earlier. "You knew about the PEDs?"

I stutter but can't get a response out.

Patrick fixes his eyes on Bucky. "Dude, what the hell? I'm your lawyer. Not to mention your friend." He pauses. "Damn. I should have known when you hit that three-hundred foot drive in Augusta. Or that time your driver head snapped off in—"

"I only did 'em a couple times!" Bucky interjects, eyes still glued to the phone. "Did you even read the article? They're talkin' about a suspension I already served. It was during your bachelor weekend." His eyes start to water for a second as he throws Patrick's phone back to him. But then he adjusts his posture, and it's like instantly turning off a valve. His face goes completely stoic. "But it don't matter. My career is over."

He shakes his head. "Fuck, man."

His pain is so visceral, it prompts my own eyes to begin crying the tears he wouldn't allow himself to.

I reach out to rub his arm. "I'm so sorry. I never meant to—"

He leans into my touch as if subconsciously seeking all the comfort I have to give. "It ain't your fault."

"Your career's not over," Patrick offers. His anger has swiftly morphed into compassion. "You can go back out there next week—"

"As what?" Bucky asks. "The *gay* golfer? The *doped-up* golfer? I'm gonna be a joke, man. I've got fans out there. They look up to me. What are they gonna think? There's gonna be comments and tweets and—goddamnit. This is a nightmare."

Patrick looks down at his Rolex. His wedding is in literal hours, and we're over here throwing a giant gay wrench into his big day. But he doesn't seem concerned.

"So you messed up," Patrick says. "You know how many of my clients have done a hell of a lot worse? You're not the first professional athlete to get dinged for PEDs...and you definitely won't be the last. You'll just put out an apology, and it'll blow over."

Patrick looks over at me and takes a breath before continuing. "And as far as the gay thing—who cares? You've already proved yourself on the course, dude. If any fans drop you because of this, to hell with 'em." He pauses. "And the world has changed since we were kids. I highly doubt people will care as much as *TMZ* thinks they will."

Patrick makes a great point.

"This could be an opportunity to gain *new* fans," I add. "If you own this moment and come out, you'll be making history as a trailblazer. You could win the Arthur Ashe Courage Award at the ESPYs."

"I don't give a rat's ass 'bout being a damn trailblazer." Bucky rubs his eyes until they're red. "You don't understand. People are gonna—"

"Remember what you always told us back at the OKB house?" Patrick says. "It doesn't matter what anyone else on the outside thinks—your brothers will always have your back. And your brothers are all here. You think Wilson and Greeny are gonna disown you just because you like dudes? You're Bucky Graham! I wouldn't be surprised if *they* start sucking dick now, too." He laughs quietly. "Shit. I'm not gonna have any straight friends left after this wedding, am I?"

Bucky doesn't seem to be amused. He ejects himself from the stack of chairs and silently finishes getting dressed. Stoic. As if Patrick's words mean nothing to him.

Which is absurd, because Patrick's words couldn't have been more supportive—such a far cry from his reaction to my coming out twelve years ago. All I got back then was a few awkward assurances that it didn't matter to him, followed by a three-year friendship hiatus.

Not that I'm jealous that Patrick has finally learned how to respond supportively. In fact, I'm proud. I'd like to think that in some way, I'm responsible for the growth he needed to get to this point.

But alas, it's not enough for Bucky.

"I'm sorry," he says to both of us. "I can't stick around for the wedding."

Patrick reaches for his arm. "Come on, man. What are you talking about? It's my—"

Bucky jerks his arm away. "If I stay, I'm all anybody will be talkin' about. I don't want all that attention. This is your day."

"Don't be crazy," Patrick protests. "You have to stay."

Bucky just stares down at the floor and squeezes his eyes shut.

"This is my fault," I say. "I shouldn't have confronted you like I did at the bar that night."

"Nah." Bucky looks up at me, his eyes finally starting to water. "I'm the one who kissed you, remember? I let myself go. I messed up."

He wipes the back of his wrist against his face and makes a sprint to the door.

"Graham," Patrick yells. "Come on, man!"

But he's halfway up the hill already.

59

The downstairs master—once the dressing room for stripping icons Kitty and Lexus—has now been transformed into a full-on bridal suite for Kate. Somehow it works great as both! Mrs. Cooper really knows how to design a versatile space.

I tiptoe through a maze of suitcases and garment bags and flower arrangements until I find Kate getting her hair and makeup done in front of a giant vanity in the expansive en suite bathroom. Her shoulders are draped in a silk bathrobe with "Bride" written in cursive across the back. Her slim, lacy wedding dress hangs beautifully on a nearby rack.

There's a camera crew from *Vogue* documenting her entire beauty regimen for a video on their website, which I interpret as a cue to get out of the way and just connect with her later. But then she spots me in the mirror.

"Dom!" She waves and turns around to address her team. "Can we cut for three minutes? I need a private convo with the best man."

Once the entourage is gone, I make a showy display of observing her hair and makeup. "Bellissima! Truly gorgeous."

She smiles gratefully before narrowing her eyes at me. "Are you and Bucky okay? I saw the article."

"I'm so sorry." I prop myself up on the marble counter to face her. "This is your wedding day and somehow it became all about—"

She lowers her voice. "Don't apologize. I'm the one who should be sorry. I shouldn't have said anything to Patrick."

"It's probably better that you did. Otherwise he would've found out from *TMZ*."

"What a trash site," Kate says. "Who would out someone in this day and age? It's so pathetic."

"I think his strength worked against him," I suggest. "Like they figured, 'Oh, he's so tough. He can handle it.' But you should have seen him. He was so visibly shattered—he disappeared right after he saw it."

Kate's face falls. "Oh, no."

"Patrick begged him to stay, but he was just a mess." I think back to that look on his face. "I feel like shit about this whole thing. It would've never happened if we hadn't—"

"It's not your fault, babe." She rubs my arm. "He'll get through this."

I shake off my emotions and sit up. "Well, today is *your* day. No more talk about me or Bucky or literally anything that isn't related to how perfect this dress is going to look on you." I gesture over at the rack. "I have a feeling you're going to be the hottest bride I've ever seen. And that's including Mariah's look at her 1993 wedding to Tommy Mottola. Marriage from hell, yes, but she was stunning."

"I *will* be the hottest bride you've ever seen." She stands up from her chair and does a twirl before stabilizing and wrapping her arms around me. "Thanks so much for everything. I know this was a bitch of a summer. But I love you and I'm so glad you're here today."

I hug her back gently, careful not to make any contact with her in-progress face. "Love you, too." My eyes catch a glimpse of the time from her phone on the counter. "Oh, shit. It's already ten." *And I still haven't written my best man speech.* "I should go get ready."

"Please shower. You smell like sex."

My jaw drops.

"Kidding!" she says. "But actually."

There's a knock at the door, which I take as my cue to exit.

Once I meander back up to my room, I get a call from Ted. He's got news about that whole fireworks drama—which I had completely forgotten about until he just reminded me.

"I wasn't able to talk them into giving us a refund," he says. "Which sucks—"

"Whatever." I don't mean to sound gruff; it's just a reflex at this point. "Can we figure it out later? I'm in Mystic—"

"Let me finish. They had another cancellation this weekend, if you can believe that. Apparently it really *is* a thing that happens a lot. So I negotiated a little bit with the manager, and they agreed to switch the fireworks to today." He pauses. "I already called Mrs. Cooper, and she's arranging it with the wedding planners. Consider it a wedding present to the happy couple. Tell them I said congratulations."

I can't help but smile at his thoughtfulness. Ted's really not so bad. Bad for me, absolutely—but not bad overall. At the end of the day, it was better for us to have a cancelled wedding than a lifetime of regret.

"Thank you," I say. "You didn't have to do that."

"It would've been silly to let the package go to waste." He goes quiet for a tentative moment. "I saw the *TMZ* post. Bucky? *Really*? I would have never guessed."

"Yeah, well." I sigh. It occurs to me that I'm going to have a shit ton of emotions to process once the show of this wedding is over and my adrenaline wears off. "Me neither."

"Is he okay? Is he—"

"Of course he's not okay."

"Damn. Never thought I'd say this about someone like him, but I feel bad for the guy. I remember what it's like to wrestle with all that." A sad little laugh. "And I wasn't an internationally ranked professional golfer."

During the entire first year of our relationship, Ted wasn't sure he'd ever work up the nerve to blow his entire life up and come out of the closet. As someone who came out in college, I couldn't—and still can't—fully relate to his experience of doing so as a grown man. But I could feel his pain. No matter when or how you do it, it's a very specific form of mental and emotional weight.

"I remember," I offer. "You were such a headcase about it."

"It was terrifying!" Ted says. "But thankfully I had you at the time. I could never have gone through that alone."

"Really? I don't remember being particularly life coach-y about it."

He laughs. "You weren't. But it was just the example you set. Seeing how everyone in your life treated you like a normal human being. Treated *us* like normal human beings. It made me realize that the world wouldn't combust if I came out to the people in *my* life. That they probably wouldn't care at all." He pauses. "Which they didn't."

I smile at the thought of my having had such a positive impact on Ted's journey to self-acceptance. But it's followed by a deep sadness for the fact that I haven't been able to provide the same level of comfort and support for Bucky.

This sadness swirls around in me for long after Ted and I hang up, making it impossible to focus on the speech I should be writing.

So instead I opt to write something else entirely.

A message to Bucky:

I know your head is probably still spinning right now, but I had to give this a shot. I think you should come back. Take it from me, as someone who almost missed our best friend's wedding due to my own silly pride, it's not worth it.

I know it's not exactly the same thing. I can't begin to imagine what it's like to be forced out of the closet as thirty-something pro athlete. Coming out—willingly—as an anonymous college kid was hard enough. But I do know that, as hard as it was, it was also the best thing I ever did. Remember the cone? You can finally take yours off now! You have all the permission in the world to scratch your itch! This metaphor still feels extremely weird, but I don't know, it's ours, so I'm using it. Anyway. I know that it hurts right now, but in time I guarantee you'll look back on your days in the closet and be so glad you ended up on the other side. And I truly believe that if you come back to this wedding, you'll find that no one will treat you any differently than they did when they thought you were straight. No one cares about our sexuality as much as we think they do. I'm still finding new ways to learn that myself. For all the drama that happened about it this summer, I can promise you we're not the gay best friends. Ultimately, for the people who really matter, we're just, you know, friends. No qualifiers needed.

And whether or not you ever feel comfortable being

out about who you are, I just wanted you to know that, as someone who got to see all sides of the real Bucky Graham...I liked him a whole lot more than the perfect pro golfer the rest of the world gets to see.

So I hope you can find it in yourself to come back. But even if you can't, please know that there are a lot of people here who care very deeply about you. Including me.

Especially me.

PS: Thanks for encouraging me to play music again. I've got a whole lot of good memories wrapped up with all the hard ones, but that's something special you gave me that I'd figured I'd never have back. So thank you for that. And for everything.

60

I'm showered, dressed, in the study with Patrick. And I still don't have a speech prepared. But it's too late to do anything about it now—our next stop is the ceremony. So at this point my only option is to just get drunk and wing it.

Patrick's got a tray set out on the poker table with a bottle of ridiculously aged bourbon and five rocks glasses to kick off the behind-the-scenes festivities. I wince as I notice that—in light of Bucky's departure—there is one too many.

Patrick stands up straight by the window, looking exactly like the candid image of a serene groom contemplating life that every wedding photographer takes prior to the ceremony.

Except the photographer left ten minutes ago.

"How you feeling?" I ask him.

"Trying not to let this Bucky thing rule my mind," he says quietly. "But it's hard, man."

I wish I had something reassuring to say, but I don't. My phone indicates that Bucky read my message thirty minutes ago and still hasn't responded. I knew it was a long shot that he'd have a change of heart so soon, but still. I hoped.

So what can we do at this point? This wedding is going to be extravagant—nearly two hundred guests. The fact that one of them happens to be embroiled in a gay sports scandal isn't enough to stop the show.

"You know what we need?" I offer. "To drink this bourbon. Where are the guys?"

As if on cue, Greeny bursts through the doors.

"There he is!" he says. Wilson trails behind him. "Mr. Kate Wallace."

"Hilarious," Patrick deadpans as they exchange high fives.

Greeny slaps my back. "'Sup Dom? What's this I hear about you getting some...uh...*golfing lessons* from our boy?"

"Dude," Patrick says. "Too soon. Come on."

"What?" Greeny asks. "I'm trying to have a sense of humor about it. He does."

"Who does?" Patrick and I ask in unison.

And then—as if staged—Bucky appears in the doorway. Fully dressed in his navy groomsman tux, the sadness in his eyes replaced with something you might even be able to call a glimmer of mischief. "I do," he says.

"You lucky bastard, Dom." Greeny rubs a hand over Bucky's bicep. "You've got this beautiful hunk of man all to yourself."

This elicits a laugh from the entire room—even Bucky, though his ears go a little pink at the exaggerated show of his friends' support.

Patrick's face lights up as he approaches Bucky. "You're really alright?"

Bucky nods in a way that suggests he is—but also that he doesn't have any desire to talk about it—and the pair engages in a quick hug.

Meanwhile, a hand grabs my shoulder from behind.

Wilson. "Hey, bro. Truce?"

"Seriously?" I ask. Not because I'm trying to start shit! It's just a knee-jerk reaction to such a startling reversal. "I mean, yeah. Truce."

We shake hands. Wilson's still an asshole—and perhaps he always will be—but I'll never *not* accept an opportunity to resolve conflict. As Kate would say, holding grudges give you wrinkles.

"Did I miss something?" Patrick asks.

"Don't worry about it," Bucky says.

"Oh, I see what's going on." Patrick cracks a smirk at Wilson. "I've been telling you to apologize to Dom for two months! But now that Graham tells you to do it, you finally listen? I see how it is, bro."

Wilson playfully punches his arm. "How about you win a PGA tournament and then come talk to me?"

Bucky and I exchange quiet smiles.

Does this mean my message worked and he's finally decided to accept himself? Does he plan on making some kind of statement confirming his homosexuality in the coming days? An *ESPN* primetime special? Or a tell-all *Golf Digest* interview? Is he going to want to try to be *together* after the PR dust settles? Or will he drop me immediately upon discovering that—as a successful out gay athlete—he can get any man he wants?

He looks away and forces himself to take a breath. I suddenly realize that he hasn't made his mind up about any of this yet. He's just trying to get through the day. And I'm well on the way to making the same sort of mistakes I always have, jumping ahead five steps before I'm even really on my feet.

Whatever happens, happens, I realize with a relaxing of my shoulders. There's no timetable on this. There's no need to rush to keep up with anyone. And when I look at Bucky, I don't see a star athlete at all, but a man I care about who needs all the support he can get.

He came back. That's as good a first step as any.

Patrick straightens his tie and clears his throat. "Alright, fellas. Gather around." He leads us all toward the poker table. "It's been a wild ride, but I couldn't ask for a better crew to have my back today."

He scratches his chin as if he doesn't know what to say next. "You know what? That's all I got. This morning gave me fuckin' whiplash, and I don't have the mental energy to give you clowns a thoughtful speech." He raises his glass and we all follow suit. "Cheers, brothers."

61

The backyard is a breathtaking postcard full of fancy paint shades: emerald grass, ivory linen, crystal sky, cerulean water. There's an enormous tent covering the dining tables and dance floor, but it's not one of those cookie-cutter party tents you'd see at just any wedding. This one is somehow both elegant and sturdy—with a constellation of skylights in the ceiling to allow the sun (and later, the moon and stars) to pour in.

As we head down to the ceremony arch, I notice that it's impossible to walk more than two feet out here without catching sight of some detailed flower arrangement. Peonies peek around every corner. It's all like something out of a high-end magazine.

Right. It actually is something out of a high-end magazine.

A squatting photographer snaps away as Patrick and the groomsmen and I line up at the altar. Shit. I didn't think about how my positioning directly beside Patrick means I'll likely be in a large portion of wedding pictures—which therefore means I'll potentially wind up in the pages of Kate's exclusive spread. From *TMZ* to *Vogue*. What label are these tuxedos? I barely even paid attention during the fitting, what with everything else going on this summer. I straighten my posture and force my face into what I hope is a natural expression that Anna

Wintour won't scoff at when she scrolls through these at her next editorial meeting.

The string quartet to our left launches into a tranquil melody.

After the parents and the flower girl and ring bearer do their little struts, Trista appears in her shoulderless teal bridesmaid gown. Looking like the golden supermodel that she is. No need for *her* to worry about Anna's approval.

Next up is Melanie, her auburn hair in an updo that highlights her soft facial features in a way I've never noticed before. Her smile is so pure, you'd never guess she's on the brink of a divorce. And then there's Paige, struggling to hold back happy tears.

The guests all rise as the string quartet transitions into a mellow rendition of "Can't Help Falling in Love."

Patrick gasps at the sight of his soon-to-be wife. She's been telling everyone her backless Vera Wang was off-the-rack, but I'm now convinced it was in fact hand-stitched around her actual body. Her hair is an ethereal mix of natural blonde waves and loose French braids, with a tasteful flower-crown-veil combo completing the look.

As her father hands her off and she steps toward the altar, Patrick wipes away the first tear I've ever seen him cry.

It's absurd that there was ever talk of calling this thing off. These two were made for each other. I can feel that in my bones. The same way I can feel that Ted and I were *not* made for each other. To think I was so eager to marry him in spite of that fact sends a chill down my spine. I almost ruined both of our lives because I couldn't grow past feeling like I was still that kid in Patrick's shadow, running to catch up in shoes that weren't even mine, desperate to measure up somehow.

This epiphany might've taken much longer than it should have to sink in, but it helps to know that all this time—all these years measuring myself against all the people around me—I've been the only one keeping score.

And so, as Patrick and Kate recite their vows to each other, I silently make one to myself. That—if and when I ever get engaged again—I will settle for nothing less than someone who accepts the real me. Whatever form that may take.

62

Midway through cocktail hour, I'm finally buzzed enough to approach Bucky.

I wait until he's alone, filling up his champagne flute by the sky-high Moët fountain on the back terrace.

To my surprise—and relief—he greets me with a hug.

"I feel like total shit about everything," I offer. "Like I said in my message to you, I can't imagine what you're going through right now."

"Thank you for that note, man. It sure did help." He exhales through a small chuckle. "You know, my granny used to have this saying—"

He cuts himself off upon noticing that a few guests from across the lawn are clearly gawking at the two of us together. He takes a giant swig in response. "I'm gonna need a hell of a lot more of this stuff."

"You and me both." I lean back on the heels of my tuxedo shoes for a few moments of nervous silence. "So, uh. You were about to share another granny-ism?"

"Oh, right." Bucky laughs. "'You can put your boots in the oven, but that don't make 'em biscuits.'"

"Huh." I roll it around in my head for a moment. He's clearly talking about the lifetime he's spent in the closet, but it also resonates with me on another level. All those years I spent trying to be Patrick when I should've just focused on being myself. "That is so true."

"It's the story of my life," Bucky says. This time with a hint of sadness. "But you know what's wild? I swear I saw today comin' ever since that first night you and I spent in the lighthouse. You stirred somethin' up in me that I always knew I'd have to deal with eventually." He pauses for a beat. "Just didn't know it was gonna be a goddamn *TMZ* scoop to beat me to it."

"Are you saying you were thinking about coming out yourself?"

"I was," he says. "Man, I'm thirty-one years old, and until this summer I never *once* took that damn cone off. I've always been so consumed with my golf game and trying to make somethin' of myself...and when you ignore an itch long enough, you can almost convince yourself the itch ain't there at all. I felt like if I caved even once, there'd be no turning back."

"I totally get that. It was over for me the first time I sucked a—" I cut myself off with a nervous laugh. "Well, you know what I mean."

He playfully punches my arm. "I'm serious. Bein' with you this summer—the way I couldn't stop thinking about you all day, every damn day—I knew I'd never be able to put my boots back in the oven. Hell, even if I could, I don't think I'd want to."

My heart grows several sizes. This would be the perfect moment for a big cinematic kiss.

"You shouldn't," I say. "I like your boots where they are right now."

Bucky smiles, leans toward me—

And then the wedding planner ambushes us from behind.

"Wedding party entrances in five!" she chirps. "Please line up behind the large tent."

We laugh sheepishly and head down together, a lightness between us that just a few hours ago would've seemed impossible.

"I'm a little worried about my best man speech," I confess. "I don't have anything prepared."

He slaps my back. "You'll be fine. Just speak from your heart."

"What if my heart can't think of anything?"

"That's the whole point," he says. "Hearts don't think. I'd say this thing between you and me is proof of that."

"Touché."

"Here's an opening line for ya, another saying from my granny: 'If you don't want blisters on your butt, ride a good saddle.'"

I stare blankly at him for a moment. "What?"

"It's a metaphor!"

"And Kate would be...the saddle...in this scenario?"

He laughs. "On second thought, maybe it's not wedding speech material. You'll think of something."

We gather outside the main tent with the rest of the wedding party.

Bucky links up with Melanie and Greeny, the three of whom are announced by the DJ first. Melanie carries one man on each arm, and the trio does a cheeky dance to the *Three's Company* theme song. Next up are Trista and Wilson, who shamelessly steal the fishing rod routine from Paige and me. *Sorry*, Trista mouths from the dance floor.

"They foiled us!" Paige whisper-screams. "What do we do now?"

"I told you we should've gotten a whip!" I lament.

Before we can say anything else, the DJ starts blasting our entrance song ("Gimme More" by Britney Spears) and instructs the guests to "make some noise for the maid of honor and best ma-aa-an: Paige Hamilton escorted by Domenic Marino-o-o!"

Paige releases a desperate shrug. "We'll just have to dance frenetically."

And then she does exactly that—looking like a cross between the Prancercise lady and Elaine in that one episode of *Seinfeld*—leaving me no choice but to do the same. I twirl her as we reach the center of the dance floor, and then we scurry to join the rest of the wedding party on the sidelines.

So that was humiliating! But also, perhaps good practice for what's to come.

The next few rituals fly by in an anxious blur—Kate and Patrick's first dance, their parents' welcome speeches—and suddenly it's my turn to take the mic.

"Just remember," Paige whispers to me. "The best man is supposed to make everyone laugh, and the maid of honor is supposed to make everyone cry." She narrows her eyes. "So don't make anyone cry or I'll cut you."

The crowd applauds as the DJ invites me up to Patrick and Kate's "sweetheart" table.

I take a deep breath. And then a deeper gulp of champagne. Patrick and Kate look up at me with eager, encouraging faces. I think about all we've been through together—how grateful I am for their friendship—and clear my throat.

"Can I just say that I love these two people so much I could puke?" I begin. Really? Vomit? It occurs to me that this is exactly why smart people prepare their speeches ahead of time. "Just kidding," I add quickly. "About the puke. Not about the love."

Moving on.

"For those who don't know me, my name is Domenic Marino, and it has been an absolute honor to serve as the best man for my best friend Patrick." I spot Bucky at our table, which helps me relax and just do what he told me to do earlier—speak from the heart. "So Patrick and I are both only children, but it's never felt like it, because really we've been brothers ever since we first met in third grade and bonded over our shared love of Donkey Kong, Devil Dogs, and Aerosmith music videos. Granted, we didn't have *everything* in common growing up. Patrick was in love with Alicia Silverstone; I was in love with...dudes." A pause. "Although I did love Alicia in my own way—I mean, the woman is a gay icon."

The room crackles with a mix of friendly and uncomfortable laughter. "We've had our differences and our ups and downs over our twenty-plus years of friendship—but through it all, he's always had a heart of gold. I'll never forget during track season junior year when he literally gave me the shoes off his feet—a brand new pair of Nike cleats—after noticing I'd been wearing the same pair of beat-up Reeboks for two seasons too many."

Paige shoots me a glare, telling me to lighten it up before I steal her thunder with the heartstring-pulling.

"And I remember the first time I met Kate," I continue. "It was love at first sight! I knew she was perfect for Patrick because she was perfect for *me*. From her encyclopedic knowledge of *Sex and the City* to her arsenal of spicy quips to her uncanny ability to always have the perfect beauty tip for any given situation—she is truly a queen. And Patrick always treats her as such.

"I remember this one time the three of us were hiking down at Devil's Den. There was this swampy, mushy puddle in the middle of the trail—at least a foot deep, with no way to get around it. And poor Kate was wearing these little sneakers—Stella McCartney sneakers, I think they were. Who even knew Stella McCartney *made* sneakers?"

The room erupts with knowing laughs, because of course Kate would show up to a wilderness hike in designer shoes.

"These sneakers were definitely not built to be submerged in mud," I continue. "So Patrick literally picked her up and carried her over the puddle! It was the most knight-in-shining-armor display of love I've ever seen." I pause to absorb a mix of swooning *aww*s and light chuckles from the crowd. "Anyway. I don't know why every touching story I have to tell about Patrick is so sneaker-oriented, but if the *shoe* fits."

This time there are more than a few audible cringes. Which is fair. That was corny and dad-ish. It's time to wrap this up.

"In all seriousness, though. These are my two very best friends in the world." Something comes over me, and I'm compelled to attempt a profound thought before I sign off. "And as with all the very best friendships, we've had our good times and bad times. We've even had times—not to get too specific, but literally this past summer—when we've gotten sucked into what Kate refers to as 'a seven-layer dip of toxic communication patterns and unnecessary drama.'"

Love how I said I wasn't getting too specific, then got entirely too specific.

Moving on!

"But no matter what we've been through, the three of us have always managed to grow *together* rather than apart—which I think is the mark of true soulmates." Soulmates? That's a very strange way to describe a three-pronged friendship. I attempt to deflect my poor word choice with humor. "Basically what I'm saying, Patrick and Kate, is that I fully expect to be invited to the honeymoon. Maldives, here we come!" I pause. "Just kidding. That would be gross and inappropriate, and we have a very healthy set of friendship boundaries, which I respect and cherish."

Am I starting to sound unhinged? I'm starting to sound unhinged. Okay—wrapping up for real this time.

"So here's to Patrick and Kate." I raise my champagne flute. "Two incredible friends and amazing people who deserve each other—and a lifetime of happiness."

63

Why is it that weddings always seem to go by so fast? One second you're popping hors d'oeuvres at cocktail hour—and then you blink and you're drunkenly fist-pumping to "Don't Stop Believin'" on the dance floor at midnight.

I've been trying to be more present at *this* wedding, but somehow it's already gotten dark out without my noticing.

"Alright folks," the band's lead singer says right as I get back to the tent from a pee-break. "Everyone head down to the beach for a special surprise from the best man!"

Kate immediately ambushes me from behind.

"Surprise?" she asks. "Domenic! What are you doing?"

My chest tightens. "I actually don't know what he's talking about."

Patrick and Bucky approach from across the floor with similarly curious looks on their faces. And then I remember the fireworks. "Oh. Right!"

"What is it?" Kate asks.

"Let's go outside," I say. "You'll see."

The four of us run down to the beach in our formal wear, feeling fully entitled to cut the line and make a scene because we're with the bride and groom.

We perch ourselves in the sand right as the first firework goes off.

"Aw, babe!" Kate shrieks as she hugs me from the side. "When did you even do this?"

I consider giving Ted credit, but decide it's not important right now. I'll fill them in later. "Don't worry about it. Just enjoy."

A constellation of giant hearts explodes in gold and silver against the pitch-black sky. The dark water of Mystic Harbor brilliantly reflects their sparkle below. Then the word LOVE is spelled out in big letters, and somehow it's not at all cheesy but instead almost makes me cry. I've clearly veered into the emotional-drunk portion of the evening.

"This is sick." Patrick throws an arm around me. "Thanks, buddy."

"I *love* them," Kate adds. "Thanks for everything today... I know it can't be easy considering there were supposed to be two weddings this year."

I nod and exhale. "But you know what? I'm glad things turned out the way they did. Something tells me the best is yet to come."

She squeezes my wrist. "It sure is."

We stare up at the fireworks show for a while. Kate and Patrick settle into a permanent embrace, kissing under the flying sparks like they're in a real-life fairy tale. Despite the joy of the moment, I can't help but feel a prick of melancholy as I think about the concept of weddings and fairy tales and love in general.

Bucky sneaks up beside me. "Incredible, huh?"

"These were supposed to be at my wedding," I blurt. "Sorry. I don't know why I—"

"You've been through a lot this year, man." He squeezes my hand as if we're not in the middle of a giant crowd of wedding guests. "Times like this, you can't help but think about when it's gonna happen for you."

"Is that what you're thinking about?" I ask.

"Sure am." He sighs. "I still got a lot of shit to figure out; I know you know that. But right now…"

"Right now what?" I ask.

He blushes. "Never mind."

"Come on."

"Alright." He smiles. "Right now all I wanna do is kiss you."

"In front of all these people?"

"Ain't nothin' the whole world hasn't already seen on the damn internet." He laughs and then leans in. "Now hurry up before I lose my nerve."

And then—right as the firework finale launches into high gear—we get lost in the big cinematic kiss that eluded us earlier. Time and space suspend themselves between our lips, which remain attached for several seconds longer than is appropriate or necessary.

And yet it's not nearly long enough.

"Hey guys," Patrick finally interrupts. "Get a room." He points over to the lighthouse and gives a theatrical shrug. "Or a shed."

Bucky snaps out of our trance and for a moment I worry he's going to tense up. But instead he just laughs. "Don't think we won't!"

The entire crowd erupts into a cacophony of cheers at the final firework. The thumping of drums and electric guitar reverberates from the party tent up the hill, signaling that it's time to get back to the reception. Kate reconnects with Paige and Melanie, who watched the fireworks from the grass behind us. Bucky likewise links up with Trista, probably to clear the air before the night is over.

So Patrick and I head up the hill together.

"Life is crazy," he says as we're halfway to the tent. "Isn't it?"

"You're cool with it?" I ask. "Me and Bucky? I mean, who knows if it will turn into something serious or—"

"Of course I'm cool with it." He smiles. "Although—actually? It just occurred to me, man. What if you guys get into a fight or something? You're my two best friends. I can't be taking sides! We'll have to implement some kind of rule."

"Wow, great point." My voice takes on a hint of a good-natured sarcasm. "I can imagine that getting caught in the middle of a lover's quarrel between your two best friends would really suck for you."

"I—" Patrick's face scrunches up as he redirects. "Touché. I deserved that." He chuckles to himself. "How about we say the rule goes both ways, then?"

I laugh in agreement as Patrick throws an arm over my shoulder. Our walking pace naturally syncs up as I reciprocate. A genuine sense of gratitude—for our friendship, our history, even our many differences—washes over me as we make our way toward the tent.

As my gaze casts itself down at the moonlit lawn, a quiet exorcism occurs. All those old feelings of comparison, resentment, and jealousy rise to the surface for the very last time. They seem so small and silly in this moment, it's amazing I held on to them for as long as I did.

And so I let them go with each step up the hill, our four feet moving in tandem, virtually indistinguishable from each other.

Reading Group Guide

1. The "gay best friend" has been a popular reoccurring trope in books/movies/television over the years. How does Domenic Marino subvert and/or affirm your preexisting understanding of this archetype?

2. Throughout much of the novel, Dom struggles with comparing himself to others—especially his well-off best friend, Patrick. Why do you think he does this? Have you ever had a friendship with a similar dynamic?

3. Mystic, Connecticut—and the Mystic house—holds a special sway over Dom. What is it about this place that Domenic finds himself so enamored by? What does it represent to him, and how does it compare (both positively and negatively) to how he was raised?

4. Much of the conflict in this novel is due to Patrick and Kate's inability to clearly communicate trickling down to their mutual best friend, Dom. Why do you think they had such a hard time being upfront with each other? What does it mean that it took so long for Kate to feel like she could be authentically herself with Patrick?

5. Dom finds himself code-switching between the bachelor and bachelorette parties—adapting to the ways his friends talk and act in order to fit in—to the point where he begins to question who he is apart from them. Do you find you can relate to his situation in any way?

6. If you were in Domenic's position at the start of the bachelor party, how would you have handled it?

7. Dom seems to let his guard down with Bucky much more easily than he does with the other men at the bachelor party (even his best friend Patrick). Why do you think this is?

8. On his failed engagement to Ted, Dom says, "I had assumed we were on the same page in thinking we could wait until *after* the wedding to address our growing incompatibility." How often do you think couples go into marriage with this mindset? If Dom and Ted had indeed stayed together and gotten married, do you think they'd have found a way to make it work? If Patrick and Kate hadn't been forced to acknowledge and address their own communication issues, would they have worked in the long run?

9. Dom seems to welcome conflict in romantic relationships, but avoids it at all costs when it comes to his friendships. How much conflict do you think is healthy? And how do you think it should differ between romantic and non-romantic relationships?

10. A key theme in this novel is living for oneself vs. living to conform to societal expectations or ideals. How important do

you think it is to make major life decisions (e.g. law school, marriage) based on what you feel you "should" do vs. what you actually want to do?

11. Bucky has a difficult time coming out, hurting Dom by denying their connection several times through the course of the book. What do you think made him finally decide it was okay to come to the wedding and be seen with Dom? Do you think he's ready to be out on a national stage, or do he and Dom have more hurdles ahead of them?

12. Incredibly, as of late 2022 there is no openly gay golfer at Bucky's level. Why do you think that may be? Do pro athletes experience pressure to remain in the closet?

13. What do you think happens next for Dom and Bucky? Patrick and Kate?

Acknowledgments

Massive thanks to the orthopedics team at Yale Medicine for saving my arm (and my ability to edit this book with both hands) after I shattered my humerus in a freak accident last year. I'm especially thankful for my excellent surgeon, Dr. Ken Donohue, and angel-on-earth nurses Sandy and Michelle, who took such thoughtful care of me before and after surgery.

Endless gratitude as always to my team of dynamo agents: Elizabeth Bennett, Samantha Haywood, Dana Spector, and everyone else at Transatlantic and CAA. And to my brilliant editor, Mary Altman, whose razor-sharp vision for this book elevated it to a level I couldn't be prouder of. Further thanks to the entire team at Sourcebooks for helping bring this book to life, including but not limited to: Teddy Turner, Alyssa Garcia, Jocelyn Travis, Meaghan Summers, Kelsey Thompson, India Hunter, Stephanie Gafron, and Tara Jaggers. And a special shout-out to Holly Ovenden for creating the most perfect cover artwork.

All the flowers to my amazing critique partners. Steven Salvatore: your (brilliant as always) edit letter for this manuscript was a true lighthouse (lol) as I figured out the direction of Dom's story. Julia Foster: this book (as with all my books) would have been a half-baked calamity without your mind-reading insights.

Dinah Alobeid: the unvarnished honesty of your beta feedback is a gift I cherish!

To the incredible authors who were kind and generous enough to read and blurb this book ahead of its publication: To Mazey Eddings and Lynn Painter—two iconic rom-com QUEENS— I'm so incredibly grateful for and humbled by your advance praise for this novel.

So much love to the community of fellow authors, readers, booksellers, librarians, and influencers I've had the pleasure of meeting over the past few years—especially all the bookstagrammers who rallied (and continue to rally) behind *Burn It All Down*. (You know who you are, mainly because I probably DMed you just this morning with a sobbing and/or gratitude-hands emoji.) And special shoutouts to Rachel and the team at Northshire Bookstore in Saratoga for being the best local indie in all the land, and to Kate and the team at Saratoga Springs Public Library for being the best local library in all the land.

To my parents and immediate and extended family, thank you so much for the endless support (and patience with my writing-related disappearances) over the years. And to my equally supportive circles of friends—whether from Connecticut, Jersey, or New York (and those select few of you *not* based in the tri-state area)—I am so very grateful for your love and support.

And finally, to my love, Graig Williams. You already know how much I love and appreciate you, but I dedicated this book to you anyway because you also know how much I love to repeat myself.

About the Author

Nicolas DiDomizio holds a bachelor's degree from Western Connecticut State University and a master's degree from NYU. His debut novel, *Burn It All Down*, was published in 2021 and praised as "unforgettable" by James Patterson. He lives in upstate New York with his partner, Graig, and their smooshy bulldog, Rocco.